PRAISE FOR J.T. ELLISON

"A genuine page-turner… Ellison clearly belongs in the top echelon of thriller writers. Don't leave this one behind."
—*Booklist*, starred review, on WHAT LIES BEHIND

"Exceptional character development distinguishes Thriller Award-winner Ellison's third Samantha Owens novel (after *Edge of Black*), the best yet in the series."
—*Publishers Weekly,* starred review, on WHEN SHADOWS FALL

"Full of carefully mastered clues… a true thrill fest that will keep readers on the edge of their seats until the very end."
—*Suspense Magazine* on WHEN SHADOWS FALL

"A gripping page-turner… essential for suspense junkies."
—*Library Journal* on WHEN SHADOWS FALL

"Well-developed, multidimensional characters and an exceptionally strong plot."
—*Publishers Weekly,* starred review, on FIELD OF GRAVES

"Shocking suspense, compelling characters and fascinating forensic details."
—Lisa Gardner, #1 *New York Times* bestselling author
on A DEEPER DARKNESS

"Mystery fiction has a new name to watch."
—John Connolly, *New York Times* bestselling author

ALSO BY J.T. ELLISON

Standalone Thrillers
TEAR ME APART (Coming Summer 2017)
NO ONE KNOWS

Lieutenant Taylor Jackson Series
FIELD OF GRAVES
WHERE ALL THE DEAD LIE
SO CLOSE THE HAND OF DEATH
THE IMMORTALS
THE COLD ROOM
JUDAS KISS
14
ALL THE PRETTY GIRLS

Dr. Samantha Owens Series
WHAT LIES BEHIND
WHEN SHADOWS FALL
EDGE OF BLACK
A DEEPER DARKNESS

A Brit in the FBI Series co-written with Catherine Coulter
THE DEVIL'S TRIANGLE (Coming March 14, 2017)
THE END GAME
THE LOST KEY
THE FINAL CUT

Anthologies with Erica Spindler and Alex Kava
STORM SEASON
SLICES OF NIGHT

J.T. ELLISON

THE
FIRST DECADE

A SHORT STORY COLLECTION

TWO
TALES
PRESS

The First Decade: A Short Story Collection

Copyright © 2016 by J.T. Ellison
Cover design and interior formatting © The Killion Group, Inc.

ISBN-13 978-0-9965273-0-9
Printed in U.S.A.
10 9 8 7 6 5 4 3 2 1

For more stories by J.T. Ellison, visit TwoTalesPress.com.

For My Mom.

Love you more.

TABLE OF CONTENTS

A NOTE FROM THE AUTHOR

I've always looked at short stories as a way to have a bit of fun with my writing. In my day job, I write psychological thrillers. I'd written three novels before I ever tried my hand at short fiction. But when I did, I discovered an entirely new world.

I spent a great deal of time telling my peers I couldn't write short stories. They kept pushing me, and pushing me, until I finally gave it a shot.

That story was "Prodigal Me." I submitted it to *Writer's Digest* and promptly forgot about it. You can imagine my surprise when I received an email from Chuck Sambuchino saying I'd won an honorable mention in their annual short fiction contest.

Perhaps I could write shorts after all.

Soon after, I attended my first writer's conference, where I met a fabulous writer named Duane Swierczynski. I asked Duane about some short fiction markets, and he suggested I send a story to his friend Bryon Quertermous, who ran an e-zine called *Demolition*. I quickly wrote another story and submitted it. Bryon loved everything but the title, which we agreed to change to "X." It was my first published piece.

My love of the short form grew from there. I began placing stories, writing for anthologies, the works. I grew to love the freedom and limitations of the form, and I still use it as a playground of sorts, a way to stretch my wings and explore genres I wouldn't normally write in.

My short stories are little slices, vignettes. Crimes of the heart, the mind and the soul. The bits and pieces that fell from my mind while I was writing long-form novels, the ideas that didn't have a place in my current work. Some are quite short, others bloomed into novellas.

With the advent of independent publishing, I decided to start my own house, Two Tales Press, in order to share these sweet little lies with you. And now, I'm so excited to have ten years of stories in a single collection, available in both digital and print. THE FIRST DECADE includes my favorites, both anthologized and written for fun, a couple of Taylor Jackson adventures, and two never-before published stories I've written expressly for this collection.

I do hope you'll enjoy the book. Thank you for joining me on this fabulous journey.

– J.T. Ellison
Nashville, Tennessee, 2016

**Want the latest news and insider exclusives,
plus awesome recipes and book recommendations?**

Sign up for J.T.'s email list at jtellison.com/subscribe.

THE STORM

The sky is transparent, a thick gray rain moving up the valley. Lightning dances, long silver-white forks hitting the ground, thunderbolts thrown from Zeus's hand.

The lights flicker as I look out the window. The wet blanket of virga slips closer and closer. The mountains hover, blue and wrinkled, old men with knowledge to share. The outcropping of rock known to the locals as Indian Head glowers at me. Hummingbirds race the wind, trying to gather one last sip of sugar water before the storm drives them to their invisible nests.

He is coming for me.

You may wonder how I know. Perhaps it's the palpable sense of heaviness that hangs over my small cabin. Perhaps the foreknowledge of inevitability. Perhaps someone who still cared slipped me a copy of the paperwork. This isn't an industry that helps one cultivate friends, but there are always people who feel sorry for you when things go south.

We don't last long in my profession. One wrong move is so easy to make. One job unfinished, one job left undone. One job refused.

Honestly, none of this matters.

The storm will blow in, bringing his acrid breath to the nape of my neck. He will stand over me. I will be powerless. The soft *pfft* of the strike will be lost to the raging winds.

If it gets that far, if he gets the upper hand, I'm done for.

Looking back is something I try not to do. I live in the moment. I am a shark, perpetually in motion, always forward, ever forward.

But in this case, a reminiscence is in order. One tends to revisit the past when the future is no longer clear.

These are the long-lasting ramifications to every action I took that day. For a moment, I wish I could go back to the early days, when my mistakes were overlooked because I was young, and being trained.

Now that I am who I am, more is expected of me.

Three Months Ago

Doing overwatch in Florence can almost be called fun. Lying face down on a rooftop for seven hours, wearing a diaper and not allowing my body to even twitch is my second greatest talent. Usually it's done in baking lands where I must be hidden beneath a tent so I don't die in the boiling sun. Florence, on the other hand, is cool and foggy today. The piazza is full of happy people, enjoying a respite from the summer heat.

The mark is expected at seven p.m. He eats at the café opposite my position every evening. He is an early diner for an Italian. He comes alone, orders a prosecco, then a carafe of chianti, eats mussels in red sauce, never touches dessert. He is fit, his legs long, the muscles rippling under his suit coat. He wears sunglasses most of the time, mirrored Ray-Bans. His hair is dark and oiled. He is a good-looking man, careful with himself.

He is also a monster.

Everyone who comes across my crosshairs is, to some extent. His monstrous activities are lauded by some and hated by others.

I don't care what he does. I don't care who he is. The money looks and smells the same regardless of their sins.

In another life, I would have killed him softly. Gently. In bed, after we were both satiated. It is my favorite way, to ingratiate myself. I get more information that way. A blunt killing isn't my usual forte.

But I can do it, and this is what the clients have asked for. Clearly a message is being sent.

I glance down the scope once more.

It is time. He has come.

And he is not alone.

Her hair, all one length down her back, the color of the pasta being served.

Her dress, white with pink and yellow embroidered flowers across the chest.

Her hand, lost in his.

She skips every third step.

Those bastards.

They sit at the table. Prosecco for him, milk for her. Milk, of all things.

This is not going to happen.

This must happen.

You don't get to choose.

Do the job.

This is a mistake.

My finger on the trigger.

The glass of prosecco explodes.

The cries and screams below carry me off the roof and into the darkness of the city.

The call went as well as I expected.

"You missed."

"I didn't miss. I chose."

"That is not your decision to make."

"I wasn't going to kill him in front of his child. I'll go back and do it myself, in the night, when she can't see."

A pause of sheer incredulity. "Don't you understand? *His* death is not the goal."

"The child is the target?"

"The child must learn a lesson. The child must be taught what happens when she speaks."

"That's what this is about? *The child?* You're insane."

"And you're fired. Clear out. The contract is pulled."

The phone went dead in my hand.

I had to move, now. They would be coming for me, yes, that was inevitable. But not right away. It was the target and his flax-en-haired daughter who were in mortal danger, immediate and ever-present.

If I could move quickly enough, I might be able to save them both.

Now

Lightning crashes. The thunder follows so quickly it shakes the house. The sensation of the floor moving under my feet reminds me of an earthquake I was in once, in Chile. Shivers of movement climbing my legs, coiling in my gut. It feels the very same.

I know who they hired, of course I do. It is my business to know these things.

He is the best, which is difficult for me to say. It's hard to admit that you may not be the most accomplished expert at what you do. But I'm a realist, and it's the truth. I have no reason to hide it from you. It's not so much that he's better than me, more a matter of his experience. He is the legend. He is the west wind. He is the assassin no one knows, no one has ever seen.

And he is coming for me. He is the only one who can.

I've reinforced the doors and windows, put a stock of weapons at hand in each room, places I will know where to look, but he won't. I don't plan to go down without a fight.

I shift, slightly. I've been in position for over an hour now. I hope I won't have to wait much longer.

The lights flicker again, then extinguish. I'm plunged into darkness. Lightning flashes in secondary increments, almost a strobe of energy, allowing me to see the huddled figured at the base of my Ponderosa stand.

It is time. He has come.

I palm my two weapons and spin away from the window. He will come in through the guest room, two floors below. I've left the window cracked to make his break-in easier.

Four paces to my left is a small alcove; to the right, the cavernous space of my office, the top room of the house: cool in the summer, warm in the winter. I hate to give the room up. I bought this house specifically because I knew I'd enjoy spending time in this bucolic space, the windows overlooking both the valley and the mountains. But I will have to leave it all behind. Once this is done, I will run, far, and they will never find me again.

I step into the shadows of the alcove, knowing the darkness hides me from sight.

I hear footsteps on the stairs. The third from the top, which creaks a single *screech* when you step to the side, is silent. He's been informed, my murderer. He knows how to approach silently, to catch me by surprise.

Truly, he is a professional.

Two more steps and he'll be in my sights. My hands don't shake. The guns are steady, pointed at where I know his heart will be. Center mass. Take him down before he can take me out. And then I'll run.

"Honey?"

I fumble the weapons. My heart, already beating ten times its normal pace, stops cold.

It is not my time after all. It is my husband.

I step out into the room, holster one weapon in the small of my back. The other I let drift to my side, hidden behind my leg.

"Robert? Jesus, I almost shot you. What the hell are you doing here? I thought you were in Seattle." I go to him, kiss his neck. He buries his nose in my hair. His arms wrap around me, pulling me close. He is damp, windblown, smelling of heather and pine.

Part his natural scent, part the storm. I pull back to look out the window again. Had I been seeing things? Was the man at the pine stand a figment of my imagination?

"This storm is terrible. And here you are, stuck alone in the dark."

"It is terrible. So loud I didn't hear your car."

"Honey, I called three times. You didn't get my messages?"

"The lines are down, Robert. All the bloody lights have blown, the whole valley is in the dark."

"Of course it is. Mountain power has never been able to sustain a storm like this." He grins, a pirate in the darkness, his teeth flashing white in the lightning's reflection. "We really should put in a generator. Where are the candles?"

I laugh, my voice still shaky, scared at how close I've come to murdering my very own husband. I put the second gun down, cover it with a magazine. I will move it when he steps away. "You know where they are. In my top desk drawer. Though I'm enjoying the darkness. I was watching the lightning. It's so beautiful."

I want to tell him the truth. *I must continue watching for the assassin who's been sent to eliminate me from this earth. And now I must protect you, as well.* But the words die in my throat. I don't like to show fear in front of my husband. It makes him uncomfortable. My power has always been my ability to be emotionless in the face of fear and danger. It is something I trained for and manifest daily. One has to in my line of work.

A thunderous *boom* from outside. The flick of a match. The room glows in an eerie, weak light.

I see Robert, lit by the blunt stub of wax, holding my 9 mm Glock. It is pointed at my chest.

The thoughts come clear and vicious.

How is this possible? How could I have not known? How could I have missed this?

A realization.

It is the only way they could make it happen.

I would never drop my guard, except for the man with whom I

share a life, share a bed. He is the man I love, the man I thought I knew. I was wrong. So very, very wrong.

Robert is the legend. He is the wind.

He is vengeance, and he has come for me.

I don't move. I don't try to flee. I stand with arms stretched aside my body, back straight, head back, a supplicant on the cross. A betrayal this deep, this sharp, is nothing to be recovered from. Deep down I know my immobility is shock, and disappointment, and treachery, but the surface thoughts render me mute and useless. My death is surety for their safety. I die so they can live.

Tenderness, fleeting, crosses his face. "I love you," he says. There are no tears of regret in his voice. It is calm and clinical. Sincere, but simple.

"You'll never find them," I reply.

"We already did," he says, and fires.

I hardly flinch when the bullet enters my chest, piercing my heart. I feel nothing.

ABOUT THE STORY

This short was written in Colorado during, yes, you guessed it, a massive thunderstorm. My overactive imagination kicked in when I saw a shadow on the hill behind the house, and my reluctant assassin on the road to being terminated was born. It began as a flash fiction piece, just a quick and dirty story, but has been expanded, and is definitely part of something bigger. Thematically, assassins run through much of my work; they are Byronic heroes, people who do the wrong thing for the right reasons. It's always a shame when one has to die, especially one who's seen the light.

WHERE'D YOU GET THAT RED DRESS?

I walk down South Congress, my heels tapping on the pavement. Saturday night in Austin, there's always something for a girl to do. I stop at the door to the Continental Club, look at the marquee.

Matinee, Richard Stooksbury. A Tennessee boy. I've missed that show by a mile. *Headliner, 10:00 P.M., James McMurtry.* Oh hell, yes.

I walk through the doors and into the darkened bar. The first thing I notice is the red velvet curtain hanging over the stage, the oval *CONTINENTAL* sign branding the space. McMurtry is up there, making jokes about being a beer salesman and asking people to buy the new CD because he forgot to remind them last night. The mood is jovial, and I swing into it effortlessly.

I take the last stool at the bar and order a dirty martini. The bass guitar whaps in time with my heart, deep and pure. My head nods involuntarily. The song ends; McMurtry launches into another. I listen with my eyes closed, sipping the cool, salty gin.

"Where'd you get that red dress?"

He croons the words, and I open my eyes, look at my breasts.

Well.

It's like he's speaking directly to me. I am wearing a red dress. The refrain courses again.

"Where'd you get that red, dress?"

I giggle.

Where, indeed?

Any woman will tell you there are few purchases that stay with you forever. There is a certain dress, one meant to be worn only once, made of silk or taffeta or satin. White. Pure. Perfect. You wear it for a few hours, then package it up, stuff it in the top of a closet and hope that sometime, someone might want to wear it again.

I had a dress like that. It reached the ground and dragged behind me, pulling on my legs until I thought I'd scream. I wore it and said the words, teared up at the appropriate moments, smiled when I was kissed. Ate food and drank champagne and danced and loved every moment of it. Then it was time to say goodbye.

He took me to the nicest hotel Austin had to offer, checked us into the presidential suite. Had chocolate covered strawberries delivered, popped the cork on a bottle of '87 Dom Perignon. Made love to me on satin sheets, relieving me of my virginity with care.

Now I'm lying. That's not really what happened. I wish it were.

To be honest, he took me to the Holiday Inn downtown, forced me on the bed, ripped my precious dress, and pummeled me until he came. Then he fell asleep and snored. It wasn't how I envisioned my first time.

But I knew who I was marrying. I was prepared for our wedding night.

I went to my overnight bag and retrieved the knife.

I just wish I'd remembered to take off the dress before I cut his throat.

The gods were smiling upon me though, because the corner 7-Eleven had plenty of those precious little dye packets, the kind you use for multicolored rubber banded t-shirts.

Back in the dingy hotel room, I dumped three packets of Deepest Rosso in a bathtub full of hot water. I placed my perfect white dress in the vermilion water and left it for an hour. Had a nice big glass of whiskey I poured from his silver flask.

It was time.

A few snips with some scissors, both the dress and my hair, five minutes with the hairdryer, and I was an elegant woman in a red dress, ready for a night on the town.

He was surprisingly heavy for a slight man. Getting him in the tub was a bitch. I sawed at his wrists a few times, made it look like he tried there first. I only spilled a few drops.

I kissed his forehead before I left.

" 'Till death do us part" just got a whole lot shorter.

ABOUT THE STORY

Music tends to inspire stories in me, and this is probably the best example. James McMurtry has a song called "Red Dress," and my husband and I take long drives in the country and play the rest of McMurty's album, *Saint Mary of the Woods*. I must say, the album is quite an excellent road companion. We must have played "Red Dress" a hundred times, but one day, riding over the railroad tracks, it hit me: where did she get that red dress, really?

A story was born, one tinged with my brand of dark humor. She got the dress honestly, I'll give her that.

KILLING CAROL ANN

I've just killed Carol Ann. Sweet, innocent Carol Ann. Her blond hair flows down her back and trails in the spreading pool of blood. Oh, God. What have I done?

I've known Carol Ann for nearly my whole life. Every memory from my childhood is permeated by the blonde angel who moved in across the street when I was five or so. Skipping up the street after the ice cream truck; getting lost in the shadows during a game of hide and seek; watching her sit in the window of her pink room, brushing that glorious hair. We were two peas in a pod, two sides of the same coin. Best friends, forever. Forever just turned out to be an awfully long time.

Our relationship started as benignly as you'd expect. I'd seen the moving truck leave, knew that a family had taken the Estes' house. When Mrs. Estes died, she left her son with bills and a dozen cats. I missed the cats. I'd wondered about the family, then went back to my own world.

Carol Ann spied me sitting on our front step, twirling my fingers through the dandelions in the flowerbeds. Mama had sent me out to pluck the poor, insignificant weeds from the ground, worried they'd ruin her prized flowers. Mama's flowerbeds were a local legend. The best in three states. At least that's what the members of the garden club said about them. They were full to the brim with the heady blooms of gardenias, azaleas, jasmine, roses, sweet peas, hydrangea, daylilies, iris, rhododendrons, ferns, fertile clumps of monkey grass, a smattering of black-eyed Susans… the list went on and on. A green thumb, Mama had. She could make any flower grow and peak under her watchful gaze. All but me, that is. Her Lily.

I was crying about something that day; I don't remember what. It was past ninety degrees, a sweltering summer afternoon. A shadow cast darkness across my right foot. The sudden shade caused my skin to cool, so I looked up to see what had caused it. A strange girl stood on the sidewalk in front of the A-frame house I grew up in. A yellow-haired goddess. When she spoke, I felt a rush of love.

"Hey, girl," she said. "Would you like to play?"

"Do I wanna play?" I answered, suddenly numb with fright. I'd never had a playmate before. Most folks' kids steered clear of me. Mama's garden club friends didn't bring their spawn to visit with me while they played canasta under the billowing tent in the backyard. The nearest child to my age lived down the street—a bed-ridden boy who smelled funny and coughed constantly. Mama made me go over there once, but after I screamed as loud as I could and pulled his hair, she didn't make me go back. There was no one else to play with.

"Are you simple or something?" the girl asked.

"Simple?"

"Oh, never mind." She turned her back and started away toward the river, skipping every third step.

She wore a white dress with a pink ribbon tied with a big bow in the back—the kind I'd only ever wear on Easter, to go to church with Mama. Even from behind, the girl was perfect.

"Wait!"

My voice rang as true and strong as it ever had, deep as a church bell. She stopped, dead in her tracks, and turned to me slowly. Her eyes were wide, bluer than Mama's china teapot. Then she smiled.

"Well. Who knew you'd sound like that? I'm Carol Ann. It's nice to meet you."

She strode to me, her hand raised. I'd never shaken hands with a girl my age before. It struck me as awfully romantic. She grasped my hand in hers, the grip strong as a man's.

"How do," I mumbled.

"Now, is that any way to greet your dearest friend?" Her voice had a lilt to it, southern definitely, but something foreign, too. She squeezed my hand a little harder, her little fingers pinching mine.

"That hurts. Stop it." I tried to shake loose, but she was like a barnacle I'd seen on Tappy's boat once. Tappy took care of the rest of the yard for us. He wasn't allowed to touch the flowerbeds, but someone had to mow and weed and prune. Mama could grow grass like nobody's business, too.

"Not until you do it right. My God, am I going to have to teach you manners as well as how to bathe?"

She wrinkled her nose at me, and I realized how sweet she smelled. Just like Mama's flowers. I was lost. I looked her straight in those china blue eyes, my dull brown irises meeting hers. I cleared my throat, but I didn't smile.

"It's nice to meet you as well."

She dropped my hand then and laughed, a tinkling, musical sound like wind chimes on a breezy afternoon. She had me enthralled in a moment.

"Let's go skip rocks in the river."

"I'm not allowed. Mama says—"

"Oh, you're one of *those*."

My hackles rose. "One of what?" Two minutes and we were having our first fight. It should have been a warning. Instead it made my blood boil.

She smiled coyly. "A mama's girl."

Back then, I thought it was an insult. I reached out to smack her one good, but she pranced away, closer to the river with each skip.

"Mama's girl, Mama's girl." She sing-songed and danced, and I followed, my chin set, incensed. Before I knew it, we were in front on the river, a whole block away from Mama's house. I wasn't allowed to go to the river. A boy drowned the summer past, no one I really knew, but all the grown-ups decided it wasn't safe for us to play down there. This girl was new; she wouldn't know any better. But if I told her that we couldn't be here, she'd start that ridiculous chant again. I didn't want to be a Mama's girl anymore.

We skipped rocks until dinnertime. Mama skinned my hide that night. She'd called and called for me to come to dinner, had Tappy look for me. Carol Ann and I were too busy to hear. We skipped rocks, whistled through pieces of grass turned sideways between our thumbs, and dug for worms. I showed her how to bait a line, and she'd nearly fainted dead away when I put a warm, wriggling worm in her hand.

Tappy found us right after sunset, took me home screaming over his shoulder. The joy I felt wouldn't be suffused by Mama's switch. Never again. I had a friend, and her name was Carol Ann.

It was the first of many concessions to her whims.

"My goodness, Lily, can't you try to look happy? You're all sweet and clean, and we'll have some ice cream after, if you're good. All right?"

"Yes, ma'am," I mumbled, sullen.

Mama had me spit-shined and polished for a funeral service at church. I didn't want to go. I wanted to run off to the river with Carol Ann, skip rocks, have a spitting contest, something. Anything but go to church, sit in those hard pews, and listen to Preacher yell at the old folks who couldn't sing loud enough because their voices were caked with age and rot.

I didn't think that was fair to them. I remember my Granny vaguely, who smelled like our attic and had a long hair poking out of her chin. She'd scoop me in her arms and sing to me, her voice soft like the other old folks. I liked that, liked to hear them whisper the words. It made the hymns seem dangerous in a way. Like the old folks knew the dead would reach out of their very graves and grab their hands, pull them down into the earth with them if they sang loud enough to wake them.

Mama wasn't hearing *no* for an answer today. We walked the quarter mile to the Southern Baptist, greeted our brothers and sisters, sat in the hard pews and celebrated the death of Mrs. O'Leary. Preacher made sure we knew that we were sinners, and I felt that vague guilt that I was alive and Mrs. O'Leary was dead, though it was supposed to be glorious to have passed to the better side.

We finished up and put Mrs. O'Leary in the ground. I tried hard to hold my breath in the graveyard so no spirits could inhabit me, but the graveside service took so long I had to breathe. I took small sips of air through my nose, felt my vision blacken. Mama pinched my upper arm so hard I gasped.

I gave up trying to hold my breath. All the ghosts had been waiting, watching, patiently hovering, anticipating the moment when I took in a full breath of air. They were inside me now; they inhabited my soul, tumultuous and gray. I tried to fight them, until I couldn't find any more reason to.

I begged to be allowed to go home, to be with Carol Ann, but Mama kept a firm grip on my arm while I cried. Folks thought I was grieving for Mrs. O'Leary. I was grieving for myself.

Mama decided homemade ice cream was just as good as the Dairy Dip, after all.

One day a massive storm came through. The trunks of the trees were black with wet, the leaves in green bas-relief to the long-boned branches. Storms frightened me—the ferocity of the winds, the booming thunder felt like it was tearing apart my very skin, shattering my soul. Carol Ann and I had taken refuge in my room. She rubbed my stomach, trying to calm me, crooning under her breath. Nothing was working. I was shaking and sweaty, low moans escaping my lips every once in a while. Carol Ann was at a loss. She stood, leaving me on the floor, and went to the window.

"Come away from there, Carol Ann." My voice sounded panicky, even to me. She turned and smiled.

"Don't be a goose, Lily. What, do you think the wind's going to suck me right out that window?"

A flash of lightning lit up the room, and the thunder shook the house. I whimpered in response, my eyes begging her to come back to me. She turned and stared out the window, ignoring my pleas.

Then she whirled around, a wide smile on her heart-shaped face. "I have an idea. Let's be blood sisters."

"Blood sisters? What's that?"

"What? You've never been blood sisters with anyone before, Lily? My goodness, where have you been hiding all these years?"

"There's no one to be blood sisters with, Carol Ann. You know that." I felt vaguely superior for a moment, but she ended that.

"We need a knife."

"Why?"

"My Lord in heaven, Lily, how do you think we're going to get at the blood?"

So I snuck out of my room, slunk down the stairs, gripping each one with my toes so the wind didn't whisk me away when it tore the roof off the house. The storm was loud enough that Mama didn't hear me go into the kitchen, get a knife from the rack next to the stove, and make my way back up the stairs to my room.

Carol Ann's eyes lit up when she saw the boning knife, the six-inch blade sharpened to a razor's edge.

"Give that to me."

I did, a sense of wrongness making my hand tremble. I think I knew deep in my heart that Mama wouldn't want me becoming blood sisters with anyone, no matter what the course of action that led me there. But that was Carol Ann for you. She could always convince me to see things her way.

Carol Ann took one of my sheer cotton sweaters, a red one, and laid it over the lamp, so the light fragmented like a lung's pink froth and the room became like thin blood. We sat in the middle of the floor, Indian-style, facing each other. She made sure our legs were touching. I was scared.

"Okay. Stop fretting. This will only hurt for a second, then it will be all over. You still want to be my blood sister, right?"

I swallowed hard. Would this make us one? I didn't want that. No, I didn't want that at all. A tiny corner of my mind said, *Go find Mama, let Carol Ann do this by herself.*

"I think so," I answered instead.

"You think? Now Lily, what did I say about you thinking? That's what I'm here for. I do the thinking for both of us, and everything always turns out just fine. Now quit being such a baby and give me your arm. Your right arm."

I didn't want Carol Ann to think I was a baby. I held out my arm, which only shook for a second.

Carol Ann was mumbling something, an incantation of sorts. Then she held up the knife and smiled.

"With this blade, I christen thee." She ran the blade along the inside of her right arm, bright red blood blooming in the furrows created in her tender flesh. She smirked, a joyous glow lighting her translucent skin, and took my arm. The point of the knife dug into the crook of my elbow. "Say it," she hissed.

"With this blade, I christen thee." My voice shook. She drew the knife along my arm, and I almost fainted when I saw the blood, dark red, much darker than Carol Ann's. Then she took my arm and her arm and held them together. We stood, attached, and walked in a circle, eyes locked, blood spilling into each other.

"Our blood mingles, and we become one. You are now as much Carol Ann as I am, and I am as much Lily as you are. We are one, sisters in blood."

Redness slipped down my elbow. Spots danced merrily in my vision.

Carol Ann's eyes sparkled. "Quick, we need to tie this together, let our blood flow through each other's veins as our hearts beat together."

She grabbed a sock off the floor and wound it around our arms, dabbing at the rivulets before they splashed on the floor of my bedroom, then beckoned me to lay down next to her. I put my head in her lap, my arm stretched and tied to hers, and she held me as our blood became one. I felt at peace. The ferocity of the storm seemed to lessen, and I felt calm, sleepy even.

"Lily!" The scream made me jump. It was Mama. She saw what Carol Ann and I had done. I didn't care. I was tired. It was too much trouble to worry about the beating I was going to get.

I didn't get to see Carol Ann the rest of that muggy summer. Mama sent me away to a white place that smelled of antiseptic and urine. I hated it.

I came back from the white place in the fall, quieter, more watchful than before. The leaves were red and orange and brown, the skies were crisp and blue. I was worried that Carol Ann may have moved away; the drive was empty across the street, the window dark. When I asked Mama, she told me to quit it already. No more talk of Carol Ann. I wasn't allowed to see her, to play with her anymore.

I went back to school that year. Mama had been keeping me home before, teaching me herself, but she figured it was time for me to leave the nest. I needed to be around more girls and boys my age. I was so happy that she sent me to school at last, because Carol Ann was there. She had moved, but only a couple of streets over. She was zoned to the junior high, just like I was.

We didn't exactly pick up where we had left off. Carol Ann had many other friends now. But I'd catch her watching me as I stood on the periphery of her group of devotees, and she'd wink at me in welcome.

Those moments warmed my heart and soul. She was still my Carol Ann, even though I shared her with my classmates.

The school year progressed without incident until Carol Ann came up with a new game. The pass-out game. Every girl in school wanted to be a part of it. We'd line up in the bathrooms, stand with our backs against the wall, hold our breath until the world got spinny. Carol Ann would cover our hearts with her hands and push. Hard. We'd pass out cold, some sliding down the walls, some keeling over. Carol Ann reasoned that it stopped our hearts for a moment, and in that brief time we could see God. That's why the teachers got so upset when they found out.

Of course, they found out when I was doing the heart pushing on a seventh-grader named Jo. I got suspended, and the fun stopped. No more pass-out game. No more Carol Ann, at least until I wasn't grounded any more.

They rezoned us for ninth grade, decided we were big enough to go to high school. I had to take the bus, which I normally hated, because it drove past the Johnsons' farm, and their copse of pine trees with the hanging man in them. I knew it wasn't a real dead man, but the branches in one of the trees had died, and they drooped brown against the evergreen—arms, legs, torso and broken neck. Mama used to drive me to Doctor Halloway on this route, ignoring my requests to go the long way past Tappy's place. I hated this road as a young girl, just knew the Hanging Man would climb out of that tree and follow me home.

When the bus would pass it by, I'd try not to look. Since I was a little older now, it wasn't so bad in the daylight. But as winter came along and the days shortened, the Hanging Man waited for me in the dusky gloom. He spoke to me, the deadness of the pine needles brown and dusty like a grave.

The next year, Carol Ann started taking the bus. Life got better. She was only on it some days, because she had a lot of dates now. Some days, after school, I'd watch Carol Ann riding off in cars with shiny, clean boys, throwing a grin over her shoulder as they faded into the gloaming. But there were times that she'd come out of the school, clothes rumpled, mouth red and raw, scabs forming on her knees. She'd jump on the bus just before it pulled away from the curb and wouldn't want to talk.

But mostly, we sat together in the back, those idyllic days, talking about boys and teachers, the upcoming dances and who was *doing it*. I knew Carol Ann was. You could tell that about her. I was fascinated by sex, though I'd never experienced it. Carol Ann promised to tell me all about it.

She snuck vodka from her parents' house and slipped it into her milk some mornings. She's share the treat with me, and we'd get boneless in the back of the bus, giggling our fool heads off. She taught me how to make a homemade scar tattoo, using the initials of a boy I liked. She took the eraser end of a pencil and ran it up and down her arm a million times until a shiny raw burn in the shape of a *J* appeared. She handed the pencil to me, and I tore at my skin until a misaligned *M* welled blood. I have that *M* to this day. I don't remember which boy it was for.

The bus driver, Mrs. Bean, caught us with the vodka–laced milk. Carol Ann wasn't allowed to ride the bus anymore. I didn't see her as much after that. I think the school and Mama really did their best to keep us apart. It was probably a wise decision. But I felt incomplete without her at my side.

Now that I'm grown, away from Mama's house, away from Carol Ann, I remember the little things.

Spilling on Carol Ann's bike, scraping the length of my thigh on the gravel. The Halloween night she pushed me into the cactus while we were trick-or-treating. The day I nearly drowned when I fell through the ice on Gideon's Lake, and she laughed watching me panic before she went for help. Carol Ann did nothing but get me in trouble, and as an adult, I was happy to leave her behind.

So you can imagine my shock and surprise when the doorbell rang, late one evening, and I opened the door to find Carol Ann, standing on my front step. Somewhere, deep inside me, I knew something was dreadfully wrong.

I live in the A-frame house I grew up in. Mama's been in a home over in Spring Hill for a couple of years now. They have nice flowerbeds, and I visit her often. We walk amongst the flowers, and she reminds me of all the terrible things I did when I was a kid. No one thought I'd ever grow out of my awkward stage, but I did. I went off to college and everything. Carol Ann went to a neighboring school.

I'd see her every once in a while, working as a waitress in one of the coffee shops on campus, or shopping in the bookstore. I learned that it was best to ignore her. If I ignored her enough, she'd get the hint and leave me alone.

But here she was, in the flesh, rain streaming down her face. Her blond hair was shorter, wet through, darker than I remembered.

She was a skinny thing, not the radiant beauty I remember from my childhood.

I was frozen at the door, unsure of what to do. She knew better than to come calling; that was strictly forbidden. We'd laid those ground rules years before, and she'd always listened.

I was saved by the phone ringing. I glared at her and motioned for her to stay right where she was. Carol Ann was not invited into my house. Not after what she did all those years ago. It had taken me forever to get over that.

The phone kept trilling, so I left her there, the door open to the night, and went to the marble side table in the foyer, the one that held the old-fashioned rotary dial. I picked it up, almost carelessly. It was Mama's nurse at the Home.

I listened.

Felt the floor rushing up to meet me.

Everything went dark after that.

When I woke, the sun was streaming in the kitchen window. Somehow I'd gotten myself to a chair. There was coffee brewing, the rich scent wafting to my nose.

Carol Ann stood at the counter, a yellow cup in her hands. She took a deep drink, then smiled at me.

"Hey, stranger." Her voice was soft, that semi-foreign lilt more pronounced, like she'd been living overseas lately.

"Hey, yourself," I replied. "You're not supposed to be here."

"You needed me." She'd shrugged, a lock of lank blond falling across her forehead. "I'm sorry about your mama. She was a good woman."

I had a vision of Mama then, standing in the same spot, her hair in curlers, rushing to finish the preparations for a garden club meeting, stopping to lean back and take a sip of hot, sweet tea and smiling to herself because it was perfect. She was perfect. Mama was always perfection personified. Not flawed and messy like me. My heart hurt.

I forced myself to do the right thing. To do what needed to be done. My heart broke a little, and my head swam when I said, "Carol Ann, you need to leave. I don't need you. I never did."

She looked down at the floor, then met my eyes. Tears glistened in the corners, making the cornflower blue look like a wax crayon.

"C'mon, Lily. We're blood sisters, you and I. We're a physical part of each other. How can you say you don't need a part of yourself? The best part of yourself? I make you strong. I've always made you strong. You need me."

"No!" I screamed at her, all patience gone. "You are not a part of me. You aren't… "

A fury I hadn't felt in years bubbled through my chest. There was only one way to get through to her. I grabbed the porcelain mug from her hand, smashed it on the counter, and swiped a gleaming shard across her perfect white throat.

She fell in a heap, blood everywhere.

As I stood over her, watching her blond hair turn strawberry, I felt a tug and looked down at my leg. Carol Ann was trying to grab a hold of my foot. I kicked her instead, hard, in the ribs. She stopped moving then.

The thought is fleeting. *What have I done?*

I've just killed Carol Ann. She was never sweet, never innocent. She was a leech, an albatross around my neck. I didn't need her. Carol Ann needed me. That's what Doctor Halloway always told me. That's what they said in the hospital, too. The white place, so pristine, so calm. They told me I'd know when the time was right to get rid of Carol Ann once and for all.

Mama would be so proud. She knew I didn't need Carol Ann; knew I was strong enough to live on my own. She always believed in me. I miss her.

The blood drips… drips… drips… from my arm. I feel lighter already.

ABOUT THE STORY

This is possibly the most autobiographical story I've ever written. There is a song by a friend of mine called "Carol Ann"—it's a love story, about a man who comes home to find his woman, asks her to put up her hair and take a drive with him. With Mr. Stooksbury's foreknowledge, I used the name and twisted the story around until the beautiful temptress Carol Ann was unrecognizable. But was she? Where I grew up, off a dirt road in the wilds of Colorado, there was a girl who pushed me to act out, to do things well outside my comfort zone. In twisting the good Carol Ann into the bad Carol Ann, I was surprised when this story emerged.

Carol Ann had become a vivid embodiment of the girl who I used to love to hate. She's gone now, sadly, a victim of suicide. Her tortured soul could never find peace on this earth. And that's a true shame, because she had a spark unlike any girl I've ever known. Had she been happy, had she known love, perhaps things would have turned out differently for her. "Killing Carol Ann" is dedicated to the memory of that girl, Noelle Holt, and all the crazy adventures we had.

X

I watched X tidy up the kitchen. The routine was familiar, comforting in its mundane, expected way. Every night, she cleans up before she goes to bed. Oh, we won't even talk about that.

I've been in that kitchen, of course. Smelled the warm aroma of clean, seen the knives lined up like tin soldiers. Each appliance in its place, each tool, each spoon, all in perfect harmony in her kitchen.

Spotless, sterile. Unlike her, actually. X is warm, strong, caring, loving. I know this because… well, I just know. Dammit, don't doubt me. I just do.

She's smiling now, and the warmth passing through my body is nearly uncontainable. It's as if she's looked me straight in the eye, her smile an arrow through my heart… oh, I see. X's cat has jumped onto the counter, is flicking its tail under her perfectly formed chin. She runs her hand along the kitty's back, purses her lips in a croon, then grabs her around the middle and sweeps her onto the floor. Okay, so I know the cat is a girl. Yes, I know her name. It's Pumpkin, which, if truth be told, I find a bit beneath this particular woman. Surely a creature so exotic, so perfect can come up with a more original name. But that really makes no difference. All that matters is X, and what matters to her matters to me.

The idiot creature had gotten out for an instant, slunk out the back door when X had her head turned. X had flown onto the deck, screamed "Pumpkin!" with such a note of panic in her voice that I had to stop and stare. How could she care so much for such an inconsequential creature? The cat must have sensed it as well, for she froze in the fallen leaves, glanced about once or twice, then turned and scurried back up the stairs and straight into the house.

I watched as X stood, hand to her throat, chest heaving slightly, the crisis averted. She looked at me, unrealizing, then returned indoors, barring the door securely behind her. An unlocked door or window would never lead me to this prize. X is too smart to be careless like that. A challenge, to say the least.

It began so simply. Just a brief flash of a smile, no teeth showing, lips in a tight line that curved up at the corners of her mouth. Gray-blue eyes snapped my direction, then slid away before she actually focused on me, saw me. She walked so tall, her ponytail bouncing as she stepped lightly toward her car. The day was warm, and she was dressed for the gym, long legs and Nikes. I stepped close enough to catch her scent—she was coming *from*, rather than going *to*. I imagined her there, glistening beneath the television sets. The deep richness of her scent invaded my senses permanently. I was lost. I knew at that moment I had to have her.

Even now, all I have to do is conjure that image, and she's there, in me, with me.

Watching was enough, at first. I wondered what she thought about in those unguarded moments. Lost in a task, staring out the window, was X dreaming of me? Wishing for the slight edge that's missing from her life?

The neighborhood dogs are a nightmare. They bark and bark. It's like being in a kennel. Are they yapping at me? Perhaps. Maybe they're just so stupid that the slightest scent, the tiniest whisper of a breeze catches their imaginations, and they respond as only a dog can, with immediate and incessant barking. There is one in particular, a deep-throated WOOF that I know drives X mad. I hear the dog start and see her roll her eyes, wondering how long the stupid beast will go on. Sometimes it will bark for hours, the chorus of hounds around the rest of the neighborhood chiming in for a midday serenade. I can tell it annoys her. I can only do one thing. If it will make my love happy, I will do it now.

The screaming is unbearable. Oh, how could X misconstrue my gift? I don't mean to scare her. Dear God, I love her! I want her. I need her.

Apparently all the women in the neighborhood have been on edge. I hear them whispering to X. They don't feel safe. They are afraid of what lurks in the night. They are afraid of me.

I hear the men talking amongst themselves. They don't want to scare the wives.

"What kind of animal could do such a thing?"

"Must have been a bear. That pack of coyotes has been hanging around, but that's a big dog to have been taken down by them."

"A bear, in these woods? We're residential on three sides. Do you really think one could get this far into town?"

"I'd think anything is possible. They get hungry enough, they'll go where the food is."

"But if it was a bear, it didn't eat the dog. Just tore it up."

"Maybe it was injured, saw the dog as a threat and attacked."

On cue, the group stared at me, lurking in their woods. They didn't see me, of course. But I shifted a bit, sending the birds on the limb next to me catapulting into the air, just to let them know I'm here.

It was when X saw me, that first time, when her eyes grew wide and her hand went to her mouth to stifle a scream, or perhaps a knowing smile. That's when the men congregated again, and decided to end my days.

I'll never forget how stunning she was at that moment.

She'd come to the fencerow to plant some bulbs.

She had a basket filled with tulips, hyacinths and paper whites, was wearing a soft oyster-colored fleece vest that complemented the shade of her eyes, sensible gardening shoes covering her bare feet.

It was warming so nicely during the day. Who could blame her for wanting to get out, to breathe in the fresh air, to taste the forthcoming softness on the breeze?

Winter was finally passing, and it hadn't been mild. Not that I minded—just the sight of her behind those quarter-paned windows had given me warmth and strength.

But to have her here in the flesh, while delightful, was unexpected.

I admit I didn't handle the encounter well. All these months, waiting for the perfect opportunity, and when it presented itself… I ran. Our eyes met, and I panicked. Thrashed off into the woods, making enough noise that the replacement dog next door started a howling cadence and was immediately matched with four other wails, one of which came from deep within X's beautiful breast. I turned for a moment in my flight and saw her back, fleeing into the safety of the house. Damn.

So our idyllic time came to an end. The men returned, this time armed. They forced their way into the forest. Found my camp. Poked through my belongings. Admitted to themselves that there was no way a bear could have made such a spectacular fire pit and hearth. But I was gone, well ahead of them. I wouldn't be back anytime soon. Give them some time to get over it. Let them call the police, search the area. Realize that I'm no longer there.

I will bide my time. X is worth it. I want her so much. I just can't live without her.

And now, I don't have to. There are new windows, a new kitchen, but everything is as it was. We're just in a new town, with new woods.

I am every bump in her night. Every creak of a pipe. I am the hair that sticks up on the back of her neck. The unexplained feeling of dread that overwhelms her, making her glance over her shoulder. I am her nightmares and her day terrors. Every time a dog barks, she knows it is because they sense my presence.

And I love her so very, very much.

ABOUT THE STORY

"X" was my very first published short story. It originally appeared in *Demolition Magazine's* Women of Crime Fiction issue back in 2006. I'd originally written it for a contest, one that wanted the basis of the story to focus on something dark living in the woods. I started it with some ironic humor, and the creature in the woods was actually a bear. But the sentience I created was so startling, so freaky, that when I looked outside and thought about that particular bear living in my woods, it gave me goose bumps. That's when I realized I was dealing with something much, much scarier than a four-legged animal.

This story has been published several times, including once in *Nashville Lifestyles* magazine in a stunning display spread, a black background with a small well-lit house on the edge of a forest. Fitting, really, because I draw on fairy tales heavily in my novels. Red Riding Hood better watch out.

THE NUMBER OF MAN

In the endless moonlight, the road was a ribbon of black, cut by a band of light two feet wide that disappeared into an unfathomably dark puddle of water. The rain drifted in and out on dark clouds, briefly inking out the moon. After twenty minutes of playing hide and seek, the showers began in earnest, drumming the ground, rhythmic, eternal.

His footsteps splashed across the pavement. A soda vapor bulb snapped on as he passed, its humming as familiar as his own breath. Newly formed puddles shimmered in the glow, but shadows still tore at the meager light. Away from the building, the luminescence bled away like a tail from a comet, trickling into nothingness.

He needed to hurry. He was running late. He couldn't miss her. It wouldn't do.

The familiar mix of shame and desire pulsed through him, a ragged tattoo in time with his steps, and he smiled.

It began in a single moment, the briefest of connections. She, in pigtails, a miniature towheaded autocrat, ruling the playground as if it were her kingdom. He, sitting desultory and resigned on the swings, the new boy, watching her cross the playground toward him, shoulders squared, prepared for battle. He was an outsider, an unknown, and therefore dangerous, and she needed to determine his loyalties. Though only eight years old, he had been at the receiving end of this conversation several times; his mother wasn't the most moral woman, had a tendency to fall immediately for a new man when her previous love discarded her, and followed her boyfriends from town to town. As such, he'd been the "new boy" too many times to count.

Imperious Caitlyn hadn't stopped walking when she reached him, just drove her shoulder into his and laughed as he lost his grip on the swing and toppled over backward. Her touch cut him to the bone, setting his arm on fire. She'd stood over him, fisted hands on narrow hips, her first words to him a demand that rang through him like a bell.

"What's your name?"

He'd thought about telling her the truth. Something about Caitlyn made him want to spill his heart onto the gravel. But he answered with the name he'd been given last night, when his mother deigned to give him a bath in the gritty, grimy motel tub, and explained how his life was now.

"Michael."

A penetrating look, one hard to fathom from an eight-year-old. As if Caitlyn saw through him, into him, and knew he was wicked.

He squirmed. He knew he was dirty. Unclean. Wrong. It was inside him, and no amount of scrubbing would loosen its hold on his soul. But he stood his ground and stared back, unmoving.

Her blue eyes pierced him. There was some ineffable movement behind the lashes as she decided his fate. He already knew she would find him wanting; the question was only how severe the punishment would be.

At long last, she nodded, curt as a judge.

"Fine. You can stay on the swings. *We're* going to play kickball." She turned, and her minions followed. As she sauntered away, giggling, he swore he heard Caitlyn whisper, "Stay away from me,

Michael."

He tried so very hard to listen.

Twenty years later, Michael stood in another lot, waiting for Caitlyn to notice him. He'd been waiting for a month, ever since he'd bumped into her unexpectedly. He, on his way to work. She, leaving hers after a hard day. Their footsteps tapped in time, echoing through the still night, sneakers and stilettos crossing the asphalt. Distracted by his ear buds, he'd nearly missed her. A flicker of shadow caught his attention, he raised his head… and there she was. Their eyes met across the darkened parking lot. They existed for a moment in the same plane, a man and a woman in this constant, perfect expanse. His breath came short. Panic, fear, and love all mingled together in his thoughts. She was still perfect. He was lost again.

He'd not been ready to see her again, not in person. She created such feelings in him, feelings he'd long ago abandoned as unworthy, incomprehensible for him. He should have spoken, said something charming, but instead, he ran, panic gripping his throat and permeating his bones.

But he came back.

He waited for her every night after that, from the shadows, not wanting to frighten her. He was shy, so afraid to approach her. He didn't know how she might react. Joy at seeing an old friend? Derision toward a lesser being? She was incandescent, and he was… Michael.

If she could only see him like she did when they were eight: just a scared young boy hoping to make a friend. She was too famous now, too important. She was always on her guard, would never let another being see inside her soul.

The Pixies screamed in his ears, words of numbers, of man and beast and heavens, and the death of all things, and he sang the chorus in his mind, knowing exactly what the song was telling him. The iPod was set to shuffle, and it was beyond fitting that this song, his anthem, had come on when he hit the Power button.

Traffic had been a nightmare tonight, aggravated by the teasing rains. He never thought he'd make it, but he did. Breath catching in his chest, heart pounding from the sudden exercise, he waited in the usual spot. Rain trickled down his forehead, running into his mouth, pooling in the collar of his shirt. He removed the ear buds, listened to the staccato snapping grow closer.

Caitlyn wasn't unaffected by the rain. She had matured into a full-fledged goddess, and with that designation came an understanding that what happened to mere mortals should not happen to her. She'd forgotten her umbrella, and he heard a trail of angry, hateful comments, but he ignored the bad language, tuned it out. A woman so ethereal could be forgiven anything, especially when she'd been caught unawares in a spring shower.

She passed right by him, didn't see him hovering in the gloom behind her car. He'd found that spot was ideal for watching.

Do it, Michael. Let her see you. Start your life together.

He saw tears tracing down her rose-tinged cheeks, and his heart broke for her.

He stood, quietly. He didn't want to startle her, send her crashing to her car in a panic.

She stopped, realizing she wasn't alone, and he froze. He was still deep in the shadows, unable to be seen, wanting so badly for her to know he was there.

Just talk to her, Michael. Just clear your throat and say hello. "Remember me? I've loved you forever..."

Her nostrils flared like an overgrown doe, as if she could smell his sweat, could taste it on the air. She glanced over her shoulder, then shook her head. He could see the thoughts run through her mind, could tell when she decided she'd been imagining things. But she covered the rest of the steps to her car quickly. The dome light flashed on, and she locked the doors of her BMW, a fitting vehicle for a creature so divine. Behind the wheel, she slammed her palms against the leather, and he saw tears again. Fury spilled into his gut. Whoever hurt her would pay.

After a few minutes, she started the car and drove away. He let her go. She'd be back tomorrow night. He would try again.

"I'm Caitlyn Kennedy, Channel 19 news. Good night, Huntsville."

"And you're smiling, you're smiling, now look at your notes, and... we're out."

Caitlyn removed the IFB from her left ear and scratched, pulling on her earlobe, trying to get the underwater sensation to dissipate. Thirty-five minutes plugged into the brain of a disembodied voice was hell on her equilibrium. When her ear finally popped, she set the IFB down on the desk, stood and brushed imaginary lint off her white skirt. Wardrobe was doing better these days, importing some of their merchandise straight from Nashville. She felt elegant in the Tahari skirt, the suit jacket tailored to nip in at the waist, the sleeveless grey shell under the jacket brought out of the grey in her blue eyes. A good combination. She made a mental note to thank Yuri, their wardrobe guru.

The disembodied voice became a series of steps, and a man materialized in front of her. Tom Stryc was their new news director, and she thought he was going to be a great asset to their little team.

"Hey, Caitie, good job tonight! You're gonna land the weekday anchor job if you keep this up."

"Thank you." She dimpled a smile at him, and he patted her arm before scooting off to his office, obviously distracted. *By what?* she wondered.

She was of two minds when it came to Tom. A young, enthusiastic director, he was breathing life into the station, shaking things up, encouraging the anchors and reporters to stretch themselves, to inject a modicum of personality into their live shots and extended reports. It was Huntsville, after all. The focus was on NASA and anything space related. The rest of their stories relied on crime and human interest, typical hometown news. That was fine with Caitlyn. She was earning her chops, anchoring on the weekend, ready to make the leap to a bigger market.

The problem was, the new director had an obvious crush on her. She wondered when he might work up the courage to ask her out, and whether she would accept. He was smart, decent-looking, and from her world. As a rule, she didn't date her bosses. Tom's predecessor felt it was his duty to sample the merchandise, and when Caitlyn didn't succumb to his advances, he'd stuck her with the most awful places and stories. In those days, she'd left the station cursing and crying more often than not. But thankfully, those days were over.

If she dated Tom, it would be as equals; she wouldn't say yes until she had the weekday slot. Then it would be both their jobs to make the station sing.

Intrigued by his distraction, she followed him to his office. He was tapping away on his computer. He didn't brighten when she appeared at his office door.

"Tom, is something wrong?"

He looked up, startled by her knock. "Oh, hey Caitie. You're sweet to notice. It's nothing, really. A family issue, not something I need to bother you with. Good job tonight. I'll see you tomorrow, okay? I need to, just… " He trailed off and looked back to his computer.

She felt dismissed, and rubbed her temples. She needed to get out of her makeup anyway. There was plenty of time to connect later.

The weekend crew hurried about, finishing their tasks. Once she was cleaned up and had changed, she took a slow walk around the studio, a hand trailing on the anchor desk. This was her station, her jumping off point. This is where she'd make her mark. This was her very own launch pad.

"Caitlyn, phone!"

A tech was standing by the anchor desk, where they actually had a working landline for call-ins. He dropped the phone on the desk, only mildly annoyed at being interrupted from his shut-down duties. Caitlyn smiled at him as she passed, took the phone and set it against her good ear.

"Yes?"

"Caitlyn Kennedy?"

The voice was male, deep, raspy. She could hear the wind whispering in the background.

"Who is this?" she asked.

The man chuckled. "I'm your biggest fan. I just wanted to let you know that I like the nude toenail polish better. That red is too garish for your coloring."

And he was gone. Caitlyn looked at the receiver, as if she could see the caller on the other end. Her brow furrowed in puzzlement. She glanced down, looking at her feet, the worn peep-toe Jimmy Choo pumps she'd bought on eBay and loved to wear. She'd gotten a pedicure last night, after she got off work. She'd done live shots for the five and six o'clock news shows, swung by the gym for a brief run, had a quick bite to eat and stopped by the salon— her typical Friday night.

And she had gone with red, feeling like a change.

She set the phone down. Great. She'd better tell Tom there was a whack job out there. The station got all sorts of strange, bizarre calls. It came with the territory. She dismissed the phone call from her thoughts, and went to her tiny cubbyhole office to see what was on deck for tomorrow's broadcast.

Twenty years, five months, and thirteen days after Michael and Caitie met, they had their first date. It took Michael hours to get up the courage to call, to let Caitlyn know he was in town again, that he wanted to see her. He needed some encouragement, something to get him in the mood. Michael was terribly shy. He didn't make it a practice to call women and ask to see them. He'd never mastered talking to an inanimate object and believing the person on the other end was real.

He made a lovely dinner—roast pork tenderloin with a mango chutney, asparagus with a lemon butter reduction, and garlic mashed potatoes. He was new to the wine scene, but with some help at his local store, he'd chosen a Shiraz from Western Australia. The wine had decanted half an hour before the meal was finished, an unnecessary step for such a young vintage, but it made him feel like an expert. The table was set with his grandmother's china, a lovely bone with etched fleur-de-lis. He'd found them at a pawn-shop in Austin, Texas. He'd remembered that etched fleur-de-lis and a small, gray woman who'd say, "This plate is fit for a king," on those rare special occasions when they used the fine dishes. Before. Before his father died. Before his mother became a trollop. Before the acrid scent of vodka permeated his world.

Now the dishes were used to serve a queen.

When the table was set, the candles lit, the wine poured into brilliantly clear globes of crystal, the food served, steaming and succulent, they focused on reconnecting. It was as Michael always dreamed. Caitlyn faced him, back straight, legs demurely crossed at the ankle under the table, a starched white linen napkin laid gently across her lap. Her manners were perfection, graceful and composed. She was a dream woman, in every respect. She told him about her day at work, the long hours, her dreams and aspirations. Over dessert—key lime pie—she confided how she wanted to move up the ladder, to be a full-time weekday anchor. Maybe get moved to a top thirty market. Maybe get to Atlanta or New York.

When he expressed dismay at the thought, she laughed that imperious laugh and said how happy she was that they had reconnected. He made her laugh. He could hardly believe how well things went.

She left shortly after dinner that night. He had plied her with a brandy, and she decided she was getting a bit tipsy. Michael was charmed. Reluctantly, he saw her to the door, sad to see her go, but invigorated by the realization that he was well and truly in love.

"Caitlyn, phone."

Caitlyn gritted her teeth, trying to quell the panic that filled her. Every bloody time she anchored, he called. It had been nearly a month now, of threats and strange platitudes, details of her off-camera life shared, so she'd know he was watching.

Tom insisted they take every precaution. She was rarely alone in the studio; someone always walked her to her car. The police had been brought in four times, and they were paying attention, but they couldn't seem to figure it out where the calls were coming from.

It was beyond an invasion of privacy. She was scared to death.

He'd been acting up lately, too. He became furious on the phone with her. He'd lash out in his displeasure, say cruel words meant to belittle and hurt.

He was getting to know more about her. Where she went on her Friday nights. Who she dined with during the week. That the report she'd done the week before some 200 miles away from Huntsville was falsely backlit because they'd been unable to get the live shot in front of the setting sun.

She varied her schedule as often as she could, but she couldn't afford the time it would take to drive across town to the other gym. There were two grocery stores she could frequent, so she switched it up. She changed nail salons five times.

She didn't want to be chased out of her life just because some nut job was stalking her. That's what Brave Caitlyn said. Inside, she was terrified. At the police's behest, she got new locks, installed a state-of-the-art security system. At Tom's insistence, she reported in whenever she went somewhere. At her mother's request, enrolled in a self-defense class, found out all the things she'd been doing wrong. It made her more fearful rather than less, and she quit.

Instead, she bought a gun. Hefting the cool weight of the metal in her hand was the only time she felt like she had control.

Michael and Caitlyn had been dating for a month when he decided he needed to tell her the truth. As with all new relationships, they'd been in the "getting to know you" phase. And now, he felt they were on strong enough footing that he could share a bit with her. And so he told her.

There were a few things he had issues with. His hypocrite mother always taught him that a lady was never brash, never put herself out there to grab attention. Caitlyn wasn't brash, not exactly, but she was drawing an awful lot of attention to herself lately, with all these people—these strangers—hovering around, and he didn't like it. She'd started off so demure and ladylike. Softly southern, feminine, so very interesting. He requested, kindly, that she focus less on herself, and more on him.

He was heartened by her response: Caitlyn was terribly distraught that she'd upset him. Promised to stop wearing those shorts out of the house, for starters. Not that he was jealous, not at all, but it just wasn't ladylike for her to leave those gorgeous long legs out for just anyone to stare at.

Their relationship was progressing slowly. They were still timid with one another, hadn't gotten into anything physical. To be honest, Michael didn't know if he could hold back when they reach that point. He had waited so long, and she was just so lovely— those ripe cherry lips, that silken hair, the alabaster, swanlike neck. When they did reach the point that Michael thought it was all right to move forward and consummate their love, he wanted it to be perfect. Caitlyn deserved perfection. He waited, patient as a monk, for her to be ready.

Tom Stryc's eyes were moist when he raised his glass.

"I'd like to propose a toast. To Caitlyn Kennedy, the hardest working, smartest reporter Huntsville has seen in years. In six short months, you've moved up the line from weekend anchor to our nightly news go-to girl. And now you've been snatched away, as we all knew you would be, to bigger and better things. You will be sorely missed, in all respects. And I, especially, am sorry to see you go."

"Hear, hear!" The shouts came from all corners of the room, a few knowing chuckles. Glasses clinked; throats were cleared. The station had rented out the Palmas Cantina for the night, closing the place down to outside customers, to celebrate Caitlyn's promotion. Over forty Channel 19 staffers were mushed into the tiny cantina, doing $2 shots of tequila every time the coal trains passed perilously close to the building, stuffing tortilla chips and gooey, guacamole-laden taquitos into their greedy mouths. The air was thick with smells—onions, stale sweat, frantic happiness, and a deeper, more ominous scent. If Caitlin didn't know better, she might say it was sex.

Caitlyn felt tears burn in the corners of her eyes. All this work. Over the past six months, she'd put everything into her job, landing plum interviews, doing undercover reporting, pushing, pushing, pushing. And her hard work had paid off. She'd worked her butt off to *be* someone, and the powers that be had noticed. She'd gotten the call.

And now she was starting over. A new city, a new station, a new crew, a new life. The nameless, faceless bastard who haunted her life for the past six months had driven her to succeed, driven her right out of the Huntsville market to a better job. In an odd way, she was grateful.

Tom stepped closer, grinning sheepishly, the jalapeño lights dangled around the restaurant making his face glow red. The blush was endearing to Caitlyn, who'd long ago discovered a few other ways to turn Tom red in the face. He turned the loveliest shade of puce when his inner thigh was nibbled. Their tryst had gone on too long; she was starting to have feelings for him—real feelings.

And he was too. Getting out now was for the best. She liked Tom a lot, but she couldn't stay here anymore.

"I'm going to miss you, you know?"

"You could come with me, Tom. The affiliate is looking for talent. You'd fit right in."

He gestured with a sweep of his hand. "And leave all this? Are you kidding?"

They shared a laugh. The station wasn't going to get any bigger, and they both knew it. Tom was a miracle worker, and the ratings had topped the remaining newscasts in town for the past four months. Losing Caitlyn was going to be a real problem for them; she was certainly a big part of the increase in viewership. But he didn't begrudge her the move.

He unselfconsciously tucked an errant piece of hair behind her ear. "Seriously, Caitie, you're going to be huge up there. And I'm gonna miss you like hell. Here's to a few months of fun, huh?"

They clinked glasses sloppily, then drank deeply. The salt of the margarita mingled with a slip of a tear at the corner of Caitlyn's mouth. Her co-workers nodded, understanding. Their star was sad to leave them.

Tom gave her a kiss on the lips, and everyone cheered. Caitlyn closed her eyes and let herself enjoy the moment, and thanked whatever God had decreed that she move to Nashville and be the affiliate's lead reporter, because it got her away from the creep.

Michael and Caitlyn had their first fight that night. Well, it wasn't a fight, exactly. He was hurt, and angry. Caitlyn admitted she wanted something different, wanted to have a change of scenery. He loved Huntsville, felt attached to its seams. He was a button, sewn to the fabric of the city.

Caitlyn didn't agree. She wanted out.

They talked long into the night, until the crickets stopped chirping. Arms entwined around each other, lying on a soft fleece blanket on the cold ground, they watched the sun rise. They'd come to a decision. Michael wasn't thrilled to leave his grandmother's house behind, but it was more important to make a new life with Caitlyn in Nashville. As long as he was with her, anything was possible.

They left the following morning, both cars packed to the gills. They shared long glances in the rearview mirrors as they drove north. The day started bright, the sky a vivid, sapphire blue. As they got farther north, the skies filled with billowing gray clouds. The rain enveloped them as they pulled in to their new home. Michael laughed while Caitlyn held a newspaper over her head to keep her hair dry, ran into the house with a grin on her face. She came back out in a baseball cap and started to unpack the car, and he felt freer than he'd felt in such a long time.

Who knew love could do that to a man?

That first night was different. They shared a bottle of wine, a crisp Pinot Grigio bought at a store down the street. Michael had learned a lot more about wine in the past few months, had developed quite a palate, and appreciated many varietals now. The wine was fresh and clean, the fresh buffalo mozzarella cheese and cracked-pepper water crackers biting into the edge of the fruitiness, giving excellent texture to a simple meal. Caitlyn stood in the gloaming, sipping the last of her wine, halo hair spilling loosely around her shoulders, her face unlined and carefree. Michael knew, deep in his soul, that they would be happy here.

He watched her standing on the deck, and realized the time had finally come. He wanted to be with her, always. He went to her, enveloped her in his arms. Caitlyn melted into him, her lips trailing across his neck, leaving a river of goose bumps in their wake. Her ardor astounded him; for months she'd been so contained, calm and poised. But when it came to actual physical contact, she glowed with passion. Lips bruised and tender, she watched Michael undress with a feral gleam in her eyes. He took his time with her blouse, shy again, fingers shaking, until she reached up, used her hands to guide his fingers. Her skin was so soft, so creamy that he couldn't contain himself anymore. He had to have her, right now.

It didn't take long.

Spent, they lay in front of the fireplace, sated with their love, so long in the making.

Michael told her then. That he loved her. That he wanted to marry her. That he wanted to spend the rest of his life wrapped in her love.

The words unnerved Caitlyn for some reason. She grew distraught, and he didn't know how to make her better. Nothing he said seemed to calm her. She yelled at him, told him to go to hell, told him to leave. He was so astonished that he did. Walked right out the door, pulling his shirt over his shoulders, her invectives stinging him like a blanket of nails.

Not knowing where to go in the strange new town, he stood in front of the townhouse for two hours, trying to get up the nerve to go back inside, to ask what he'd done wrong.

The curtains were drawn. The lights went out. She'd gone to bed without him, gone to bed mad. That was always a big mistake.

The change came over him in an instant. She'd dragged him here, accepted him into her life, into her body, and when he'd done the right thing, told her his true feelings, asked her to marry him, she said no? Exploded, and tossed him out like a piece of trash?

She'd ruined everything.

His heart became hard, a rock in his chest. How could she? How *dare* she?

"I'm Caitlyn Kennedy, Channel Two News. Good night, Nashville."

"And you're smiling, you're smiling, now look at your notes, and... we're out."

The cameras shut off, and Caitlyn had that moment of déjà vu she experienced every time she wrapped. New city, new studio, new crew—same old, same old. Reporting the news was the same everywhere.

"Great show, Caitie. You've really got something special behind that desk. The camera goes on and *bam!* You're on fire."

She smiled at Kevin Claueswitz, the Channel 2 news director. He was a good guy, ready to take a chance on her from day one. She'd found out later that Kevin and Tom were friends, had gone to journalism school together. Tom never mentioned it. She thought that was good of him.

"Caitlyn, phone!"

Her heart skipped a beat. Surely not. There was no way. She raised the receiver to her ear.

"I hate the red polish, Caitlyn. I've told you that. Why do you continue to defy me?"

She smashed the phone down, heart so suddenly in her throat that she ran from the room, barely made it to the ladies' before she chucked up her meager dinner in the toilet. She sat carelessly on the hard tile floor, after, with her head against the cool tiled wall, and cried.

Michael hadn't seen Caitlyn for a week. He knew she was still upset with him, though he'd apologized a thousand times. He wasn't schooled in the moods of women, couldn't figure out exactly what she wanted from him. Hadn't he declared his love properly? Didn't every girl want to get married, to have a family of her own? Was he so bad in bed that she wasn't willing to do it again, and didn't want to hurt his feelings?

He was offering her the world, and she'd shunned him. But Michael couldn't help himself; he loved her too much to just walk away. He wished he could take back that night, undo the passion they shared, start over anew. He racked his brain. How could he unwind the clock?

Flowers. Women loved flowers.

He went to the shop down the street and spent too much money on a multicolored spray of irises and roses. Left them on the front porch without a note. She'd know who they were from. She'd always known.

Caitlyn sat on the edge of the chair in Kevin's office.

"I know you're scared. But Caitie, I promise, I'm not going to let anything happen to you"

"Kevin… "

"I talked to a couple of homicide detectives. The laws are ridiculous. Basically, he has to hurt you before they can do anything. I know that's unfair and makes no sense, but technically, he's not done anything to harm you physically."

"And emotionally? Somehow, being terrorized day in and day out is okay, and we're all supposed to just wait until he breaks into my house and murders me before they'll do anything?"

He gave her a painful nod. "Like I said, the laws—"

She stood, interrupting, her voice nearly a shriek. "What am I supposed to do, Kevin? How long am I expected to let this go on? He's going to hurt me one of these days, and we all know it."

Kevin nodded slowly, the sunset glimmering off his hair. "I do know it, and trust me, I'm not willing to let it get to that point. So here's the name of a guy. He's one of the best private investigators around here. I think he can help. At the very least, he can find ways to keep you safe. We don't want to lose you, Caitie. You're a great reporter and a fabulous anchor. We'll figure this out. I promise."

Caitlyn took the small beige rectangle from Kevin, holding it gingerly in the palm of her hand. She glanced at the gold embossing—*William Goldman, Private Detective*. She stashed the card in the back pocket of her jeans, dashing away tears from her cheeks. She hated to show weakness like this, but damn it, she was scared. There was no more feigning nonchalance.

The moment she left Kevin's office, Caitlyn's phone was out.

Goldman answered on the first ring.

Michael went by the house with more flowers, Gerbera daisies and tulips this time, her favorite, but the door was locked. A new gold deadbolt was affixed to the door. Defeated, he sat on the front steps, shredding the flowers into bits.

He wasn't sure what was happening. Things were so far off track, and he didn't know how to get them back. Two things he knew for certain—they'd made love, and she'd suddenly turned cold, distant. Like she didn't love him anymore. But that couldn't be true. Michael had seen the look in her eyes as he entered her, watched her pupils dilate in pleasure, saw the tiny vein rise in her left temple, felt her breath quicken and her muscles spasm around him. He may not be well versed in the ways of love, but biological responses were impossible to fake. You can't react like that, so organically, and make it feel like a lie.

Maybe it was too soon. Maybe she wasn't as ready as she'd told him. Or maybe, just maybe, he was wrong about her.

Maybe she was like his mother after all.

And with that thought, a small spike of blackness reared up inside him. He'd been controlling it for so long, he almost didn't recognize the moment his confusion and pain coalesced into fury.

He would have her. Or he would kill her.

Goldman looked like a private detective in a comic book: large head, sloping shoulders, a cauliflower nose flushed with rosacea. He wore a fedora and lumbered when he walked. But his eyes, round blueberries tucked into the folds of his cheeks, were kind, and sharp, full of intelligence and mischief. Caitlyn felt safe with him.

They met for the first time in a dark bar next to a strip club.

When she parked in the lot, she was worried about how it might look—a nice, fresh, new female anchor hanging out in the seedy part of town, then decided she'd play it off as an investigation and walked in with her head held high.

Goldman arrived late, breathless, covered in a sheen of sweat. Caitlyn wondered if he'd taken the advance payment she'd couriered over the day before and had himself a moment next door.

Turned out, hot and fast and out of breath was just the way Goldman operated. He was a quart high, ran a little warmer than the average bear.

They went over it all that first night. How the calls had started. How her stalker expressed dislike for anything that made her "look like a whore." How he hadn't stopped calling for weeks on end. The things he said, little tidbits shared about her day. A comment about the brand of tomato juice she'd bought. A recommendation that she fill her Beemer at the gas station two blocks from her house, because the prices were better.

He'd noticed when she switched from lattes to green tea because the caffeine, coupled with the stress, was eating her stomach apart. He even knew about that brief little scare two months ago, when she worried she and Tom might be together forever, and her career would be over before it really began.

"Going through your trash," Goldman said, which made it all worse.

The Huntsville police hadn't been able to do much. He'd used multiple disposable cell phones, and they couldn't trace the numbers. They didn't have the personnel to have a constant presence, but they'd watched her at odd times, hoping to catch a glimpse of her stalker. It hadn't worked. And now the Nashville police were saying they couldn't do anything either.

She was tired of being scared.

Caitlyn started to cry. Goldman reached a meaty hand over and patted her shoulder awkwardly.

"It's gonna be okay. We'll keep you safe. Don't worry about a thing."

Michael's fury drove him.

He'd had been patient, and kind. He'd been more understanding than a man could ever be expected to. He'd sent flowers, written beautiful love notes. He'd called, he'd dropped by the house. He'd put more effort into their relationship than anything he'd ever done before.

Caitlyn refused to accept any of his overtures. She wouldn't see him. Wouldn't acknowledge him. She looked right through him, cringing a little when he spoke to her.

He *knew* having sex so soon into their relationship was a mistake. Maybe he shouldn't have proposed. Maybe the ring hadn't been big enough. Maybe he hadn't been.

Caitlyn had disappeared into an alley. After forty minutes, she reappeared, eyes red. He watched her turn and walk up Union Street, determined, shoulders squared. She looked different to him now. He didn't see the little girl who'd bossed him on the playground, or the woman he'd fallen in love with. He saw his mother's back in her carriage. Determination, and hate.

He followed slowly, watchful and wary, as always. She slid into her car and drove away, and he could have sworn she looked straight at him as she went by, really saw him, for the first time in weeks, and smiled.

It hit him deep in his gut, like an arrow.

She'd smiled at him.

His anger melted. He'd lost her once, but this... invitation made him want to try all over again.

He would give her one more chance. It was the right thing to do. The adult thing to do. The manly thing to do.

Goldman had a plan. He and Caitlyn met in the Starbucks near Vanderbilt, off West End, someplace where she could go in dark glasses and hide from the eyes that bored into the back of her neck at all hours, and not look out of place. She was completely anonymous among the co-eds and socialites and joggers and hippies and worker bees. The chairs were filled with a cross-section of Nashville, a slice of the Southern life. It wouldn't be polite to stare.

The detective had found some sort of new 007 device that could trace the calls she was receiving via GPS. Even if they couldn't get the cell number, the illicit company who made the device could monitor the calls, triangulate the caller's whereabouts using the mapping software. It was cutting edge. That's what he told her. She didn't care about the details. Caitlyn just wanted the damn phone to stop ringing. She wanted her life back.

They decided to try the very next night. She made sure to paint her toenails vermillion and wear open-toed shoes. Bait.

Goldman came to the studio, watched her do her bit. He had the device hooked up to the phone.

Like clockwork, the creep called as she wrapped the show. When she answered, he asked why she was meeting strange men for coffee during business hours. She felt the fear crawl up her spine. So much for anonymity. He knew. He knew everything. He was inside her head. Knew what she'd think next, what decisions she'd make, where she would go, what she would do.

She flubbed their planned script. "What do you want?" she screamed into the receiver. He simply hung up. Goldman shook his head. Not enough time for the GPS to trace him.

"We'll try again tomorrow. At least you know he'll call back." Goldman said. He patted her on the back and walked her to her car, eyes swiveling around the parking lot. As she climbed in her car, he said gruffly, "Give me your phone."

She handed it to him, and he gave her a spare. "Don't worry," he said. "I'm watching now, too."

Michael had been wrong. Yet again, he'd been wrong. She hadn't smiled in invitation. She thought she was smarter than him. Fighting his fury, he paced, trying to decide what to do.

It was time. Time for Michael to pull out all the stops. He needed to see her. He dressed carefully, certain to look his best, yet able to blend into the night. He went with black head to toe: a fine cashmere turtleneck, wool gabardine slacks, soft-soled shoes in fine Italian leather. Slimming, and tasteful. If Caitlyn was going to be this woman—this whore, this slut—then she'd have to answer for it. Michael had turned his entire fucking life upside down for her, and this was the way she repaid him? No. He wouldn't stand for it. She would be made to understand what she'd done.

He made his way to her house. Stood on the street outside the house and called her cell phone. The phone rang and rang and rang. No lights came on. No shadows moved.

She didn't answer.

Out of the corner of his eye, he saw a darkness moving closer. A black sedan.

He left the phone ringing, dropped it in the bushes. Casually walked down the hill, away from Caitlyn.

There was time. There was always time.

Goldman had watched all night, all day, got her safely from home to the studio. He didn't answer when she asked if her phone had rung overnight. Which told her all she needed to know.

She did the news, smiled for the camera, feeling empty. Knowing what was to come. The moment the cameras went dark, the studio phone rang.

Caitlyn's hands were shaking. She needed to play this just right. She took a deep breath and answered.

"Hello?"

"Nice show, Caitlyn."

"Thank you." She hesitated for effect. "You've been calling me for months. We know each other so well now. Why don't you tell me your name?"

"I've got him, I've got him," Goldman mouthed to Caitlyn, making a rolling gesture with his hand, silently telling her to keep him talking.

The caller barked a laugh in her ear. "You don't need to know my name. All you need to know is that I love you. Isn't that enough? I call you all the time, just like a boyfriend should. I compliment you. I give you flowers, write you notes. I make sure you know what I like, I give you advice on your career. After all this time, Caitlyn, do you really want to keep playing this game? Why do you think a name will make any difference?"

"It's not a game. I want to know your name. It means a lot to me." Her voice was small, pleading. Just how Goldman wanted her to play it.

"I'll tell you my name, Caitlyn. My name is—"

There was a click in her ear.

"Oh shit! I lost him. Goddammit it to hell, Caitie, we had him. Let me see, let me see... "

Goldman's eyes were transfixed on the little LED screen. Caitlyn put the receiver down on the table, a small trickle of sweat slipping between her breasts.

"Gotcha, you son of a bitch."

"You found him?"

Caitlyn was upset at the note of fear in her voice. She sounded like a mewling kitten rescued from a drainpipe. She hadn't been faking it after all. She felt weak, worn. Exhausted, and overwhelmed. The bastard had beaten her down, stolen all the joy and happiness from her life.

She squared her shoulders and shook her head. Damn it, she wasn't weak, and she wasn't a damsel in distress.

Goldman was smiling, his potato-shaped face split by the grin. Relief streamed through her body, so overwhelming that she needed to sit down. This freak was trying to ruin her life. Now it was time for payback.

"I got him. I got him. 4679 Old Hickory. Jesus, Caitie, he's calling… ”

A coldness went through her.

“From my house.”

The house smelled different. The window was open now, the breeze blowing in the screen, carrying in a hint of skunk and burned leaves from down the street. Michael walked through the familiar rooms, as strange to him now as if he'd never seen them. He stopped in the living room. There was a picture of Caitlyn in a cap and gown on the end table. She looked so damn happy. So beautiful. So aloof.

He picked up the frame. Ran his fingers along the curve of her lips.

The pain in his chest was crushing. She was happy before he came into her life. How was that possible? Could it be so? Could she have been happy without him? All these months, Michael knew every smile was for him, every hair flip, ear touch, lip compression, tongue lick. It was all for him. Caitlyn had stared out at Michael from that television screen, and loved him.

Hadn't she?

Goldman drove. Caitlyn looked out the window at the city, knowing everything was about to change.

When they reached her neighborhood, Goldman pulled his car to the curb two blocks from her house. “Are you sure you want to do this?” he asked, loading a fresh magazine into his backup Glock.

“Just give me the goddamn gun. I'm a big girl.”

Goldman handed the weapon to Caitlyn. She hefted its unfamiliar weight in her right hand. A good, solid piece of metal. A life taker. Perfect.

"Caitlyn, we can call the police. They'll be here in less than five minutes."

She faced him, her features softened. "Goldman, you know they won't help until he hurts me—that's why I had to bring you into this. This ends *now*. If you don't want to be there, if you want the deniability, I suggest you leave. Because I'm going into my home and stopping him once and for all. I won't ever be free unless I do this. He'll keep following me, keep calling me, keep stalking me. God knows where it's going to lead if I don't stop him." Her voice shook on the last note and she cleared her throat. "No. I won't let this go on any longer. Are you coming or not?"

Goldman nodded. "Of course I'm coming. Wouldn't want anything bad to happen."

They got out of Goldman's beat-up maroon Thunderbird, shutting the doors quietly behind them. She could feel the caller in the air, that palpable sense of foreboding she always got when he was near.

The house was dark. The light in the living room was off. She never turned it out, kept the switch on the wall taped to the on position so it couldn't be accidentally shut off. That one light kept the darkness at bay, kept him away from her life. She knew that he must be in there, pawing through her possessions, making himself intimate with her things. How many times had he done that, she wondered? Five? Ten? A hundred?

How many times was the recurring nightmare she had—the one where he stood over her and watched her sleep—how many times had that been a reality?

She took a deep breath. Felt the metal of the gun biting hard into the soft flesh of her hand.

She was in control now. This had to end.

Emboldened, she stepped up to the front door. It was unlocked, slightly ajar. If he knew they were coming, he would have shut it behind him. Right?

She eyed Goldman, nodded, and pushed open the door with the toe of her boot. It swung wide into the gaping darkness.

She slipped through, waited for her eyes to adjust to the light.

A shadow moved. She turned to face it. Extended the gun toward the outline that was her waking nightmare.

"Don't do that, Caitlyn." The bastard's voice was gravelly, familiar. It crawled around her body like a sinuous cat, curling around her legs, working its way up her spine, over her shoulders, around her neck, into her mouth, down her throat until she thought she would choke.

"You don't have to do this. I forgive you. I understand. We can try again. Maybe a new town, fewer distractions. You don't have to work. I'll provide for us."

"Jesus Christ," Goldman whispered.

Caitlyn took a step toward the voice. "Go. To. Hell."

The shadow moved to the right, and without warning, Caitlyn fired. The muzzle flash blinded her for a moment, but she fired again, and again, and finally, when her fingers went numb, she heard Goldman yelling at her to stop.

The rage dissipated. The lights came on. Caitlyn saw the man who'd done his best to ruin her life lying on the floor. He stared at her as if she were the only person in the world. He looked vaguely familiar, but she brushed that away. He didn't deserve her concern.

She watched the puddle of blood spreading across the hardwood, catching the edge of the carpet, and smiled.

"You're never going to bother me again."

Michael stared at the face of his love in awe. He'd made her happy at last. He could see it in the manic smile, the fire in her eyes. He'd been forgiven. He knew now that she was truly, madly, deeply in love with him. At this moment, she adored him. He was complete.

And so it was done.

He sang himself to death, the words he'd written for her whispered into the ether as the world went black.

"If God is one, and man is six, together they make seven. I loved you, darling, loved you long. I'll wait for you in—"

"This is Kelly Mokler, sitting in tonight for Caitlyn Kennedy. As we've been reporting throughout the day, Caitlyn was forced to shoot and kill and intruder in her home last night. Caitlyn returned from work to find a man who has yet to be identified in her living room. He attacked her, and she was lucky enough to be able to retrieve her personal protection weapon and shoot the intruder. We are so grateful that she was unharmed in this incident. And look forward to having her back in the studio.

"In other news, storms blew through Nashville last night—"

The police brought her to the Criminal Justice Center, and sat her in a soulless white interrogation room with cinder block walls and a decrepit table. They asked the same questions, over and over and over. She told them the story, again and again. That the dead man had been harassing her for months. That she had the gun for protection. That the man had broken in, crazed, and gone after her. That she'd shot him in self-defense.

Goldman backed her up, and they were finally forced to let her go.

Michael. His name was Michael Everett. It had taken her a while to place it—and eventually, she remembered. A quiet young boy from her elementary school. A friendless waif. There had been rumors about his mother, his family, but she'd been too young to understand the whisperings. The following year, her parents moved, and she never saw the boy again.

She had no idea how he'd found her, why he'd decided to focus on her.

In death, Michael managed what he tried to do in life. He became a permanent part of Caitlyn's world. She would forever remember the moment the gun bucked in her hand and the bullet embedded itself in his flesh. The mad glee she'd felt at stopping him.

She was no better than him. But she'd always know that.

Goldman walked her from the CJC. The sun beat down. The Nashville sky was cerulean blue, free of clouds, a hint of a cool breeze playing in the trees. It was a perfect day.

A perfect day, and Caitlyn was free.

And the shadow of the man she'd killed followed her as she walked to Goldman's car.

ABOUT THE STORY

This story first appeared in BASED ON: Words, Notes, and Art from Nashville, a collective work of Nashville artists. If you ever visit Music City, you'll notice we have a lot more going on besides country music. Writers, artists, thespians, and musicians (of all genres—we do alt-rock, punk, and world-class classical, too) all call Nashville home. You should come visit sometime.

But watch your back. You never know when unrequited love will be lurking around the corner...

CHIMERA

I do not sleep anymore.

I can't take the risk, not again. I won't survive it again.

"I'll see you in hell."

These words are rooted in my brain. They aren't even words, exactly. Not enunciated and pronounced, but hissed and lingering, seeping into my skin and settling into my bones, my heart, my mind.

The room is dark, silent and reproachful. I've forgotten the nightlight again, and the gloom is penetrating, the white walls lost in the dark abyss. There is no boundary to the room; it is infinite, black and salty. I can't smell the sulfur, even though I've been told I would. It is more like the scent of the sea, slightly brackish, over-ripe, dead fish and seaweed making it putrid.

The hissing begins again. "I'm here to take you. It is your time."

I realize this has happened before. I've been in this bed, this room, this murky gloom when the demon came to me. How many times have I fought him off?

I turn to face him. He has come through the shuttered window. The night air blows behind him, sweet jasmine and bougainvillea overpowered by his rankness. He doesn't resemble anything I've seen before, any depiction drawn or imagined. He is taupe, nearly translucent, his skinny ferret-like body supported by long-boned feet, hands ending in claws that drip a viscous liquid, the remnants of bitter souls from his earlier catch. I'm not sure how I know he is male; there are no external clues to his gender.

"Tiiiiiimmmmeee." That sibilant voice again. I feel a drop of slime hit my forehead. His hands are past my shoulder now, reaching around to scoop me in his arms. His mouth, crowded with sharp teeth, spit trails stringing between upper and lower jaws, grows wider, bigger, and I feel the claws rake across my back. He is pulling me in, consuming, sucking. I feel my soul depart from my heart and begin to leave my body.

No. I will not let him take me.

I take a breath so deep that pieces of his spittle fly into my mouth, and I scream louder, longer than I ever knew I could. My body convulses; the flesh of my throat begins to rip, tiny tears marring the surface. And still I scream. I know, deep in my heart, that he will leave if I continue.

The demons do not like screams.

Flashing a look full of hatred, of lust and regret, the demon is sucked back through the shutters. They bang closed, startling me with their vehemence. My scream trails off.

I am safe.

I sit up and turn on the light.

My worst fears are realized.

I have not escaped lightly.

The Chimera has come again.

He sits in the chair, feet tucked under him like a pleasant cat. He raises an inky eyebrow, strokes two fingers through the obsidian silk of his goatee. He flashes a smile at me, teeth so pearly against the darkness they're nearly blue. He doesn't say a word.

Stroke, smile.

Stroke, smile.

"Bastard," I whisper.

He laughs silently, deep in his chest, and the sound reverberates around the room like thunder.

We made a deal, he and I. It was a long time ago. I was too young to know any better; he was hunting the night for victims. A match better suited to novels and nightmares. But he likes me. Enough that the deal we struck benefits us both.

I murdered. I sinned.

He took.

It was that simple.

Fetial declarations aside, he takes from everyone. Good, bad or indifferent. The indifferent, mostly. He signs for the souls of his victims without their knowledge. It's that last glimpse, when they assume they'll see the light, that shocks the living hell right into them. And the Chimera laughs as he greets them down below.

But the lost souls aren't my problem. The Chimera is my problem. We're friends in a strange, make-a-deal-with-the-devil kind of way. Like I said before, he likes me. He's a fallen angel like the rest of them, still wanton in his desires. I guess I fit with his image of a partner.

He's here to collect. Anytime, anywhere. That's our deal.

And with our agreement in place, I don't have to go straight to hell.

He possesses my body. Gives a whole new meaning to burning desire.

He knows that you're most vulnerable when frightened. That's why he sends in the demon first, to soften you up. He's a true sadist.

I do have a choice in the matter. God gave us free will, the ability to choose which path to follow. My path is forked, two roads less traveled. I can accept the demon's proposal, go with him the next time he comes to me.

It's a toss-up, sometimes, which is worse. The Chimera or the demon. Love, or the blankness of death?

I could resign myself to never sleep again. It's not like I get any rest. Every time I close my eyes, start toward that REM stage, they appear. Never sleeping again is a comforting idea.

I wish I could take back that night, ten years ago.

The Chimera was there, though I didn't know it at the time. I thought it was just the two of us, alone in the alley. That no one heard my screams. That I was abandoned. That I wrestled the knife away at the last minute with my own strength. That *my* fingers grasped the hilt. That *my* muscles forced the tip of the knife into the man's gut. That the blood spilling onto my arm, my torn dress, my shoes, was untainted.

He could have let me die. It might have been easier.

The yin and yang of his world are too complex for me to comprehend. Suffice it to say that while I was being raped and then strangled, he stood and watched. Waited. Knew that he could give me the strength to overcome the man and stop the attack, which he did, but not until after the man finished grunting and scraping at me.

When the knife appeared, the Chimera stepped in, silent, transparent. He grasped my hand, grappled with the knife. Using my strength, he stabbed the stranger in the stomach, driving the blade in so deep that a warm spill of intestines gathered in my hand.

He turned with that luminescent smile and said, "You owe me one."

As we were driving our deal, the Chimera had the audacity to point out I should thank him for saving my life.

What kind of life is this?

Labyrinth assassin, fevered dreams, the warm copper spice of lifeblood pouring through my hands. The Chimera, possessing me night by night, the length of him buried deep between my thighs, his scorching desire blazing inside me.

He comes to me, insatiable, unfulfilled. Takes me, over and over. Drives me onward. Over the brink, where the madness of climax allows me glimpses into the raging inferno that awaits.

He is the cause of my reckless journeys, my wasted relationships, my never-ending string of dead-end jobs. He is in the drugs, the alcohol, the cigarettes. The lush, provocative nights and the solitary days. He never leaves my side, but only appears when I sleep. He and his demon familiars.

I'm a lucky girl. I'll never be alone again.

ABOUT THE STORY

"Chimera" came to me in a dream. A very, very bad dream. I was watching the movie *Constantine* with my father right before bed, and the movie came to life in ways I could never imagine. The demon came for me. I knew, with the absolute clarity that comes from your unconscious, that this had happened before, and if I screamed, he would go away. My poor parents were awakened by the bloodcurdling shrieks echoing through their house. My father rushed outside, positive a young woman in the neighborhood was being murdered. Finding no one, he came back to the house, realizing at last that it was me. I've never screamed aloud in a dream before. Even though I've captured the demon, put him on the page where he can't ever hurt me again, I still sleep uneasy in that room.

GRAY LADY, LADY GRAY

The corridor was empty. A small mouse nibbled in a corner, whiskers covered in dust, his gray fur nearly translucent in the dark. Preparations were being made below. She could hear them. Scurrying, simpering, slutting. Wood brought in for the fireplaces, which meant the attics would become unbearably hot as the warmth rose from floor to floor. Winter flowers and the deep Scottish weeds tended in the gardens outside, what was left of them, anyway. Balustrades polished, floors washed and waxed, carpets vacuumed, bedding changed.

A wedding, if her long ears didn't deceive her.

A chance.

The lips on her decrepit face pulled back from long, taloned teeth into a semblance of a grin.

"Dolon," she called, delighting in the fright it gave the cook five floors below, who heard the wind whistling through her kitchen and smelled the odor of sulfur on the breeze.

He appeared before her, summoned by her use of his name.

"Yes, Lamia?"

"What have you been doing?"

"Eating the late lambs. They are so succulent this time of year."

She looked closer—her vision wasn't what it once was—and saw the little bits of flesh hanging from his beard, the gray stained black with blood. Blood. Blood on the corner of his mouth. With sight came smell, the rising odor forcing her to salivate like a rabid dog.

Her loins throbbed.

"Come here, my sweet."

He obeyed, and she flicked a long, pointed tongue around the edges of his mouth, catching flesh and blood and the musk—he'd eaten the lambs from the ass first, the beast.

Just that little bit of essence was enough—Dolon became solid in front of her.

A handsome man, Dolon. Simple, driven by needs not unlike her own, banished to this castle at birth, forced to grow up under Lamia's tutelage. She loved him in the only way she knew how to love, which was filled with hate and fear and loathing and manipulative desperation.

"That was lovely, darling. Now you must do something for me. It seems we have visitors arriving."

"Yes, I saw. They will have to go to the next farm for the lamb shanks."

He laughed, uproariously. His joke, so simple, so crude. Just like Dolon.

She ran her fingers along the slick flesh of his forearm.

"Pretty, please pay attention."

"What is your wish, my lady?"

Her tongue curled round her mouth. "Bring me all the information, Dolon. Leave nothing out."

Elizabeth wanted to be a princess.

From the time she was five and grasped the concept of the Cinderella myth—that any woman could capture the heart of her own Prince Charming—she set herself on the journey to become a princess. She didn't seek a royal throne—no, that was best left to those who would squabble over the scraps and look cross-eyed down their long, nebbish noses at lesser beings like her. She didn't want a crown.

Elizabeth sought the only real path to princessdom. She sought true love.

And she'd found it in the form of a wonderful man named Edgar, who looked at her with sunshine and roses in his eyes.

They'd met at a softball game, of all places. Opposing teams. She was sweaty and covered in dust from the pitching mound and a long slide into third; he was sweaty and covered in the dust she kicked up when she slid. They emerged from the cloud coughing and laughing. He'd helped her to her feet, and she'd been lost. Gone. He had blue eyes that sparkled and a strong jaw, not to mention legs like tree trunks and an ass that would make a grown woman cry. He knew how to use it, too. His voice was soft and melodious, and had never been raised in anger toward her. Edgar was an infinitely patient man, one who would bite his lip and walk to another room if she were ever shrill or annoyed. Which wasn't often. He gave her no reason to seek connubial combat.

Edgar, quite simply, made her happy. So when he'd asked her to marry him, down on one knee, a clear glistening stone nestled in a bed of gold in hand extended, she hadn't hesitated. Within weeks, they'd decided to have the wedding in Scotland, at a castle, to fulfill Elizabeth's lifelong quest. Only princesses married in castles, after all.

Elizabeth stood in the parking lot outside the castle keep and raised her hand to her eyes, blotting out the sun. It had been cloudy and rainy since they'd landed in Edinburgh, but the moment she'd arrived on the estate, the sun had boldly forced its way into the sky, as if it too wanted a piece of her happiness. It was too bright now; she stepped to her left so the tower of the castle would help block the incessant rays.

Something moved behind the highest window. The breeze picked up, and Elizabeth's sullen brown hair whipped into a frenzy, then fell limp against her ears. She felt… odd. Filled with longing, her pulse beating hard between her legs. She wanted to bed Edgar, *now*. She blushed and felt her breath come fast.

"Edgar, did you see that?"

"See what, dear?"

Elizabeth focused on the window again, and saw nothing. She let her breath regulate. Nerves. It was just nerves. She'd been a bundle for days now—the pressure of the trip, the planning, the knowledge she would be binding her life to his forever; it all had her on edge.

"The sun is playing tricks on me, I suppose. Shall we go in?"

A small party had been planned as a surprise for Edgar and Elizabeth. Unbeknownst to them, their wedding attendants had all flown over a day early to have things prepared.

When they entered the long corridor to the castle keep, the hall was lined with white roses and bedecked with ribbons, and a small white sign with a hand drawn arrow pointing down the hall read *This Way*. It was quite fetching, and Elizabeth commented as such to Edgar, who agreed, though he was quite preoccupied with their baggage at that moment, and was startled when Elizabeth screamed in delight.

Hands grabbed at them—parents, friends, sisters and brothers, hugging and kissing and showering the couple in rose petals. Elizabeth cried prettily, and Edgar was also moved. To have such love surrounding you is something to treasure, and Edgar wasn't the kind to dismiss strong emotion when it overcame him.

He handed Elizabeth a tissue, and took one for himself. Once they were done with the tears, they were ushered into an intimate dining room, seated in the middle of the long, grand table, looking toward the window that spread the gardens before them like a fertile green blanket, and tucked in to a light lunch. Elizabeth simply glowed, and Edgar couldn't resist leaning into her begonia-scented aura and slipping in a kiss.

The crowd cheered and clicked their forks against their champagne flutes in thrilled response.

Edgar deepened the kiss, letting his tongue touch hers—so warm, so wet, so perfect. God, he loved this woman. He wanted her. His mind saw her splayed facedown in front of him, legs spread, wide and pink and moist and wanting.

He felt a quick breath of air, fetid and warm, at his right ear, and opened his eyes a fraction. He was a rational man. His mind didn't allow him to see the bearded face, twisting slowly two inches from his own, dark skin rippling with maggots and roaches. His mind allowed him to feel momentarily uneasy, as if something were watching him, or a goose had walked over his grave, but he dismissed the smell as old meat left in the sun and put another arm around Elizabeth.

When they broke free, accompanied by hoots and hollers, the castle staff filtered in and their wedding planner gave them the schedule for the following two days. Edgar did his best to pay attention.

Dolon mounted the stairs slowly. He knew what was waiting for him. Lamia was once a beautiful, cunning woman, sought after by men across realms. But she had become something less than real, something full of hate and spite. He didn't blame her. Not really. He was simply annoyed that he was tied to her, forever. All gray ladies were assigned a demon, for they were unable to leave their earthly rooms without a demon's escort, and needed something that could travel through the air, move through walls, lift into the breeze and delve into the souls that fed her existence to make that happen.

It was just… Lamia was so old. Even when she received the essence, became the glorious woman she once was, even then he knew that she was crinkled up like an old parchment inside. It interfered with his abilities, it truly did.

He reached the top of the stairs and slid through the wooden door into her rooms. She was asleep in her chair, facing the fire, a fur throw around her shoulders. Her gray skin sagged, and a fine line of spit dripped from her sharp, hollow teeth. At least she still had them.

He stood for a moment, repulsed. She would be furious with him for watching her sleep. He slipped back through the door and made some noise in the hall, a warning to wake her. When he moved through the door again, she'd straightened in the chair. The fur throw was in her lap now, and she was smiling at him. Her cataracts made her eyes the color of sludge.

"What news, my sweet?"

"A wedding, Lamia. Just like you thought. Between two very young, very impressionable beings. You should have seen the female when you called to her—she turned red in the face like a baboon's ass. And him, my love, he is strong, but also susceptible. We have a chance."

Lamia leapt briskly from her seat and went to the window. "When is the ceremony?"

"Tomorrow night. Seven. We should have enough time."

"Yes, we will." Lamia turned back from the window to face him, and Dolon could see the vestiges of the beauty she had once been. Even she, old and cruel and severe, could be transformed by joy.

"We will."

The dress Elizabeth wore was simple and elegant. The base had been her grandmother's, a wide bell-shaped skirt of thick satin. The bodice and lace were current additions, making the dress modern and sophisticated. It had a cathedral-length train, and though it was much too long for their purposes in the small castle chapel, shortening it was a concession she refused to make.

Princesses had cathedral trains.

She swished about in the heavy skirt, feeling the slick fabric mold to her legs. She was rapturously happy. She checked off the list in her head.

She was in a castle.

She was about to marry the most wonderful man alive.

She was wearing part of her grandmother's wedding gown, which brought her back to life, in a way.

She looked beautiful. Her skin was clear, she didn't have her period, her dress fit like a glove. Even her hair had gotten in line and was piled on her head in glorious waves.

That was plenty for one girl's wedding day, she thought.

There was rustling in the antechamber.

"Lizzie, it's time. Are you ready?"

Her father. Tears pricked her eyes. *Oh, my God.* Her whole life she'd been waiting for this moment, and now, here it was. She took a deep breath.

"Ready, Daddy."

She opened the door and admired her handsome father, resplendent in his white tie and tails. He twitched a bit, uncomfortably humbled by the scrutiny.

"You look gorgeous, Daddy."

"So do you, my dear. Shall we get you married off? Remember, it's right foot first."

There were forty-nine stairs. She counted each and every one as they went down.

The castle was decorated to the nines. She wondered which mice had descended upon the rooms to make it happen.

Before she had a chance to think anything more, the planner handed her the flowers, a simple spray of white roses and hydrangea, then opened the doors to the chapel.

It all went very quickly from there. The trumpet voluntary sprang to life, her guests rose to their feet, and she saw Edgar, standing at the other end of the room. It was all she could do not to break free and run to him, to throw herself in his arms.

She floated down the aisle to gasps of appreciation. She attributed the crawling, goosebumpy sensation running down her spine to nerves. She couldn't see the two uninvited guests standing at either side of the altar, waiting for her with blood risen.

Her father stopped walking, so she stopped as well. Edgar looked ready to cry. She fought the urge as well.

Words.

Words.

Words.

Her father squeezed her hand. And then it was time. The priest was a homely man with wads of white hair spilling from his ears. *Mawwiage…* She stifled a giggle. He spoke in a clear bell voice that snapped her back to sober.

"Elizabeth, will you have this man to be your husband; to live together in the covenant of marriage? Will you love him, comfort him, honor and keep him, in sickness and in health, and, forsaking all others, be faithful to him as long as you both shall live?"

"I will." Elizabeth brushed a single tear from the corner of her eye.

The priest turned slightly with a rustle of cloth as dark as a raven's wings.

"Edgar, will you have this woman to be your wife; to live together in the covenant of marriage? Will you love her, comfort her, honor and keep her, in sickness and in health, and, forsaking all others, be faithful to her as long as you both shall live?"

Edgar's voice carried to the back of the hall.

"I will."

"Will all of you witnessing these promises do all in your power to uphold these two persons in their marriage?"

There was a chorus of confidence. "We will."

Elizabeth glowed.

"It's time," Lamia whispered. "Their fidelity has been pledged. The moment is ours. Go, Dolon, go!"

His disappeared from Edgar's side. It was easier for Dolon—as a demon he was built to enter the host seamlessly. Lamia, on the other hand, was forced to choke down a potion whose recipe was of unknown origin, one that she'd gotten the chance to make only four times in her existence. She unstoppered the bottle and dropped the contents on her tongue. It was most powerful; only three drops were needed. She swallowed quickly, before the taste of soot and hellfire registered fully, and shut out the voices of the consecrated blood spilled for her formulary that screamed in her head.

She willed it. Willed herself into the body of the girl. Into the sweet nothingness that resided in the girl's blood.

She was getting smaller, her features softening, her hair growing and weaving onto her head, her nails shortening, her skin smoothing, her eyes clearing, and then she opened her conscious being and stared into a blue abyss with a slight brownish cast over it. She felt the girl kicking against her liver, drowning in the bile of her body, crying out for release.

It had worked.

Lamia resisted the urge to lick her lips. Her tongue was very long. It might look wrong.

Less than ten hours. That's all she needed.

Edgar took her hand.

"In the name of God, I, Edgar Allen Gray, take you, Elizabeth, to be my wedded wife, to have and to hold from this day forward, for better, for worse, for richer, for poorer, in sickness and in health, to love and to cherish, until we are parted by death. This is my solemn vow."

Speak, Lamia. It is your turn.

Her voice was astonishing, pure and only slightly wavering. "In the name of God, I, Elizabeth Banks Morton, take you, Edgar, to be my wedded husband, to have and to hold from this day forth, for richer, for poorer, in sickness and in health, to love and to cherish, until we are parted by death. This is my solemn vow."

Lamia smiled serenely, and a small red tear formed in the corner of Elizabeth's right eye.

The officiate blessed the rings. There were more words. A single gold band was slid onto her finger, and Lamia felt the power of the metal course through her. She knew she was shimmering, feeding upon this, the love Edgar had for Elizabeth. It was powerful and good. If she could just make the dawn, sleep and awake in the body of the child, the transmogrification would be complete.

"Then by the power vested in me through the Lord, our God, I now pronounce you husband and wife."

The priest leaned in and said quietly, "You may kiss your bride."

Dolon's face flashed through for an instant, a leering grin, then Edgar was back, solemn and steady. He leaned in slowly, savoring the moment, staring into Lamia's eyes. His lips pressed to hers, and the flood of innocence brought blood to her tongue.

"To the dawn," she whispered.

Edgar looked surprised for a moment, then smiled knowingly. "To the dawn," he replied.

A cheer went up as they turned to face their new world as husband and wife.

The party went on into the wee hours.

Neither Edgar nor Elizabeth seemed to be in any hurry to get to their marriage bed, instead choosing to dance and carry on. Their friends and family loved it. Seeing their son and daughter, their buddies, let loose, the pressures of the wedding behind them, was just the ticket. The alcohol flowed. The music took on maniacal proportions, going faster and faster until the band members themselves seemed to melt from the sweat pouring off their bodies, yet they continued to play, louder and quicker and more insistent.

Bridesmaids found themselves in dark corners with groomsmen they'd never before found attractive, rolling with wave after wave of orgasm as they were penetrated with all manner of appendages and penises.

The whole castle thrummed with a primal rhythm, the bodies and heartbeats bumping in time to the music.

And when the music stopped, they didn't even notice.

Edgar even took a quick turn in the bathroom with one of the waiters, and was thoroughly amused when Elizabeth walked in on them and slapped his hand in response.

But at three in the morning, after watching their bacchanalian with an emotion bordering on contentedness, Elizabeth edged up to Edgar and said, "We must go."

They left the wedding party writhing in ecstasy and mounted the stairs. No one noticed them leaving.

This was the tricky part. There were so many conditions on the spell, so many different ways it could go wrong.

Lamia and Dolon needed to exit the bodies they possessed and consecrate the marriage, each to the other, Elizabeth to Dolon, Edgar to Lamia. A very intense glamor was needed to make their appearance deceptive enough. Then each must sleep for one hour in the arms of their lover, and as the dawn broke the sky, the transformation would be complete. Lamia would become Elizabeth. Mortal, for a time. For all time.

Lamia into Elizabeth was the most important. Dolon into Edgar was somewhat of a moot point. Dolon could inhabit Edgar any time he wanted. Dolon, as a demon, could enter bodies and exit them, be them, whenever he pleased. But he was doomed to his fate: nothing, nothing would change him from a demon to a human. But Lamia, having been cast into the role of gray lady nearly fifteen centuries earlier, had a real chance at escape.

She had to trust that Dolon would uphold his end of the bargain. She knew he didn't love her. But she thought he'd want to be rid of her more than he wanted to take revenge on her for his plight.

But demons… they were hard to predict. And Dolon was a stubborn bastard at best.

Lamia tried to focus on the situation at hand and not worry about what might happen later. She'd only had four other chances like this in hundreds of years, and she wanted this to go smoothly. So far, Edgar and Elizabeth had proved malleable and perfectly willing to be hosts. She didn't pray any more, but felt a small part of her being lifted up.

But first, they needed two separate rooms, and impeccable timing.

They'd spent the day creating the identical bridal suites, one on either side of the castle. Dolon was quite handy with the details. She'd never known him to have a flair for decorating before. If this didn't work….

The stairwell was dark. Dolon had unscrewed all of the electric light bulbs. Alcohol would only make their hosts so blind; darkness was needed as well. Edgar and Elizabeth moved as one up the stairs, the remnants of their possession making them compliant. At the very top, fear began to emanate from one of them.

"Now," Lamia whispered.

A shimmering glow filled the air. Lamia felt the sweetness that was Elizabeth cover her like a gossamer blanket. The glamor was in place. Dolon winked at her as he shimmered into Edgar, taking Elizabeth's hand and pulling her toward the west bridal suit, as Lamia pulled Edgar to her side and continued down the hall.

"Wait," Elizabeth said, but Lamia coughed and made Edgar walk faster.

"I can't wait to be with you," she whispered, running her hands around the front of his trousers.

Edgar laughed, a throaty, drunken sound. "Not going to last long, sweetheart. I think I've had a bit too much to drink."

Lamia smiled her most feral grin. "That's fine, darling. Once is all we need."

Elizabeth woke just before dawn. She was horrendously sore between the legs. She blushed at the mere thought of the things they'd done. As drunk as she'd been, she was willing to try most anything. And Edgar, Edgar had tried most everything.

Oh, God. She had a horrible hangover. Bile rolled in her stomach, her head pounded. But she'd had the strangest dream. Her grandmother had come to her. She wanted her to drink saltwater upon rising. The woman had been dead for twenty years; Elizabeth rarely dreamt of her. But when she did, she always knew to examine the dream, what fleeting bits she could remember of it, then think to whatever pressing question had been weighing on her mind. Dreams of her grandmother signaled a decision would be made. Sometimes when she didn't even know she was struggling with a question.

Saltwater. Yuck. But she'd learned never to question, only to do. She went into the bathroom, looking for a glass. Her grandmother had been a wise woman.

Maybe there'd be salt on the table?

Edgar, curled in the bed behind her, looked exactly like hell. His skin was tinged with green, his hair spiked to one side of his face. He even looked like his beard was growing in. That was strange. Edgar wasn't a heavily furred man.

She spared him one last glance, then went to the window. She heard waves crashing. She hadn't realized the beach was so close. The castle perched on the edge of a cliff, with a long, rickety staircase leading down to the rocky beach below. In the waves, she saw a man swimming.

It looked like… no, that couldn't be. It looked like Edgar. But Edgar was in the bed behind her. Wasn't he?

A strange pull began in her stomach. She heard a voice calling her name.

"Elizabeth. Come to me."

She held her hand up in front of her face. It was transparent. Clear with the morning sun, she could see directly through her forearm and hand to the sill below.

The pull grew stronger. Panicked, she turned to call for Edgar, but there was no one there. She was alone in the room.

She fought her way to the window again, breath coming hard in her throat. There were two men swimming below now, one riding the back of the other in the waves. They were body surfing, two men, together as one. As she watched, they caught a wave and rode it in to the beach, then clambered out of the water. The man was Edgar, and the man attached to him was… Edgar, too.

Her breath began to fail. She didn't know what was happening.

"Come to me, Elizabeth. Come now." The voice called again, summoning. She had no control. She looked in the mirror and saw only a wisp of herself as she vanished into thin air. She was gone.

Edgar was exhilarated. He didn't know what possessed him to drag out of his warm bridal bed and go swimming in the cold surf, but he was glad he had. It cleared his head. He felt wonderful. Starving, in fact. And wanted to see Elizabeth. He wanted to see his wife *now*.

He grabbed the towel and dried off briskly, then started back up the wobbly wooden stairs. He had so much energy. So much power. My God, Elizabeth had done things to him he'd only read about. He had no idea she even knew those actions existed. Saving it for the wedding night, she was.

He didn't think they'd gotten more than an hour's sleep. Then he woke to the note—*My love, go for a swim. I'm getting us break-fast*—and thought to himself, *Yes, that's exactly what I'll do. I'll go for a swim.*

He bounded back to the castle, up, up the stairs to the bridal suite. He flung the doors open.

Elizabeth was on the floor under a large gray mass. She wasn't moving, but the mass was, sinuously sliding up and down Elizabeth's body.

"What is this?" he demanded, completely uncertain what to do.

There was a deep hissing noise, and he felt the room contract into coldness. Extreme fury pushed at his chest, making him fall back against the wall. A breeze began, one that smelled like sulfur, whipping his hair and drying the last drops of salt from his arms, and he heard the words falling through the air like the hiss of daggers.

"Dooooolllloooooon. Stooooop hiiiiiiiim."

Edgar looked away from the writhing mass for a moment and saw himself, standing on the far side of the room, arms crossed, a small grin on his face. Enjoying the show.

A small squeaking caught his attention. It was coming from Elizabeth. That thing was killing her.

Edgar tossed a glance at his twin, then threw himself at the thing. He smelled himself on her—his sweat, his semen—and realized he hadn't lain with his wife at all. The thought sickened him.

The thing wailed and fought against him. It was like wrestling smoke. Punches and kicks were ineffectual. Elizabeth's squeaking grew fainter.

With no full realization of what he was doing, he stood and rushed at his twin. Edgar laughed at him, moving out of the way slightly as he drew near.

How could this be? The real Edgar saw a mirror behind the thing that looked like him. Deviating at the last second, he ran smack into the mirror, causing it to shatter into a hundred pieces. He grabbed the largest from the floor and plunged back into the fray, stabbing at the gray thing with the shard.

"Elizabeth! I love you!" he screamed.

A deep, shrieking howl rose from the floor, and blood began to splash. Edgar slashed, and slashed again, until his could raise his arm no more, and his breath gave out.

The scream was earsplitting. The windows shattered. The walls began to shimmy. The bed rocked, and the wardrobe fell over. It was as if an earthquake had struck the room, accompanied by cries of such intensity Edgar felt himself going mad.

And then it stopped.

The silence was deafening.

It took a moment for him to realize he wasn't moving. And another to feel the smallness beside him.

"Elizabeth!" he cried.

She was no longer translucent, but rosily painted in the thing's blood. Her eyes were closed, and the parts of her skin that weren't red were deathly pale.

They were alone in the room.

He scrambled to his knees. "Elizabeth, can you hear me?"

She moaned, and his rational mind took over. Blood. There was so much blood.

It had to be hers.

He was rough with her, pulling her body to and fro, until he found the shard of mirror wedged deep within her arm. Blood was pouring from the wound; it must have struck an artery. He needed a tourniquet.

He grabbed the towel from the floor and wound it around Elizabeth's arm. She was going gray.

"Don't leave me, baby. Hang on."

She opened her eyes. "I. Love. You." Her eyes lost their focus.

He started CPR on her, fighting, pushing air into her lungs, pounding her chest. He didn't know how much time had passed. He just knew he couldn't give up.

"She's gone, you know. You can stop now."

The voice startled him. He looked up, and saw himself standing by the end of the bed. Only this version of himself wasn't covered in his love's blood.

"Who are you?"

"My name is Dolon."

"What have you done with Elizabeth? Why did you kill her?"

"I didn't. You did. You did a wondrous job of it too. Just look at her, won't you?"

Edgar glanced down. Elizabeth's eyes were open. The blood was gone. She was breathing. The horrid open wound in her arm had closed. She started to sit up, and Edgar, lost, bent to help her.

"Edgar, what happened?" She caught sight of Dolon, still looking like Edgar, and shook
her head. "I'm dreaming."

Dolon changed forms, just to show them he could, then disappeared.

Edgar rubbed his eyes. He knew he hadn't just seen what his mind said he saw. "I don't know. Something is very wrong with this place. We need to get out of here, right now. Can you stand?"

"I think so. Edgar, you were swimming. And my grandmother

told me to drink a glass of saltwater. I couldn't find the salt. I feel awful. Oh, God. Hold on..."

She turned to her right and retched onto the floor.

When she was able to stand upright again, Edgar searched her face.

"Elizabeth, what's wrong with your eyes?"

"What do you mean?"

"They've changed color. They're gray."

She rushed into the bathroom and looked. He wasn't lying; her beautiful brown eyes had turned a murky gray.

"I don't know what's going on, Edgar. Just... get me out of here."

He was backing away from her, a look of horror on his face.

"That thing... the thing that was eating you, it's inside you."

"Edgar, don't be silly."

"Elizabeth, you died. I saw it with my own eyes. I think... I think I killed you."

"Edgar, I'm very much alive. Look at me. I'm talking to you, aren't I?"

She was talking to him. But it wasn't her. He could tell. He could see the shadows of the woman he'd slept with last night, the details coming back to him in a rush. The teeth, long and pointed; the bat-like ears; the flesh hanging off her body; the vertebrae sticking out like armor.

"You," he said, voice hushed and terrified.

"Me," Lamia replied, her perfect pink tongue caressing her new pink lips. "Let's go home, husband."

ABOUT THE STORY

I spent several months of 2010 researching and writing about a castle in Scotland. The castle itself was fictional, cobbled together from multiple visits into Scotland, brochures and obsessive Googling of haunted castles. But it came alive for me on the page, as did its secrets. My castle, you see, was haunted.

In the way of all haunted castles, there are multiple tales, legends, sightings, and horror stories that accompany the structure. In a country whose history is so bloody, it's fitting to have remnants and echoes of those battles seep onto the page, whether between hundreds on Culloden Moor, or simply one on one, when bared, softly-skinned throats are slit in silent, stone-walled bedrooms.

Are the legends true? Are the castle ghosts of Scotland real? All I know for sure is I would sprinkle salt across my threshold and along my windowsills before I'd spend a night alone in Dulsie Castle. They say there is a gray lady who lurks in the attics. Her name is Lamia. The questions is, who, exactly, is she? And what does she want with you?

I'll never tell....

PRODIGAL ME

He's not speaking to me again.

It's happened before. I think the longest we've ever gone without some sort of verbal communication is two weeks. But that was back when he thought I'd tricked him and let myself get pregnant. I hadn't, but he didn't want to hear that from me. I remember it was two weeks because when I started to bleed, he started talking. Apologies, for the most part. The black eye had faded by then, too.

So I don't usually become alarmed when he quits conversing. I'm just not sure why I'm getting the silent treatment. I wonder how long it's going to last this time? It can actually be quite nice, not having to make conversation. We can sit at the kitchen table, each sipping from our respective coffee cups. I have many cups. I decide which to use based on my mood each morning. Today I have one of my favorites, decorated in loops and swirls of color—abstract, joyful. That's how I woke this morning: content, but feeling a bit out of place. This was the perfect chalice to represent my feelings.

Yesterday it was the bone white with the geometric, triangular handle. All sharp edges and uncomfortable to hold. No elegance there, befitting the dark nastiness that I'd felt when I got up.

But today was different. Better. Happy. Even without speech.

I watched him from under my lashes, tasting the bitter brew. He'd made the coffee before I arose. He'd been doing that lately, and it was unusual. Normally I was the first to the kitchen; the coffee was my responsibility. I certainly made a better pot. I wondered if that was why he'd designated the coffee to me in the first place, because his was lousy.

He was snapping the pages of the paper, passing through them so quickly that I knew he wasn't really reading anything. He knew I was watching him. He heaved a sigh and laid the paper flat on the wood of the table.

He looked at me then, finally. His eyes were bloodshot. Not attractive at all. When we'd first met, he had the most beautiful blue eyes, a shade that matched the sky on a crisp fall day. Today, they were muddy, a hint of brown in the azure depths. He didn't meet my eye, just stared at my shoulder. I slid my silk dressing gown down just a bit, enough for the smooth white skin above my collarbone to show. He dragged in a breath, swept up his cup, and threw it at the kitchen sink. It shattered, and I rolled my eyes.

Typical for him, communicating through violence. For a smart man, he was so very stupid.

I glanced at the clock on the stove; it was well past time for him to leave for work. I sat back in my chair, ignoring him. The sooner he was out of here, the sooner I could clean up his mess and start my own day.

He didn't leave right away. He'd walked out of the kitchen right after his temper tantrum, but went into his study instead of heading out the front door. He generally preferred that I stay out of his study. Even our maid, Marie-Cecile, was only allowed in twice a week to vacuum and dust, but she was never allowed to touch the desk proper. Those were his rules, and Marie-Cecile stuck by them faithfully, even while she muttered Haitian curses under her breath. It always gave me joy to see her in there, hexing him for his transgressions.

It struck me that I hadn't noticed Marie-Cecile's car in the drive. She arrives every day at 9:00 a.m. like clockwork, with Sundays off. Don't judge. With a house this size, you have to have someone to help with the work.

Besides, all of our friends had someone come in. Personally, Marie-Cecile was the best of the lot, but perhaps I'm bragging.

Today was Thursday, and it was already nine-thirty. Normally,

I'd be at the club; my Tuesday/Thursday golf group tees off between seven and nine. But I'd slept later than usual, and I wasn't in the mood to play this morning. I decided to join them for lunch instead.

I set about making the kitchen right, wondering where Marie-Cecile was. It wasn't like her to be tardy, to miss a day without letting me know in advance she wouldn't show up for work. She'd only done that about three times in the three years she'd been cleaning for us. Marie-Cecile was very reliable.

No matter. I was certainly capable of straightening up. The cup had been made of heavy fired clay, and though it had broken into about fourteen pieces, they weren't shards and slivers, but well-formed chunks, which made them a cinch to gather. That done, I wandered back to our bedroom.

Sunlight spilled through the windowpane, enhancing the patina on the buttery walls. I'd designed this room myself. The decorator had commandeered the house, overloading the rooms with her personal touches, but I wanted one small place that I knew was mine, and mine alone. Guests didn't get to venture into this part of the house. It was my own little refuge, even more so now that he was sleeping in his study. Eight bedrooms, and he chooses a hobnailed leather sofa. To each his own.

The bed wasn't made, which was odd. I knew I'd put it together before I made my way downstairs this morning. I always do. It's the first thing that happens when I wake up. I slide out the right edge, pull up the covers and plump the pillows. Maybe he had come back into the room after I went downstairs, pulled the covers back to tick me off. Typical.

I made up the bed, humming to myself. That's when I found the hair. It was his, there was no question about it.

I must have had too much to drink last night.

He'd slept in the bed with me, and I didn't even remember. Perhaps that was the cause of his silence. Things hadn't gone as well as he hoped?

It's hard to explain, but he does come to me, in the night. I let him, mostly because it's my duty to perform, but also in remembrance of a time when I welcomed him without thought, joyful that he'd chosen to be with me. It wasn't that long ago, after all.

Bed made, I showered and dressed in khaki slacks and a long sleeved Polo shirt. I threw a button down over my shoulders in case it was still cool out. Layers for my comfort, layers for their perception of how I should look when I walked into the club. The official dress code was undiluted preppy.

He was gone when I passed the study on my way to the foyer.

It simply was not meant to be my morning. My Jag wouldn't start. And Marie-Cecile was nowhere to be found, so I didn't have a ride. We lived on the golf course though, so I detoured through the fourteenth fairway and wandered up the cart path on the eighteenth. We're not supposed to do that, but I timed it well—right after the ladies group had finished and before the senior's group made the first turn.

I arrived at the front doors a little breathless, more from the chill than the exercise. I'm in good shape.

As his wife, I have to be. It's expected. Not much of a challenge for me; I'm naturally tall and willowy, but I still work with a trainer three times a week. Like I said, it's expected.

My friends and I have a standing luncheon on Tuesdays and Thursdays. After our round, we gather in the Grill Room, settle our bets, eat some salad, and gossip. Some of the older ladies play bridge. I've always wanted to learn; I just haven't gotten around to it. There is something so lonely about them, sitting in their Lilly Pulitzer capris, their visors still pulled low, shading their eyes from the glare of the multitudes of 60-watt bulbs. Sad.

My usual foursome was sitting along the back wall today. Bunny (that's actually her name, I've seen the birth certificate) had the farthest spot, the place of honor: back to the wall, viewable by the whole room.

My spot.

She lounged against the arm of the chair, her feet propped on the empty chair facing the window, looking for all the world like a queen ready for coronation.

My punishment for missing the round this morning, I suppose. Bunny glistened with the faint flush of exertion. She always looked like she'd just rolled out of bed, freshly plucked and glowing. No wonder there; she was sleeping with half the married men in the club, as well as most of the tennis and golf pros.

Probably a couple of the high school caddies and college kids, too.

Tally and Kim rounded out our little threesome, both looking a bit peaked. Tally was short and brunette, a striking contrast to Bunny's wholesome blondness. Kim was blonde, a little dishwater, but since she'd moved to Bunny's hairdresser, she'd been getting some subtle highlights that worked for her complexion.

Kim was fiddling with her scorecard, probably erasing a couple of shots. We all knew she cheated. We let her.

Tally sat with her back barely touching the chair, ramrod straight. Uncharacteristic for her; she usually slouched and sprawled like the rest of us. The chairs were suede-lined and double width for our comfort, and they served their purpose well.

I approached the table, expecting Bunny to see me and drop her feet off my newly assigned chair.

Instead, she was talking about me.

I stopped, indignant. They hadn't even noticed I'd come in. Bunny was so caught up with whatever maliciousness she'd intended for the day that she didn't realize I was standing barely five feet away. I could hear her clearly. Talking about me. Gossiping about me.

That little bitch.

I started for her, then stopped. Maybe I'd eavesdrop a little more, see what I could use against them later.

Don't get me wrong, I'm not naïve enough to think that a group of women friends aren't going to talk to one another about the missing person. But there's a big difference between talking about a friend who's absent and publicly dissecting that friend's life. We're all somebody, the four of us. Which means that there are multitudes of fodder, plenty of grist for the communal mill.

There are some things that are sacred, though, and an open discussion of my disastrous marriage is one of them. You just don't do that.

I started toward the table again, ready to give Miss Bunny a walloping with the side of my tongue. A short frizzled blond with mismatched socks beat me.

Damn. Shirley.

Shirley was one of those people. You know the ones I mean. Not to be mean, but they drift around the periphery of any tight knit group, waiting like a dog for the table scraps. Shirley wanted to be a part of our group, but that would never happen. She was just too annoying.

Yet Bunny's face lit up when she saw the diminutive disaster headed to the table. She swung her feet off the chair, rose like Amphitrite from the depths, and hugged Shirley. Physical contact with a barnacle? That was well known to be strictly forbidden. What in the hell was going on today?

I had become persona non grata without a clue as to why. No one would look at me; each woman kept her eyes from mine. Busboys and waiters wandered right past me, no one asking to help me, no one offering me a refreshment. After my long walk to the clubhouse, I could have used a nice Chardonnay.

That was it. It was time I let my presence be known to my so-called friends.

I glided to the table, mouth slightly open, deciding which opening I'd use.

Hello girls, waiting for me?

You lousy bitches, how dare you speak about me behind my back?

Bunny, you look divine today—whose sperm are you carrying? Kim, I think you need a quick trip to Alberto's. And Tally, darling, do try to sit back—you look like you've got a pole stuck up your ass.

But all my words died in my throat when I saw what Shirley had brought as an offering to my group of friends. The newspaper unfurled, bearing a special edition logo, the headline seventy point.

GUILTY, it screamed.

I stormed through the house, searching.

How dare *he. How could he do it? What was he thinking?*

I wasn't finding what I was looking for. I needed to stop and think. I was in a black rage; I couldn't even see straight when I was this worked up. So I sat on the bottom step and took a few breaths. That helped.

My husband was not a foolish man. He wouldn't have left a trail, or a bunch of clues. I had all night to search. The rest of my life, if it was necessary.

I'd start in the obvious place. The basement.

I'd had a very difficult time reading the article Shirley had brought to my friends in gleeful attribution.

She was a lawyer, one of the few women in our circle that actually worked for a living. A prosecutor, at that. Assistant District Attorney Shirley Kleebel. She paid her dues, if you know what I mean. She wasn't married to, or aligned with, a man of the club. *She* was the member, one of the few singles to join. That's part of the reason she'd never make it into the right circles. We had nothing to gain by being around her.

Really, even meek and mild Tally had her signature on the checking account of the largest footwear mogul in the country. Shirley had nothing, except her name.

So I'd been a bit skeptical when I'd read the article. If I'm being totally honest, I didn't believe it. Not that it was outside the realm of possibility. My husband could be vicious when he chose.

It lauded Shirley as a genius, having resurrected a trial that was not only lost before it began, but achieving a guilty plea from the jury. I ran the article over and over in my head as I searched. According to the reporter, this had been done already. Several fruitless times, in fact.

But it's a big house. There are places no one would think to look simply because they wouldn't know they were there. Passages between floors with unseen staircases, a tunnel in the basement that accessed the freestanding garage. Escape routes. I thought them charming when we'd bought the house, then put them out of my mind. Now I needed to comb through them, because I knew I'd find the truth in one of those dark, dank places.

Either way, he wouldn't be coming home tonight. There wouldn't be any more arguments, no broken coffee cups, no unmade beds.

The bed.

He'd slept in the bed last night. And he'd cried. I remember that now. He sobbed winningly, and told me how sorry he was. That he'd never meant for it to go so far. That he loved me, he truly did. He'd cried himself to sleep, then gotten up in the middle of the night and wandered away.

I hadn't understood the night before. Now I'm afraid I might. But I had to see for myself.

The basement reeked pleasantly of cool and damp. I sensed nothing unusual, no odors, no sights that gave me cause for alarm. I crept around the corner, slipping silently through the gloom. If what the article said was true, if my friends' gossip was accurate, I'd have ages to find all of the little passageways in this house. I think there's one that goes all the way up to the clubhouse, but I've never found it.

The one I did know about was just ahead. A false wall, easily misleading without the exact knowledge of where it should be. If you looked closely, you could see a crack in the foundation, like the floor is settling. The fracture runs up the wall, and if you push just the right brick…

There.

The wall swung open to reveal a small passageway. When the house was built over two hundred years ago, the original owner wanted to be buried in the house. That's right, *in* the house. The crypt was the logical place to look.

I couldn't describe the emotions I felt when I saw it. It was a sloppy job. He knew no one would ever find their way in here by accident. He thought he was safe.

So pale.

I'd always loved my hands, long fingered, smooth skinned. Sticking up out of the dirt, though, they didn't look quite as nice.

The article said it was Marie-Cecile that testified against him. She'd seen it all. Seen his hands around my throat. I wonder why I don't remember that part.

Son of a bitch. I hope he rots in jail.

Maybe I'll go visit him.

ABOUT THE STORY

They say you never forget your first. And isn't that the truth? This is the story that started me along the path to writing short-form fiction. I'd been hounded by several friends who wanted me to try writing a short story. I wrote this basically on a dare—I'd never tried to write anything under 100,000 words before. But I finally caved, and tried. This is what came out.

I liked it. They liked it. So I took things a step further and submitted to *Writer's Digest* for their annual fiction contest, then forgot about it and moved back to the novel I was writing. Imagine my utter shock when I received a letter telling me I'd placed. The story was a hit. I revised it to use for the *Killer Year: Stories to Die For* anthology, and received my first ever review—they called the story "Hitchcockian."

That's all the impetus I needed. My career as a short story writer was born.

So this is the story of my heart. My first, on many levels.

THE OMEN DAYS

Christmas
Nashville, Tennessee

Mercy Lounge. Heaving masses of bodies writhing back and forth in time with the heavy bass beat, yelling and screaming, happy faces locked on the stage, eyes lit up and mouths stretched into manic grins. It smells like teen spirit, and brimstone, and cold iron from the overhead girders, which are sprinkled with fake frost, all overlaid with the thick, sweet scent of liquor. Guilty Pleasures are playing a Christmas show. I am drinking. Heavily.

I hate Christmas.

It's not only the weather. Christmas in the South is hit or miss. Some years, it's eighty degrees and we're playing football in the backyard. Others it's cold enough for snow, light dustings of white crystals shadowing everything. Most years, though, it's freezing cold, and bleak, and empty. Slate skies with nothing falling but the temperature and my mood. What's the point of Christmas without snow?

But that's Nashville for you. Utterly unpredictable. Especially during the holidays, when the kids are off from school and the parents are high on rage and champagne and tinsel and greed, loaded with murderous intent.

Thinking about it, maybe *hate* isn't a strong enough word. I loathe Christmas. I despise it. I would rather dig a hole the first weekend of December and emerge again with that poor groundhog in February, when the insanity and water-cooler talk of the holidays are truly over.

Maybe it's because I don't have a family nearby, and I'm not religious, and as low man on the totem pole, I usually get stuck on call. There's nothing like being an undercover cop on Christmas. You see everything humanity has to give at the holidays. It's like the full moon: it brings out the worst in people, and it brings out the best in others. I rarely see the best, though. Nature of the beast.

Maybe it's because people are harried, tired of the year and the demands of their lives, or because they're ready to turn over a new leaf, to start fresh, start again. It does feel like we're all simply going through the motions.

And not maybe, truth: spending the holidays alone sucks.

What I do sort of like are the days *after* Christmas. That time when all goes quiet: silent night, holy night, all is calm, all is bright. A certain peace steals over the city, as if everyone's breath is held in anticipation of the new year.

The calendar didn't used to have an exact number of days, and it ran according to the sun. The long nights and shorter days of winter meant there were always a few days at the end of the sun year that didn't fit in with the calendar. This is a mystical time. If you look at your Greek, Norse, or Roman mythology, this is when legends are born, when gods and goddesses spring forth, crossing the veil of the two worlds, blurring the lines between mortal and immortal. This is where the twelve days of Christmas really comes from—not silly gifts of French hens and lords leaping and partridges. It's those lost days at the end of the year.

The Omen Days.

I think it would be better if we called them by their true title. It's more fitting, really. You can figure out a lot about your life in those twelve days after Christmas, when the old year dies and all its highs and lows become a memory.

But whatever you call it, or I call it, I can't find the joy in the season. Not anymore. It hasn't been a real Christmas since I lost her.

So I count the days until the season draws to a close and do everything I can to distract myself. Like tonight's bacchanalia on Cannery Row.

Grimey shouts something and the band switches gears, going full bore into "Cruel Summer," and the girls from behind the bar jump on the stage and dance. I'm dancing now too, throwing my left arm in the air, trying not to spill the drink in my right hand. I have enough whiskey in my system to let me relax a bit. The band plays on and on, mining the best hits from a bygone era. With each new tune, I scream the words at the top of my lungs, feel the enmity leave. The crowd melts together into the most raucous sing-along yet. "And I'm gonna keep on loving you... "

I gulp more of my old buddy Jack with its tiny splash of Coke for fizz, let the blessed numbness calm my tortured soul.

The band shifts to Journey, and I'm believing, all right. I'm taken back to our first prom. The whiskey threatens to come up, so I have some more. I'm rocked now, completely drunk, limbs loose, vision off. On stage, if I'm not mistaken, someone has joined the band and is wearing a codpiece. Ballsy.

My shift today was long and sad and full of unhappy people doing stupid things, and tonight I am trying to disappear into the fabric of the city and let it consume me. I order another drink. I will feel exactly like hell tomorrow, but tonight... tonight, I can try to forget.

I'm here with my two best friends, Stephen and Jim. We used to be roommates until my undercover gig made it awkward for me and too dangerous for them. I needed room to be by myself, roaming town as the lone wolf, busting drug dealers and pimps, but I miss the days at the townhouse, the three of us howling at the moon together.

Friends are a good thing to have when you're alone.

Jim is a patient advocate lawyer, and Stephen is a writer. They're both good at their jobs: Stephen won an award for his debut novel this spring and is writing a new book, and Jim got a partner offer last week. The three of us couldn't be more different. We met at Vanderbilt freshman year, in Dr. Tichi's English Comp, and have been thick as thieves ever since. They got me through the breakup, for which I'm usually grateful. Usually.

These two men are good to their cores. I wouldn't be the man I am without them. Though at this moment, their actions are questionable. They are dancing, unsteady and silly, jumping up and down, heads bobbing. Jim is carelessly spilling beer down his arm, soaking his blue Brooks Brothers button-down, but he's too drunk to care. Stephen is drinking whiskey, like me, but at a slower pace. He has to meet up with family tomorrow and doesn't want to spend the day puking and green. He is sliding around from side to side, creating enough space in the crowd to do the moonwalk, the "Thriller" dance, the works. He looks like an idiot. I love him. I love both of them.

We are moving as one, the crowd and the guys, and the music is pumping and I'm almost, almost, at a place I could call happy when I turn my head to shout at Stephen's antics. . . and that's when I see her. The world screeches to a halt. The music fades. The room stops heaving.

Autumn is here.

Autumn Cleary was my first everything: friend, kiss, car ride, football game, dinner date, blow job, sex. We met in kindergarten and spent the next eighteen years either fighting or kissing, and sometimes both at once. We had plans, man. White picket fences and two point five kids and a dog. The whole American dream.

But soon after we graduated from college, Autumn broke my heart.

It was a clean break. She looked at me one night two weeks before Christmas, when we were getting ready for bed, and said, "I'm leaving in the morning. I thought you should know, in case you wanted to talk about it."

"What do you mean you're leaving? On a trip? To where?"

Brilliant of me, I know. No one ever said I was smart.

She sat down on the side of the bed, her blond hair falling in waves around her shoulders. She'd gotten it cut two days earlier, taking her waist-length hair to a long bob, a *lob*, she called it, and it was so different. She was so different.

She must have seen some sort of recognition of that in my eyes, because she smiled sadly and touched her hair self-consciously. "I know it's strange. I needed a change, and this wasn't enough. I need to do something else. I love you. I'll always love you. But I want to be by myself for a while."

A desperate wave of fear and hurt and panic started to rise in my chest. I wanted to roar, to scream, to beg and plead. My worst fears were being realized, my very worst nightmares coming alive. Losing Autumn would kill me dead, as sure as a bullet. My heart rattled against my ribs, and I took a deep breath, somehow managed to hold the tidal wave at bay.

"Did I do something? Say something? What in the name of fuck is wrong, Autumn?"

She smelled of cinnamon. She'd been decorating the apartment— *why would you decorate if you were planning to leave, Autumn?*—and I had the insane urge to push her down and roll on her body like a dog, get her scent all over me before it was too late: cinnamon and cloves and lavender and that soap she used on our clothes, the organic stuff that was safe for the environment and smelled like rain. It was a heady perfume, and I didn't want to forget it.

Perched on the edge of our big bed, she said the words that tore us asunder. "Baby, if I knew the answer, I wouldn't have to leave. Something's wrong. I don't know if it's you or me, but I'm going to give us some space and find out. I don't want to end up like our parents. I refuse to do that. You remember how..."

Remember? How could I not? Autumn's mom had pretty severe clinical depression one year, got sadder and sadder, and she started to drink, and her dad ignored them both, spent all his time in the basement or the golf course, until her mom finally decided enough was enough and hung herself in the bathroom. Autumn was eight. She never got over it. Not that anyone expected her to.

Autumn was still talking. "... and I don't want that to happen to us. I'd rather remember us as perfect than spend a minute unhappy."

"You're unhappy?" I'd whispered, confused, so confused.

"Yeah, I think I am." She'd reached out a hand and grabbed mine, her long white fingers so elegant and soft against my blunt ones. "You're not happy either. You just don't want to admit it. Trust me. This is for the best."

Then she drew me down and kissed me, and we made love, hard and wet and furious and desperate, and in the morning, when I woke up, she was gone. My soul was broken in two, and nothing, nothing, could ever fix it.

All I've dreamed about for the past seven years is finding her again. Holding her in my arms, warm and fragrant. Having the life I'd always envisioned, the one where we're together with our kids and our dog, our happy, perfect dream. It was always us against the world.

And here she is. She's standing by the door, a drink in her hand. As far as I know, she hasn't been back to Nashville since she left. She wasn't close to her dad after her mom's death, had bounced around her girlfriends' houses and mine until she moved in with me permanently sophomore year of college, our first apartment.

I assume she still has friends here. No one speaks Autumn's name to me. Ever. It is an understanding I have with my whole world. We were the "Most Likely" couple. Prom king and queen, most likely to get married, most likely to get pregnant in college, everything. When we broke up, it was like a bubble of hope and comfort burst for everyone who knew us. Everyone hates her for what she did to me, how she left me—all of a sudden, with no real warning, and no real explanations. No one understands what happened, least of all me.

From what little I know, Autumn has gotten on with her life. I haven't, not really. Don't think I've lived a monk for seven years. There have been other women. None have touched my soul the way Autumn did. No one ever will.

Face it: I'm a heartbroken asshole who can't get over his first love.

A first love who is now moving toward me. Almost like she's making sure I see her. She's getting closer.

Is she going to come over here and talk to me?

Panic rises in me. I have the insane urge to run away. I don't know what I'll do if she tries to talk to me. I'm torn between hugging her and hitting her, which is a very bad way to feel when I've consumed half a bottle of Jack.

I'm not a volatile guy, but this woman ruined me.

Breathe. Breathe. Breathe.

She's watching me. She looks sad. Thin. The blond hair is even shorter now than when I saw her last. It grazes her chin, the front longer than the back, the ends flipping toward me like a ski jump.

Stephen and Jim notice me staring away from the stage. Stephen says, "Dude, what is your damage?"

"Autumn," I manage to spit out.

Jim overhears this news, sobers immediately, puts a hand on my arm as if to hold me back. He cranes his neck to see over the crowd. "Where? I don't see her."

"By the door. Her hair's short."

"I still don't see her. I'm going over."

"Shit, no. Don't. Stay here. If anyone should go over, it's me."

Autumn is still staring at me. I take one step toward her, ignoring the cries of my friends. Another. Then a big guy wearing a flannel shirt and Dr. Martens steps to her side. She smiles up at him, gratefully, I think, casts one last glance at me, almost as if she wants to be sure I'm watching, and leaves with the lumberjack.

Autumn leaves. She walks out without saying anything to me, and I am struck dumb and nearly blind by the pain.

The guys shuffle me over to the bar, dump me on a stool covered in questionable stains, and shove another drink in my hand. Seconds later, it is gone and another replaces it.

One of them asks, "You okay, dude?"

"Did you see her?" I choke out. "Who was that douche she left with?" I am slurring. I am making no sense.

Stephen's eyes are grave. "I didn't see her, man."

"Me neither," Jim adds. "She must have chickened out when she saw you. I didn't know she was back in town. I thought I would have heard."

If anyone would have, it was Jim. He'd always had his finger on the pulse of our crowd, and his girlfriend Joy had been Autumn's best friend back in the day. They'd kept in touch for a few years, probably more, but I'd asked not to be informed when they heard from her. It hurt too damn much.

Stephen is looking at me with concern. "You're pretty fucked up. Maybe we should bail."

"You stay. I want to be alone." I manage to stand up, though my legs are wobbly. I hear Jim murmur, "Is he carrying?" and Stephen say, "Is he ever not?" and Jim comes to my side and says quietly, the word a demand, "Gun."

A pretty girl with wads of blond dreadlocks whips her heads around. A wave of patchouli stings my nose. She's gone white, instantly terrified, is staring at Jim, ready to spring away to save herself.

"Fun!" Jim yells, waving her off, then walks me to the door. I see Stephen eyeing Patchouli; he's always gone for the hippy types. Good. I like it when he's occupied. He'll go home with the girl instead of sleeping on my couch. I wasn't kidding when I said I want to be alone right now.

Down the stairs, out the doors. Half the crowd is out on the sidewalk and balcony smoking. I slur my way into bumming one. Jim helps me light it, then walks me into the parking lot.

He makes sure we're alone. I use a vintage Beetle covered in stickers to hold myself up.

He points to my ankle holster, hidden beneath my jeans and boot. "Do you need to leave that with me?"

"Naw, no reason to. There's more where that came from."

"Not funny, dude. I don't want you doing anything stupid."

"You're a good friend, man." I slap at his chest, missing, hitting his bicep instead. "Yeah, I'm good. Gonna walk. Walk it off."

Jim looks worried. He's thinking he should make sure I get home in one piece.

"Don't worry," I tell him. "I'm a grown man. I've grown up, man." This strikes me as funny, and I start to giggle. Jim purses his lips like a teacher about to scold me, and it sets me off in gales of laughter. He rolls his eyes. He's not sober, not by a long shot, or else he'd never send me off alone, but I am in luck. He's drunk enough to let me go.

"Okay, tough guy. Call me in the morning. Don't be a dummy. Walk straight home. Don't drink anything more."

"Yes, Mom. I will not pass Go. I will not collect two hundred dollars. I will not eat pancakes with a fox. I will not linger with the lox."

"You're a fucking idiot." Jim starts to say something else, then squeezes my shoulder and heads back inside. It feels good to be alone.

A chick in angel wings and thigh-high boots walks past me, smoking.

"Hey. Can I buy your pack off you?"

She gives me a look, then tosses it to me. "Looks like you need them more than me. Merry Christmas, beeyotch."

I nod gratefully. Merry fucking Christmas, indeed.

I walk. The city is quiet, and there's glory in this.

I head toward Broadway, past Cummins Station, giving it a dirty look as I go. They're ruining the historical building, and it hurts to see my town growing and changing the way it has in the past few years. We're being overrun. I think the crane-to-person ratio is at an all-time high. They have T-shirts with cranes in the Nashville skyline now. We have totally jumped the shark with all the new construction. Soon enough it will be a ghost town again, the new buildings only partially full, because the millennials are getting knocked up and moving to the suburbs for better schools. Wax and wane. The story of any city.

When I pass the Frist and step onto the sidewalk on Broadway, I realize I don't want to be out anymore. Seeing the changes is going to depress me. I want to go home, climb into bed, pass out. Say goodbye to this fuck-awful night. I turn back, swing over to Demonbreun, walk down 11th, barely keeping my balance on the decline.

My apartment in is the Gulch, in a one-way alley behind Bar Louie's and The Pub. I'm right in the midst of the action, and it's usually packed with people, but tonight, it's empty, quiet, eerie. One brave soul is out walking her dog, a big-ass Aleutian something that I've seen around before. I give her a little wave, then head into my building.

My apartment is cold and quiet. I grab a beer from the fridge and sit down, hard, on the couch. I slug down the beer, toss the can toward the kitchen, then half fall, half roll onto my side, cheek against the cheap leather. The lights outside blink incessantly, and I put my hand over my eyes.

Autumn.

Even the thought of her name sends a spike of pain through my body so intense it numbs me.

And then I'm gone. Gone. Spinning and drifting and trying like hell to get her out of my mind, slipping into sleep when I hear a voice, soft and elegant, saying my name, over and over, like a prayer.

Zachary. Zachary. Zachary.

I open my eyes and she's there, sitting on the coffee table. Autumn still looks sad, but she's alone.

God, I am so drunk I'm manifesting my ex-girlfriend in my living room. What was in that whiskey?

"Zack. Wake up."

And… bonus. She talks, too. Great. Okay. Maybe this is a dream.

Maybe it's a dream come true.

I sit up, wiping my lips. I taste awful, cigarettes and beer and whiskey. She smells good, like cinnamon and cloves. Yep, it's a dream. I'm going to wake up with my hand wrapped around my cock, like I do so often when I dream about Autumn. I play along.

"Autumn?"

"Hey." She reaches over and brushes a strand of my too-long hair off my forehead. She used to do that when we were together, and she's done it in all the dreams I've had of her since.

Except this isn't a dream.

I sit bolt upright and scramble back into the couch.

"Jesus Christ. You're here. How'd you find me?"

"Calm down. I followed you from the bar. You left your door unlocked. For a cop, you aren't very cautious." She looks around, smiling. "This is a nice place. I'm surprised you live alone."

"The guys were sick of me."

"I meant without a girlfriend. Or a wife."

Silence. She smiles again. Her hand drops back into her lap. She's sitting on the coffee table, facing me, smiling and talking, and I can't decide whether I've gone round the bend or she's actually here.

"I'm glad," she says. "I would have been jealous."

"You don't have the right to be jealous. Not about this."

She nods, her hair flipping with the movement. "You're right. I don't. Honestly, I'd be happier if you did have someone. I wouldn't feel as bad about… everything."

"Oh, you mean bailing on me, on us, on our life and plans? *Now* you feel bad?"

I stand up, brushing past her, and go into the kitchen. My apartment is pretty nice. Reclaimed wood, exposed brick, lots of glass. The kitchen is a decent size. I like to cook, like to nest. Autumn gave me those gifts. She showed me how important it was to have a home, not a place to crash at night.

I grab another beer from the fridge. Slam the door. She's watching me. With a sigh, I gesture to the beer. She nods. I hand it to her. Our hands brush, and it's like a lightning strike. I jump back and move to a stool at my breakfast bar, keeping fifteen feet between us.

"Why are you here?"

"I wanted to see you and—"

"You don't get to make arbitrary decisions with my life anymore, Autumn. Showing up out of the blue isn't cool."

She ignores my interruption. "—and say that I'm sorry. I shouldn't have left. It was a dumb mistake, made by a dumb kid who didn't know herself very well. You deserved better. Deserve better. I am so sorry, Zack. I know you are furious with me, and you should be. But I couldn't let things end on such a horrible note. I had to tell you how much I miss you. How sad I've been without you."

I am floored by this speech. Floored and angry. "Seven years? And now you decide to show up and throw this at me?"

"My dad died. Did you know?"

"No."

"It was a couple of years after I left. He didn't want a funeral or anything, he was cremated. I came back for the ashes, drove around. I'd been miserable since I left, and I wanted to come back. I went by your place with the guys that night. You were with someone, a girl with black hair. On the front porch. You were smiling, holding her hand. You seemed happy. I didn't want to ruin it for you."

"She meant nothing."

"How was I supposed to know that?" She's being snappish, and I almost laugh. Almost.

"What would you have done if I was alone that night?"

"I would have thrown myself on the floor at your feet and begged you to take me back."

The pain of this admission is almost too much to bear. "So you disappeared again, didn't even bother to try and reach out?"

"Yeah. I went back to Austin—that's where I am now, outside of Austin—and tried to get on with my life. Dated a couple of guys, nothing serious. I couldn't get you out of my head, that moment in time with you holding another girl's hand. Who was she?"

"Honestly? I have no idea. No one's ever mattered to me but you."

She sighs then, and it's a happy sound. A sigh of relief, I think. "I'm glad to hear that. I've missed you so much. I felt so stupid, and I didn't know how to come back, how to ask for forgiveness. And then, time passed. The days went faster and faster. I got a job I liked, met some friends, real friends. I told myself you were my past, that Austin held my future. I was wrong. I was so wrong. Without you, I have no future."

She begins to cry, soft and gentle. I go to her without thought, pull her into my arms. She feels so thin, so insubstantial. It's weird, but I figure it's been seven years and I've had a lot to drink, and besides, this is a whopper of a dream—I've changed my mind, it *is* a dream—so I tuck her head under my chin and hold on tighter.

It doesn't take long for her to stop crying. She raises her head and looks up at me with those intense blue eyes. I do the only thing I know to do. I touch my lips to hers, gently at first, but when her arms go around my waist and she sinks into the kiss, I let go. Seven years of pain and fury and love and fear and loneliness go into that kiss. It is epic. We have never kissed this way before, as if we know stopping will untether us forever.

She's small, Autumn, and I easily scoop her into my arms and carry her to my bed, all without breaking the kiss. Her shirt buttons down the front and they come free with a single pinch. The soft cotton slips back over her pure white shoulders. She isn't wearing a bra, and my hands find the warmth of her breasts.

She has the buttons on my jeans undone now, and I am inching hers down. I don't want to rush; it's been so long, but she's yanking down the fabric, running her hands along my thighs and grabbing ahold of me. She breaks the kiss with a gasp and drops to her knees. Soft, so soft. I gather her hair in my hand and do everything in my power not to give up, not yet.

She laughs when she feels me tense, and that sends me over the edge. I pull her up, stumble backward to the bed with her in my arms, my lips locked on her again. She wraps her legs around me and slides onto me.

Time stops.

There is something about the way we fit together when we're making love that I've never experienced with another woman. I've also never dreamed about it. This feeling, this sensation that I'm buried in the depths of the universe, hasn't happened since the night she left me.

My hands are in her hair, and she's going faster and faster until we're both out of control. It lasts a long time. I am not ready to give up, to give in. I want this to go on forever.

The sky is lightening when Autumn untangles herself from me and goes to the bag she left on the coffee table. We haven't slept a wink. I am sore and she is sore, and we've laughed and loved together for hours. She's back, she's back with me, and I am complete once more.

I watch her small body cross the room.

"Get back here," I say, but she shakes her head.

"I can't. I have to go back."

"To Texas? Not without me."

She drags on her jeans and her top, steps into her shoes. She returns to the bed, sits on the edge. I feel the familiar horror of the situation, know the happiness we've shared tonight is about to come to an end.

"Don't leave. God, Autumn, don't leave me again."

She leans over and kisses me, fragrant and lovely. When she draws back, she's no longer smiling. "There's something I have to do. This is not over, you and I. I promise." She reaches into her leather bag and draws out a watch. It is a nice watch, a dark blue face with heavy silver links. There is a logo on the top, but I don't recognize the brand.

"I want you to wear this until I get back. Promise me you won't take it off. It's important, Zack. You can't take it off."

"Hey, you haven't given me a gift in a long time. I won't ever take it off." I take the watch and snap it onto my wrist. It is a perfect fit.

She looks relieved, as if she were worried the watch wouldn't fit or I wouldn't like it. And it's a little weird, that she's making me promise not to take it off, but I love this woman, and it seems like a simple request. If it makes her happy, I'll comply. But I don't want her to go.

"Give me a minute to pack a bag, and I'll go with you."

She hugs me, hard and long, then steps back. "I have to do this alone. I love you, Zack. Always have, always will."

She heads toward the door. I'm out of the bed now, striding after her. "Wait!"

She has her hand on the doorknob. She turns and blows me a kiss.

"I'll see you soon. Promise." And the door shuts behind her.

The sun is coming up in earnest now. There are flashes on the sterile buildings opposite me; the intense glare of glass and metal makes me squint. I run my fingers over my lips, glance at the watch. I feel good. Better than I have in years.

I check the time on the watch against my phone. It's almost 7:00 a.m. I have three missed calls, all from the past hour. I guess I turned the ringer off when we went to bed, or maybe when I got home. Whatever. Jim and Stephen both have called to check on me.

I go into the kitchen, make a cup of coffee. Take it with me to the bedroom. The sheets are rumpled. The room smells of Autumn. The weight of the watch is heavy on my wrist. It wasn't a dream. She was actually here. She loves me.

I wish she hadn't run out of here like she needed to do the walk of shame. But the things we talked about in the night come back to me. I trust her. She said she'll be back, and I'm sure she will.

All is right in the world. Or it will be, as soon as I have her in my arms again.

My phone rings. Jim, yet again. This time I answer.

"Dude, I'm fine, I'm fine. I'm…"

"Shut up and listen to me. I don't know what the hell is going on, but I got a call. Autumn Cleary is missing."

"Yeah, about that. She was here most of the night. She followed me home from the bar. Felt bad. Wanted to talk. And other things."

There was silence.

"What? Don't even tell me I shouldn't have done it. She followed me home, man. We're getting back together."

"Zack, she lives in Texas. She went missing from a bar last night. In Austin."

"I know, she told me. That she lives in Austin, I mean."

"She wasn't in Nashville. She was in Austin last night."

"Then she drives like a bat out of hell, to get here so fast."

"Dude, you aren't hearing me. She went missing at midnight. Walked to the bathroom, didn't come back. Her friends are going wild."

I suddenly have a headache, and the pain pulses like a gong. "But that's impossible. We saw her at midnight. She was at Mercy Lounge with that big motherfucker."

Silence again. "We didn't see her, man. And you were really drunk."

"This is ridiculous. There's been a mistake. I saw her clear as day. And she's been here for hours. She gave me a watch, for God's sake. An apology watch." I tap the metal. Yes, the watch is very real. "Someone's made a mistake." I am repeating myself, as if saying it multiple times will make it true. I don't have any other words. Can't think any other thoughts. There *must* be a mistake.

"I think I should come over," Jim said in the tone he usually reserves for the mentally ill clients he represents.

The watch catches the light from the sunrise, sending graceful beams dancing across the apartment. "This is too weird for me, man. There's some sort of mistake."

"Zack, it's all over the Internet. She's some sort of bigwig in Austin now, does merchandising for a record company that has all kinds of musicians through there. The label has put up a reward for news of her."

"What are you saying?"

"I don't know, man. You tell me. You claim you saw her, you spent time talking, but at the same time, in another state, twelve hours away, she was hanging out with some girlfriends at a bar, and went missing. She couldn't get here that fast, there's no way. And she can't be in two places at once. Something's not right."

"No kidding. Fine, whatever. Come over. I'll prove she was here." I hang up.

Either I'm losing my mind, or... no. That's not possible. Not at all.

I ran a hand across my mouth. The taste of her lingers on my lips.

I flip open my laptop, scroll to Google News. My heart stops. Literally skips and stops beating. I suck in a breath and refresh the page, my heart hammering as fast as a thoroughbred's hooves thundering down a racetrack.

The picture of Autumn is current, based on what I saw last night. The haircut, the impossibly big blue eyes, the thin frame, the tender smile.

Above it, in huge, 24-point font, the headline screams:

AUSTIN WOMAN MISSING

I shake my head. This is impossible. She was here. There is no question in my mind that Autumn spent the night in my apartment, in my bed, in my arms.

I am a police officer. I am a logical, realistic human being. The love of my life spent the night in my apartment, but she also is missing from her hometown.

What if it wasn't really her? What if Jim's right?

An eerie sense of loss fills me as I do the math.

There's only one way a woman could be in two places at once.

And Autumn couldn't be a ghost.

Could she?

The news of Autumn's disappearance goes national two days later, when the Austin police find a traffic cam that shows her walking out of the bar, down the street, and disappearing into the night. Moments later, a tan Camry can be seen peeling away from the dark spot in the video. The police surmised she either got into the car willingly or was forced into it by an assailant. There are BOLOs out on the car, but without a license plate, it is going to be hard narrowing it down. All the sex offenders are being checked on, par for the course when a young woman goes missing. So far, there is nothing. Autumn has vanished into thin air.

I've been trying to work, but my heart isn't in it. I can't get my mind off the blond goddess who'd visited me Christmas night. The things she'd said. The way she'd moved. The feeling of her lips pressed against mine, her legs wrapped around my waist.

She hasn't been back, but I am still wearing the watch she gave me and begged me not to take off.

There are many strange things about our time together, yes, but I am in pretty hefty denial until Stephen and Jim sit me down and force me to watch the time-stamped video.

Seeing the incontrovertible evidence makes me break down and admit they are right. I have to trust the forensics. Everything, from witness statements to fingerprints to DNA swabs to this video, is telling me that Autumn was in Austin on Christmas night.

So how the hell was she with me? Have I finally lost my mind, been driven crazy by grief? Did I have some sort of acid trip flashback? I swear to God the woman was with me, in my apartment, in my living room, in my bed. I am wearing the watch she gave me.

Nothing makes sense. I'm a rational guy. Yes, I was drunk, totally-wasted drunk. But I have a tangible item on my wrist. Proof that she's been to my place.

There is only one other explanation, and I don't think I rolled someone on my way home from Mercy Lounge on Christmas night. I am slowly coming to grips with the idea that maybe, just maybe, something I can't explain is happening.

The guys treat me like I'm some sort of mental patient for the next couple of days. The search for Autumn is heating up. Autumn's friends are all over television, doing very serious, heartfelt interviews. And still, there is nothing.

Time keeps passing.

A week into the search, on New Year's Eve, the 24/7 news cycle finds another juicy murder story to latch onto, and Autumn Cleary disappears from television sets nationwide as well.

Though I am really not in the mood, I agree to go out on New Year's Eve with Stephen and Jim. We start the night in awkward silence, have a couple of drinks at my place, then walk down to Lower Broad and watch the guitar drop. It is cold and dreary, the skies overcast, the early dark oppressive. I can smell snow. Usually New Year's in LoBro is a blast, but I'm not feeling it. There is a sense of dread hanging over the evening. Nothing seems right. I can't have fun. Not when I don't know what's happened to Autumn. I am back at my apartment by 12:30 a.m., sober as a judge, the TV on but muted, staring out the window at the chilly night. Thinking. Again.

I'd like to think Autumn and I have some sort of connection, that even though we haven't seen each other in seven years, I'd know if she were in trouble, or hurt, or dead. I can't help but obsess about her visit. Since there are no rational explanations, I finally allow myself to think in less realistic terms. If she were a ghost, and she appeared to me, that means she must be dead.

The very idea squeezes my heart and makes my breath come short. Losing her all over again is killing me.

Accepting I am probably on my way to a straight-jacket, I take the watch off my wrist and stare at it. I don't know anything about watches, except they tell time. This is a nice timepiece, not gaudy. It looks expensive. I pull out my phone and finally Google the brand: TAG Heuer.

Shit. These fuckers are expensive. Where in the world did

Autumn come up with the money to buy me a gift like this? I turn it over and realize the back is engraved. I feel a little better now. She got it used. I'm glad. I wouldn't feel comfortable knowing she'd spent six months' rent on a present for me.

Engraved in the silver back is a stylized star, and inside its borders there is a monogram with the initials *TWH*. The *W* is bigger than the other two, it must be the last name. *T* is the first, *H* the middle. I wonder who owned the watch before, why they gave it up, where she found it. Do ghosts wear watches? Do they need to tell time?

I don't know, if I were going to spend eternity floating through life, I don't think I'd want a watch constantly reminding me of time's never-ending passage.

I put it back on my wrist. Try to wrap my head around my thought process. If she's a ghost, she's dead, and the last thing she did was bring me a present. Not only the watch. She gave me forgiveness. She gave me love, her body. She gave me closure.

And I finally understand what's happened. She is gone. But she found a way to let me know she still loved me and regretted what happened between us.

I can't believe what a gift Autumn has given me. Despite myself, I start to cry. I have to find out where she is, what happened to her. She's counting on me. I know she is.

And then it hits me.

The watch isn't a present. It's a clue.

Day ten after Autumn went missing, I take a few days of vacation, happily sanctioned by my boss, who is (rightly so) concerned about me getting myself shot on the streets if I don't get my head back into the game. I drive to Austin, fast. It takes me a little over twelve hours, with two breaks.

This is even more confirmation I had some sort of drunken vision the night Autumn disappeared. There's no way she could have gotten to me in the timeframe we're talking about. Not as a human, that is.

I've never been to Austin before. It reminds me of Nashville. Thumping music downtown, tony neighborhoods, restaurants galore. My GPS takes me to police headquarters on 8th Street, and I go inside, show my badge, and ask to speak to the detective working Autumn's case, Mario Torres.

He comes out of the bullpen immediately, hand outstretched. Torres is a big guy, barrel-chested, with jet-black hair and a luxurious mustache. When he speaks, it is with a sense of contained joviality. He reminds me of one of the sergeants I work with in Nashville, Bob Parks.

"I'm Torres. You Aukey?"

"Yes. Call me Zack."

"Zack. Don't know how much help I can give you, this is a local case, you know. But come on back, and let's chat."

Torres is humoring me as a fellow cop, and I can't say I blame him one bit. It's not usual for cops from other jurisdictions, other states, to come in on a case without first being asked, and without anything to add to the mix.

We walk by a break room and he gestures to the coffeepot. I nod and he pours me a cup, thick and black. I dump in four sugars; I need the boost. I am tired. So tired.

He leads me to his desk, pulls me up a chair, and drops a pen on a clean yellow legal pad.

"So, Zack, tell me what Austin PD can do for you, now that you've come all the way from Nashville. I take it you used to date Ms. Cleary?"

Go careful, Zack.

"That's right. We broke up several years ago." I take a deep breath. "This is going to sound crazy, but I saw Autumn in Nashville Christmas night. Around the same time that she went missing, as a matter of fact."

Torres leans forward, his dark eyes searching mine. I can tell exactly what he's thinking, which he confirms a second later.

"Is there something you need to tell me, Zack?"

Boom. In one fell swoop, I've made myself a suspect in her disappearance.

"Yes, there is, but it's not what you think. I'm not here to confess. I didn't have anything to do with her disappearance. I'd never hurt Autumn. I love her, man."

Torres's voice is thoughtful. He unconsciously plays with the snap on his cuffs. "Afraid I'm a bit confused, partner."

"This is going to sound absolutely insane, and if you toss me out on my ear, or throw me in the pokey, I will completely understand. But roll with me."

"I'm listening."

"About an hour after Autumn was seen on the video, she showed up in my apartment in Nashville."

I sit back in my chair and take a drink of the now cooled coffee. It is terrible. I set the cup down and wait for Torres to either cuff me or kick me out.

Instead, he's looking at me with undisguised curiosity.

"What do you think this means, Zack?"

In for a penny, in for a pound, as my grandmother used to say.

"I think Autumn's ghost came to visit me. And I think she's given me a clue about where I can find her. I know it sounds crazy, but she was in my apartment. We were together for several hours, and she gave me a really expensive watch before she left."

Torres is staring at me like I'm going to bite him. "Wow. That's…"

Oh, it's definitely time for me to leave. I stand up. "I get it. Sorry. Forget I was ever here."

"Sit down, dummy."

He gestures toward the chair and I'm startled by his tone. He sounds almost… friendly. I sit. I have nothing left to do.

"You say she touched you?" he asks.

"Yes. Several times." She'd done a hell of a lot more than touch me, but I wasn't going to tell a stranger I'd had sex with a ghost.

"And she gave you a watch?"

I unsnap it from my wrist and hand it over.

He looks at it, gives it back.

"Amazing." And he means it.

I can't help feeling surprised. "You believe me?"

"You're talking to a guy who celebrates *Día de los Muertos*. Of course I believe you."

"No idea what you just said, man. I took French in high school."

"Idiot," he replies companionably. "*Día de los Muertos* is the Day of the Dead. The first of November, the day after Halloween, we celebrate our ancestors who are no longer with us. The whole idea is to encourage a visit from them, to see them again. So yeah, I believe in ghosts."

I must look shocked because Torres starts to laugh. "Dude, I'm Catholic and descended from Mayans. I believe in most everything, from miracles to visitations." He stops smiling, and his voice is gentler now. "I'm sorry that things are shaking out like this, because if she's a ghost, she's…"

My chest squeezes tight. "Yeah. I'd figured out that part for myself. Unlike you, I don't believe in this stuff, so I'm having a hard time wrapping my head around it. I mean, we broke up years ago, and we haven't talked or seen each other since. I'm kind of flattered she came to me."

"You're a cop, dude. She probably assumed you would try to investigate and find her body. That's what cops do, you know."

"Yeah. I figured that part out, too. So here I am. What can I do to help?"

Torres is staring at my wrist. "Let me see that again."

I hand over the watch. My wrist feels cold without it there. "There's an engraving on the back. Initials."

Torres flips the watch over, puts on his glasses, holds the watch under the lamp. Hey, he's older than me. Not everyone can have cat vision.

I'm about to make a joke about detectives and magnifying glasses when he turns white and lets off with a string of what I assume are curses in Spanish. He jumps up, out of his seat.

"What is it?"

"Come with me."

"Wait, you recognize this?"

He doesn't answer, marches toward the hall like a bull charging a red cape. I follow, heart starting to beat a rapid tattoo.

We bolt up a flight of stairs to the third floor and down a long hallway, into the quiet executive offices of the Austin PD.

Ignoring the protests of the chief's young secretary, Torres opens the door and strides into his boss's office.

The guy who I assume is Chief Acevedo is in a meeting with a three men in suits. They all look surprised, which is no wonder, considering the way Torres is advancing on them. He gets to the desk, tosses the watch to the chief, who catches it. Torres practically growls, "I know where Autumn Cleary is."

On the last of the Omen Days, Epiphany, we drive west in a caravan of cars and trucks. It is before dawn, in the darkest hours of the night. The Texas skies are crystal clear, and out here, there are no lights, no city brightness to hide the stars. I don't think I've ever seen anything like it, this vast openness, the constellations easily discernible. Stars litter the sky, diamonds cast onto a black velvet canvas. The brightest star, Sirius, seems to have a halo of light around it. Polaris is to my right, giving me perspective on our travels.

I'm queasy worrying about what we might find. SWAT is already in position; they've been watching the ranch for the past twenty-four hours, trying to determine if Thomas Holden Winchester III is on site.

Winchester, it turns out, is a young guy who comes from some serious oil money. His grandfather was a famous wildcatter and struck oil on what is now their extensive property. Winchester the Second continued the tradition, but went missing a few years back. According to Torres, there have always been rumors that he was killed by his kid and dumped down a well on the property, but Austin PD never had any proof and they couldn't get warrants to search.

Torres gives me the rest of the rundown as we drive.

"T.H. Winchester, as he's known, is rich and ruthless. There's always been this thing about him maybe bumping off Dear Old Dad, but we also think he's running coke in from Mexico. He's funding the coyotes who bring illegals across the border. They come in near Laredo, and Winchester's people drive 'em up to the ranch with the drugs. On his property, they can find food and shelter, but the price is hefty. No drugs and you're dead. Considering the number of illegals we have coming through here? I'd say they're happy to pay the price."

"And you haven't arrested him for it?"

"It's a hard situation. We haven't been able to get close enough to catch him in the act, and with a guy who has this much money, nothing less than the proverbial hand in the cookie jar will do."

"But you were able to get a warrant easily this time. Why?"

"Judge Crater is hard on kidnapping. Had a daughter killed when she was a teenager. Body showed up after a few weeks on the side of the road. Dumped. She'd been killed elsewhere."

"How?"

"Strangled. Raped." He paused. "She had some broken bones. The works."

"Do you know who did it?"

"Nope. Not officially."

And Torres goes quiet. A meaningful silence. He watches me with his dark eyes, made black by the empty sky, waiting for me to put the pieces together.

"Are you telling me Winchester might be involved in the Crater murder?"

He looks out the window.

"I'm telling you there are a fair number of girls who have gone missing from this area over the past ten years. Five have shown up again on the side of the road, broken and strangled, like Crater's daughter Rose. The other three are still missing."

"Is Autumn one of the three?"

"Yes."

I take a deep breath, try to swallow the bile rising in my throat. "We're talking a serial killer?"

"In my opinion, yes. The cases have been documented in ViCAP. A couple of FBI profilers gave us some leads a few years back. I've never bought their profile—one of the women was from Vermont, so they think it's a truck driver dropping bodies during a long haul. I disagree. Whoever's been doing this is smart and local. Crater's daughter is the only victim who was a native. The rest of the women were all transplants to the area, without family nearby. I've always thought T.H. was involved. Call it a gut instinct."

"And now you have his watch. Which we can't explain."

"Well, we have one explanation. Your ex managed to get it to you the night she went missing. Let's pray it's not too late."

Word has gone around about the way Torres and I came up with a suspect. The Austin cops seem nonplussed by the idea that a ghost visited me and gave me a watch belonging to her murderer. I'm thinking if they are this open-minded, and I ever need a change of scenery, Austin might not be a bad place to work.

"The thing about T.H.," Torres continues, "is he won't go easy. We're T-minus ten minutes to the ranch. I want you out of the way, and out of the fray."

I don't argue. This is their rodeo. I'm lucky they've let me ride along, considering the tie I have to the case.

Torres's phone rings. He answers it, listens, then hangs up and smiles, mean and sinister. He is a different man, one primed for action, serious and deadly. I am suddenly glad he's on my side.

"SWAT confirms T.H. is on the property. They spied him walking to the barn." He smacks me on the shoulder. "It's gonna be our lucky day."

It might be their lucky day. All I know is there is a better-than-average chance I'm going to see the love of my life dead and broken, and I don't know if I want that image of her to be my last.

Suck it up, Aukey. If Autumn can manage to cross the veil to give you a clue, the least you can do is face whatever she went through to do it.

The sun is breaking in the east when we drive through the gates of the ranch. I'm not used to the openness of the land here, the vastness, the flat scrub brush and shifting sands. It feels too big, like there's no way we'll find a small woman like Autumn. I swallow back the fear and frustration, and hear a series of gunshots. Small arms fire.

Torres is on his phone immediately. "What happened, what's going on? Son of a bitch!"

He slaps the cover closed and jacks a round into his Glock. "SWAT had to engage. T.H. saw them and ran." He launches a volley of rapid-fire Spanish at the driver, a guy named Hernandez, and the man veers off the main road. A choking plume of dust follows us into the field.

"Where are we going?"

"Coming around back. Maybe we'll get lucky and he's fleeing this way."

I rearrange myself to look out the window. Adrenaline has started pumping through my system. I pull the .38 from my ankle holster. Torres watches impassively.

"Sorry, man, but I'm not walking in there unarmed."

He nods, reaches over the back seat and yanks out a vest. "Put this on. I don't want to be responsible for you getting dead, not on my watch."

I shrug into the bulletproof vest and keep watch out the window as we bump and slide through the scrub. This is happening, and all my thoughts are for Autumn. Torres hands me a monocular. I jam it to my eye and start scanning the landscape.

"There," I say, pointing. "Dust rising to the south."

Hernandez jerks the wheel and we plot an intercept course. Torres is shouting into his phone.

After a few minutes the dust plume stops. "He's gone on foot," I call, but I see quickly that I'm wrong. There is a maze of buildings in the middle of this emptiness. Barns. I catch a glimpse of lush green land in front of us. There is a small lake, marshy with cattails and scrub.

"Out here, they only water the land they need to keep the stock alive," Torres says in explanation. "Winchester's always kept horses. Thoroughbreds. He races them, likes being the big playboy at the track. SWAT is coming. They want us to stay put."

Hernandez pulls the truck over to the side of the road, one hundred yards from the barns. We wait. I am jittery and holding the gun too tightly in my hand. My knuckles are white. I release my fingers, try to relax.

Torres stiffens next to me and swears. "Did you see that? The fucker ran through the corral."

Hernandez says, "SWAT's five minutes away."

"She could be in there," I say, and my hand is on the door and then I'm out, into the chill, onto the marshy land, my legs pumping as I run toward the barns. Torres is right behind me, saying things in Spanish I assume aren't complimentary. We run low and fast, trying to avoid getting ourselves shot.

When we draw closer, he grabs my arm and steps in front of me, starts signaling with his left hand. "Go around the front," his gestures say, "I will cover you."

I move slowly this time, my feet touching the ground lightly and quickly as I move to the entrance of the main building. There are six outbuildings. The bastard could be in any of them.

Torres signals he's going right, I should go left. I do. I step into the barn, hugging the wall. There are horses, I can hear them nickering and the air is redolent with manure. There is a long cement channel in front of me, tack hanging on the walls, the stall doors shut all the way down.

The hair rises on my arms.

I am not alone. I can feel the eyes on me.

I dive to the left a second before the bullet hits the spot I was standing in. Torres ducks right, behind the door to one of the sixteen stalls in the barn.

I hear trucks and shouts. SWAT has arrived to save the day. But I know how they work. Set perimeters. Assess the situation. Time.

Time. Time.

I don't want to be a hero, but I don't want to wait for hours, either. The bullet came from above me. I'll be safer with the horses.

I run down the row, find the first empty stall, throw myself over the top. I land hard in fresh straw. But I am alone, and alive.

Turning back to the cement interior, I scan the area I've run from. I have a new perspective on the barn's entrance. There is a ladder by the door. A hayloft. He must be up there.

There's only one way to do this. Using the stall door as cover, I swing it open gently. A shot hits the wood, and another, and another. But now he's given his position away. I can see him. T.H. Winchester has red hair; he looks like a strawberry in the hay.

He ducks his head back in and shoots again. But it's too late for him. I step from behind the door, and I don't hesitate. I walk forward, aiming for the spot I've seen him disappear into, hoping the flash of white and red I saw a second earlier is his forehead. I squeeze the trigger, and a muffled thud tells me I've found my mark. I shoot again, and once more. Winchester falls out of the loft at my feet, dead.

It is over, less than three minutes after it started.

Torres is there, pressing fingers into Winchester's neck, knowing already there will be no heartbeat. He looks up at me with genuine respect.

"Nice shooting."

"Yeah." My hands are strangely cold. I've never killed anyone before. And now I've shot a man without ever saying a word to him, in anger or curiosity or fear. He is dead, and I am glad.

"Is that him?" I manage.

"It is." Torres still has his gun out. "I need to tell SWAT and my boss what's happening before they come in here cocked and loaded, and we need to search this place."

"You talk. I'll search."

"You sure, man?"

His dark eyes are full of concern, but I nod. "I'd rather be the one who finds her."

"Listen… stay here a minute. Let me brief them on what went down, then we'll do it together."

I nod, but the minute his back is turned, I start down the row of stalls again. There is a reason Winchester fled to this place. There is something here of value to him, something he wanted to protect.

Seven of the stalls have horses, spooked and stomping and white-eyed, all freaked by the shootings. The eighth confirms my deepest fears.

I open the stall door, and I see her in the gloom, on her back, her empty face staring at the heavens.

"Autumn!"

She doesn't answer and I realize life as I know it is over. She is dead, lying in the hay in the thoroughbred's stall, her legs bent at a strange angle, as if she tried to ride one of the horses to safety but fell off. Or Winchester left her that way, arranged her awkwardly, as if he'd used her then forgotten her. I want to shoot him again, but I leave him to Torres and his crew and go to Autumn's side, steeling myself.

It's been twelve days since she went missing. I expect there to be a strong stench around her. And while I catch the scent of ammonia and feces, there is no decomposition.

Her face is so white. I can see the veins running under her skin. She is thin, so thin.

Oh God, I pray, not knowing any more words. *Oh, God.*

And her eyes focus. Her head turns toward me. She looks at me and something like love flits across her face. Is she a spirit?

Her mouth moves. "Zack," she whispers.

Dear God, she's alive.

"She's alive," I scream, running to the stall window. "Torres, she's alive! We need a medevac, STAT!"

Shouts go up around the ranch.

I fall to my knees by Autumn's side. Her face is bruised from a beating, and it must hurt to do it, but she smiles.

"Zack. I knew you'd come." Her voice is torn and thick, like she hasn't had water in a very long time.

"I'm here, baby. I'm here. You're safe now. Can you get up? I want to get you out of here."

And it hits me, the way her legs are splayed, so unnatural, so odd. Her back is broken. He has broken her back so she can't run away. Rage fills me. I am so glad I was the one to kill him. I am so glad I've taken some small measure of revenge for us both.

"I can't walk," she whispers, but her hand snakes up and touches my forehead, brushes back the hair from my eyes. "He made sure I couldn't walk first thing. Don't worry, Zack. It doesn't even hurt."

"That's okay, baby. That's okay. I'll carry you. I'll always carry you."

We're both crying, and I hear the *whump whump whump* of a helicopter's rotors.

Seven years ago, I lost the love of my life. And now I have found her. She is cradled carefully, gently in my arms, pale and still, broken in two, but breathing, her chest lifting lightly. Autumn is alive. And I don't know what to think about anything anymore.

The sun is shining, masking the bitter cold outside. I didn't know Texas could get so cold, but I'm wearing a North Face fleece and damn glad I packed it, because it's colder than a witch's tit down here.

The Omen Days are over. There has been a requisite rebirth; the season's requirements are met. My life has changed, altered. I will never be the same again.

Autumn is still in the hospital in Austin, but is better, much better. The break was lower than we first thought, and the doctors think the damage to her spinal cord is temporary, that she'll be able to walk again. She's already getting feeling back in her toes. They think the trauma of the broken vertebrae caused swelling, and that's what's shutting off the signals to her brain that her feet really do work. It is a miracle. Torres finally told me the details of the other bodies they'd found. They all had their backs broken. Winchester's gruesome signature: he paralyzed his victims so they couldn't run away or even fight him. He was a coward.

We haven't discussed what he did to her over the course of the twelve days he had her. She'll tell me when she's ready, and I will listen, knowing I've meted out the justice she deserves.

Late that first night, I did ask how it all happened, how she managed to find me. I was holding her hand and she was trying, and failing, to sleep. We talked, quietly, low.

"How did you get me the watch?"

She looks distant and eternal, like she's touched the sky and the stars and they've left a mark on her.

"I don't know. Not really. It was like a dream. He took it off the... the first time, put it on the dresser. When he started to hurt me, I fought back. He slugged me, flipped me over onto the floor and stomped on my back, and I got all kinds of floaty. That's when I had the dream. I dreamed of you, Zack. And I knew you could help me. I got up, walked away from him and the things he was doing, took the watch and... found you. I know it doesn't make any sense."

"I don't care if it makes sense or not. I am so proud of you, honey. So proud."

I'm not kidding. It doesn't matter how she managed to leave her body and find me. All that matters is that she's going to be okay, and she's going to be mine.

Torres and his team have already found six bodies buried on the ranch property, plus the bones of a male Caucasian in an abandoned well three miles from the barns. It will take a while to sort out who is who, and the ranch covers so many thousands of acres they will be searching for a while, but they are calling the mission a success. A sad success, but so many families will finally know what happened to their loved ones, their lost girls, because my brave Autumn found me, and gave me the piece of the puzzle they needed to take down a prolific, sick serial killer.

Autumn has made a request of me, so I've left her in her room and am off to fulfill her dearest wish at the moment, to find some obscure Austin ice cream she loves.

This morning, when I walked in, she was smiling and humming to herself. When she saw me, I swear there was a sparkle in her eyes again. Last night she told me she wants to come back home. Not only to Nashville, but home to me. Home to our interrupted life.

I don't know what Christmas miracle has occurred between us, but I welcome every minute I get to spend with Autumn. Maybe being apart so long has given me a deeper appreciation of what love is, and how bleak life is without it. Maybe the girl outside Mercy Lounge really was an angel, and when she gave me her smokes, she gave me some sort of blessing, a new lease on life, or opened a plane that allowed Autumn through. I will never know.

I find the ice cream shop. It is next to a jewelry store.

The old me, the Zack who doesn't believe in miracles, would walk right past. But I go inside, happy for the warmth of glassed-in store. A dark-haired woman is working behind the counter. She looks up and smiles as I approach.

"Looking for something special?"

"I am. Something pretty. It's a late present. A very, very late Christmas present."

Twenty minutes later, I have a small velvet box in my front pocket and a carton of salted caramel coffee crunch ice cream freezing my hand off. The walk back to the hospital isn't quite as cold.

Autumn is clean and fresh, smiling widely when she sees me. Her hair is glistening. "The nurse let me have a shower. I had to stay lying down, but I feel human again."

"I'm glad. I like your hair short, by the way."

"I don't know. I was thinking about growing it out again. For old time's sake." She spies the ice cream. "Oh, Zack, you found it!"

I present it to her, with the small wooden paddle spoon attached. "I am a miracle worker."

Her eyes meet mine. The bruises are fading. Soon she'll look like she always did, peaches and cream and freckles. There are a few new lines around her eyes. I like them. She's gone to hell, and she's come back. She's going to get better, and I will love her no matter what happens, and what choices she makes.

Her hand reaches out and catches mine, and she squeezes, hard.

"Thank you for not giving up on me."

"I never have, Autumn. And I never will. Now eat your ice cream."

"I love you, Zack. I've always loved you. I want you to know that." She nods once, as if resigning herself to her fate, then opens the top of the ice cream. It comes off easily. She gasps.

The ring is nestled in the ribbon of caramel. Hey, it's an impromptu proposal, don't judge. I'm thinking on my feet here.

Autumn is crying and laughing through her tears. I have never seen her look more beautiful. I drop to my knees by her bed and say the words I've wanted to utter for a decade.

"Merry Christmas, Autumn. Will you marry me?"

Oh, in case you were wondering, we got married on Christmas Day, at St. George's in Belle Meade. Guilty Pleasures played the reception. Autumn and I danced all night.

Have I ever mentioned how much I love Christmas?

ABOUT THE STORY

For months now, every time I get on a plane, I start my music and listen to Airborne Toxic Event's excellent song "Sometime Around Midnight." There is something about this song that lends itself to story. I have used it on several of my book soundtracks, and for each book, the song inspired different aspects of the story, of character development, of setting. It's a universal tune, one of great love and extreme pain. I think we've all been in the position of losing someone we love and seeing them soon after, when the hurts are soothed but not forgotten, with someone else. It's heartbreaking, and a universal pain. It's become, in many ways, my favorite song.

Earlier this year, when Amy (my co-publisher on Two Tales Press) asked me to put together a Christmas short story, I immediately thought of my song. I've mined the hurt and fear and angst and bad decision jeans that go along with it, but I'd never written something directly inspired by it.

Right around this time, I re-watched a favorite movie—*500 Days of Summer.* Starring Joseph Gordon Levitt and Zooey Deschanel, it's a great look at how love changes people, for better and for worse.

So armed with tons of breakup angst, I set out to write a story worthy of the emotions of young men broken in two by women they love. I knew only three things: There had to be a ghost. It had to revolve around Christmas. And since this is a J.T. Ellison story, it had to have a twist.

Now I just needed a title. Something unique. Something cool. Something Christmasy but uniquely me.

I had heard of the Omen Days—Twelvetide—the origins of the twelve days of Christmas, during my research on THE IMMORTALS. Some quick research brought the legends back to the fore, and I knew immediately what my story was going to be, and how it was going to happen. And THE OMEN DAYS was born. Autumn and Zack and Jim and Stephen and Torres and that bastard Winchester—they paraded onto the page and told me their tales.

I'm also especially excited that this is the first story I've written expressly for my publishing house, Two Tales Press. If you liked this one, I encourage you to leave a review and help me spread the word. And feel free to check out my others on the website. Because without you, there are no stories.

Lastly, if you ever get a chance to see Guilty Pleasures play in Nashville, do it. They are they bomb! For your enjoyment, we've put together a Spotify playlist of all the songs mentioned or referenced in the story, and some more from Guilty Pleasures' show playlists over the years.

Merry Everything to you and yours!

MAY GOD HAVE MERCY ON YOUR SOUL

"In this, as in all things, may God have mercy on your soul."

The intonation echoes in the chamber. The priest closes the Good Book, the leather covers slapping together like birds' wings. Dark birds, ravens and crows, the harbingers of death. Death has come. I feel it lurking in the corner, a gap-jawed beast, ready to take me away.

The priest hasn't met my eyes. Is he worried what he might see reflected in them? The Devil? God? A poor, lost soul? No, if he thought that, he wouldn't be avoiding my gaze.

Come to think of it, no one has met my gaze for the past twenty minutes. My life is about to end. I'm a little concerned about that; I'm not really ready to give up the ghost. But there's not much that can turn back the clock now. I've had all the lasts: the food, the blessing, the IV—the latter shoved carelessly into my vein. A small trickle of blood pools in the crook of my arm. I hear the patter of it hitting the floor.

It reminds me.

I look to my left, try to anyway. My head is tethered to the table. Four people bustle about, preparing. I ignore them, focus on the sheet of dirty windows. They'll be pulling back the drapes any moment now.

There's two of us being put down tonight. Not unheard of. After all, in the old days they'd line up the convicts and make them watch as their brothers were hanged by the neck, one by one. Bowels loosened in fear, flies buzzed in the hot sun—the stench was overwhelming. That won't happen to me. They shoved a damn douche up my ass earlier, cleared me out so I wouldn't have that last indignity.

They did Garcia too. I bet he liked it.

We sat in the adjoining cells after our Right Stuff moment, eating our meals with gusto. I had the full menu—fried chicken and okra, cornbread as sweet and crumbly as my grandmother used to make, a thick slab of apple pie. These prison kitchens weren't all bad when it came to the last meal. Some ordered out, but ours, well, they figured it was the least they could do. Nothing like being executed in the South.

Garcia was a Catholic, and assumed with the nonchalance of someone who had no real idea that he was going straight to hell. His eyes got a little wild when I asked him if he really believed he would burn.

Me? There's nothing out there. No way. You have one chance at this life. One chance to be good, or evil.

I'd screwed that pooch early on. I was condemned. There was no hope for me. If there was burning to be done, Garcia would certainly be first in line. I'd watch, and laugh. But then I'd be alight alongside him.

Garcia and I ate, and talked. He was a squirrelly fucker, down for serial murders. He had a thing for blondes—used to tie them up, cut off their breasts, and eat them, baked in the oven like chicken. He wasn't right in the head, I'll say that. They found thirteen bodies in his backyard, buried in a cement pit and covered up with lime. He'd been working for at least six years before he royally screwed up.

They caught him with the last one. He'd left her nipple in his glove compartment. Stupid fool got drunk, weaved his way out of town, where Johnny Law was waiting for him behind the Welcome sign. Lights flared, a siren wailed, and Garcia was pulled over. When he went for his registration, the damn nipple fell out on the floor.

Garcia loved to tell the story, how the officer who'd pulled him over took one look at the piece of flesh and vomited right in the window, all over Garcia. Garcia shot him, of course. A man has a right not to be barfed on.

Make that fourteen.

What did I do to deserve this treatment, you ask?

Well, I never ate anybody. Me, I'd just killed the one.

"So, you gonna tell them?"

I humored Garcia. "Do you think it would do any good?"

He wiped his nose with his fork hand. "Mebbe. Might buy you a few more days, at least. You could have another douche and another meal."

A few more days. "Now, why would I want that? I've been stuck in this hellhole for nearly fifteen years. This is my ticket out."

He sniffed, and I realized he was crying.

"What's wrong?"

"I don't want to die."

"No one wants to die. The women you killed, did they want to die?"

"Yeah. They did. They begged me to." And he grinned.

Like I said, the man wasn't right in the head.

"So are you?" he asked.

"Am I what? Afraid to die? Of course I am."

"No, are you going to tell them?"

Would I tell them? I wouldn't know until the moment it happened. The secret has been locked inside my tongue for so many years I don't know if the words will come out, even if I try to speak them aloud. Even if I whisper into the void.

No, I'm waiting. Waiting to see who comes to watch me die. Then I'll make up my mind whether to talk or not.

"We'll see."

We finished our meal. They took the plates. Garcia whimpered like a cowed dog. These serial jackasses, they're all cowards. Get themselves all worked up, go out and kill a bunch of people, get caught, then spend twenty years pulling every trick in the book to get out of it. No dignity in that. If you're gonna commit a murder, have the balls to stand up for it.

That's what I did. I never ran, never denied. I just didn't tell them where the body was.

My vision is impeded; I'm stuck staring at the ceiling. I focus on a string of spider web that keeps floating in and out of my line of sight. When the air conditioning comes on, the web flutters toward the center of the room. When it shuts off, the silk disappears from view. We're getting closer now, I can sense the anticipation building in the room. A face appears above me. The eyes of the doctor witnessing my death are cold and hard. I'd once been in a bar fight with a man who looked at me with dead eyes. He stared at me, pupils pinpoints, the flat eyes of a snake, no intelligence, just a predatory gleam. Wasn't my fault I broke his arm in four places.

That's how the doctor is looking at me now. I suppressed the urge to rip out his throat.

"It's time."

He loosens my head strap an inch. With a *whoosh*, the curtains swing back.

She's come.

It's almost impossible to see into the antechamber, but I can feel her there. I can smell her. Her honey blond hair will be pulled into a ponytail, cornflower blue eyes shimmering with tears. Midwestern corn-fed hips will be jammed squarely into the hard institutional plastic chair. Her back will be ramrod straight, her nails buffed and clipped square, hands in her lap, one holding the other tightly. I've seen this pose from her so many times I don't need to see it for myself to know that's her presentation.

I fell in love with her the first time I saw her, sitting like this, and my heart has grown with each subsequent meeting. I feel a deep, unending sorrow. Our lives could have be so very different.

If it weren't for her, I wouldn't have any second thoughts about the needle. But the chance to win her love one last time, well, I can hardly pass that up, can I?

A loud ringing. Everyone freezes. The doctor answers the phone, listens for a moment, hangs up. Shakes his head. People resume bustling around the room. It's really happening. There's no stopping it now.

I continue staring into the darkness, at the shadow of her, debating. I could tell them. I could. And my love would be able to bury her daughter.

The year was 1987. I'd been out of college for two years, working myself to death at two jobs that barely supported my habits. There's nothing to make you feel like less of a man than not being able to provide for your family. My wife, a pert cheerleader whom I'd met my junior year of college, had spent the last six months of our marriage fucking a richer, better looking guy. Thank God we hadn't had a kid yet. It made leaving her that much easier. I found myself divorced at twenty-four, working two jobs for practically nothing, and lost. There, I've admitted it. I was lost. I was desperate for something—love, honor, machismo. Anything to make me feel like I wasn't an abject failure.

It was a bright, sunny day when I saw her for the first time. I was walking between jobs. I didn't have enough money for a car after the alimony payments. Every day, I hoofed it from the bakery to a night job two miles away in a dank elementary school, where I cleaned the shit of babies out of toilets. Apparently, their mommies hadn't taught them how to flush. It was fitting, really. My life was in the toilet; there was no better place for me to stew.

That day, when I saw her, I almost kept walking. That would have been the right thing to do. Just keep walking toward my dead-end life, and be done with it. Instead, I stopped to watch. The girl wasn't more than four at the time, a bright angel playing with a pile of rocks. Stack, stack, stack, until they tumbled down. Where a lesser child might get frustrated, she chortled with delight. So I stopped and watched as she did it again and again, and felt something I hadn't felt in a long time. Joy.

It was later that I found out they'd just moved to town. That there was no father in the picture, just a mommy and a little girl, cut from the same cloth, both towheaded, cornflower, corn-fed girls. My favorite kind.

Somewhere in the days after I saw her, I realized I was walking a little slower by the house. That I was looking for the sunny child, knowing that a glimpse of her would brighten my day, make me forget, for a moment, what a failure I was.

She's staring at me. There is no hate in her eyes, not anymore, just a tired resignation, a sorrow that can't be supplanted. I took her child away, and she is marked by it. Marked and unable to move on. My death won't help her. She knows this. Knows it deep in her soul. And yet, when they ask if I have anything to say, an atavistic gleam begins. I can actually see her eyes shining through the dirty window, sense her shifting forward slightly.

"Any last words (and don't you dare antagonize that sweet woman, ya shit, have some decency, be a man) you want to say before you die?"

Before you die. Before you die. Before you die.

The words, hollow, tasteless, formless on my tongue.

We're all dead together. We all die alone.

Even sweet-tempered little girls with sunny blond hair.

I find some spit and manage to swallow.

"Yes, I have something to say."

I didn't hurt her. Not on purpose. This I swear. I loved her. Loved her and her mother. They were all that was right in the world. Happy and brave. Strong and good.

I was a reject, society's dreg, the long-abandoned coffee in the pot, scorched and blackened to the bottom of the earth. All I wanted was five minutes of humanity.

Amber—that was her name, and how appropriate for a child of the sun—came with me for a walk. That's all it was. A walk. We chatted about the clouds and the birds in the trees. She was so cute, so sweet. She climbed the steps to the bridge like a clambering goat, fast and clumsy, then walked along the flat edge of the girder. I called for her to get down. She laughed and skipped. When she fell, I was five feet away.

There were rocks below. The water was shallow, the sandy bank exposed. She'd landed wrong. She was dead before I got down to her, less than a minute after she fell.

And I panicked. I grieved. I slapped my head and pulled my hair.

How could this happen? How could I have lost her?

I will never understand the urge I had to hide her. It was as if a command was shouted in my brain. I spirited the body away, into the woods. I buried her. And then I walked away.

It was not rational. It was not wise. It ruined everyone's lives: mine, hers, her mother's. Everyone who knew us, everyone who judged us. All were derailed by my stupidity.

And yet, once it was done, I couldn't undo it. I didn't want to undo it. It was a secret between me and the sunny child.

We expect the horrors of society to come from those less fortunate. When one with means, with a future, with an understandable past, commits the unthinkable crime, the world stops on its axis and rallies together.

Maybe it was the attention. Maybe I knew if I didn't speak, I'd at least keep contact with her mother. Maybe I wanted to die. Maybe I wanted someone to suffer as I suffered. I don't know.

I am long past psychoanalyzing myself. My stubborn, chilling self. All I know now is I finally, finally want to come clean.

"She's fifty feet from the bridge. Under the green willow. You searched there once, and I moved her so you wouldn't find her. She's there again. You'll find her there."

I hear the wail through the window. The succor is a balm to my soul. I seek those blue eyes, shining at me in the murky glass. "I loved her. I never hurt her. She fell. I swear."

The burn begins. The spider web shimmers.

I hear the words again. *May God have mercy on your soul.* I hear them whispered, softly, the caress of a warm breeze, of a mother's love. The voices of the dead and the damned are pushed away for a brief time as I bask in the glow of their glory.

As the pain comes, rushing, burning, I spare a moment's thought to Garcia, weeping into his chicken dinner, and know he will be burning. I, I will be nothing. No one. Nowhere.

Then darkness comes, the sting of the drugs forcing their way to my heart, and I'm consumed by the glow of a sunny smile, the feeling of—

ABOUT THE STORY

On June 27, 2006, in the state of Tennessee, at Riverbend Maximum Security Prison, there were two killers in adjoining cells with back-to-back dates with the death penalty. One was scheduled for June 28 at 1:00 a.m., the next scheduled at 2:00 a.m. Their names were Sedley Allen and Paul Reid. And I couldn't help but think to myself, *What would the conversation be? Two men, facing death for their crimes, sharing a last meal together. Would they admit their crimes? Would the beg forgiveness?*

I threw down a few paragraphs, knowing where the story was going. The evening didn't go as planned. Only one execution took place. And I never finished the story, until now.

Ten years later, the remnant found, I knew how it had to end. Sometimes, there can be justice.

BLOOD SUGAR BABY

A TAYLOR JACKSON NOVELLA

CHAPTER 1

Nashville, Tennessee

He was lost. His GPS didn't take roadwork into account, nor roads closed to accommodate protests; he'd been shunted off onto several side streets and was driving in circles. He finally made a right turn and pulled to the curb to get out a real map, and as he reached into the glove box—shit, he needed to get that knife out of there—he saw her. She was on the concrete sidewalk, sprawled back against the wall, a spread of multicolored blankets at her feet, staring vacantly into space. Her dirty blond hair was past limp and fell into dreadlocks, matted against her skull on the left side. He drove past slowly, watching, seeing the curve of her skull beneath the clumps of hair; the slope of her jaw; her neat little ear, surprisingly white and clean, nestled against her grimy skin. Her eyes were light. He was too far away to see if they were blue or green. Light irises, and unfocused pupils. High, perhaps, or starved, or simply beyond caring.

Perfect.

No one would miss her. And he could rid himself of this nagging fury that made him so damn antsy.

He closed the glove box and circled the block. There she sat, just waiting for him.

A sign.

A gift.

It had been a bad day. The fat ass he'd started med school with, Heath Stover, had called, wanting to get together. Stover was a classic jock gone to seed: flakily jovial, always over-the-top, clearly trying to compensate for something. JR had run into him last month in New Orleans, been forced into drinking hurricanes at Pat O'Briens, and had stupidly told Stover where he worked.

He shook his head, the scene replaying itself over and over and over. Stover bragging and braying at the top of his lungs about his hugely successful practice, his new BMW, his long-legged, big-busted bride, his offer of tenure at Tulane. The only thing off in his brilliant, wonderful life, Stover confided, was his piece on the side, who'd been pushing him to leave his wife.

In the moment, bolstered by alcohol, the camaraderie, the over-whelming need to fit in, to be accepted, to look as palatable to the real world as this fuck-up, he cast sanity aside. Arrogance overtook him, and he revealed his own career path, one that had taken him up the ladder at Bosco Blades; he was a salesman extraordinaire. No Willy Loman, though he perhaps looked and sounded a bit like the sad sack, but that was all a part of his act. He was better than that. Better than good. He was the best the company had: stock options, access to the corporate jet, the house in Aspen, all of it.

"As a matter of fact," he'd told Stover, "I'm headlining a conference in Nashville next month. Talking about the new laser-guided scalpel we've developed. Hell of a thing."

"Hell of a thing," Stover had replied. He was counting on the fact that Stover was far too drunk to recall the name of the company, and he gave him a fake number to write down, and a bogus email.

But the stupid son of a bitch had remembered the company name, had called and wormed JR's personal cell number out of his secretary, and managed to put himself on JR's calendar. In a couple of hours, the sloth would be waiting at a restaurant several streets away for an instant replay of their recent night in the Big Easy.

If only Stover knew what had really happened that night. About the knife, the silent scream, the ease with which the flesh accepted his blade.

He needed someplace quiet and calm to prepare himself for his night out with a "friend." He needed a drink, truth be told. Many drinks.

But the woman would do just as well. She would turn his frown upside down.

He parked a few blocks away, pulled a baseball cap low on his head, and walked back to the spot. A marble and concrete sign said he was at Legislative Plaza. The War Memorial. The Capitol rose to his right, high against the blue sky, and the small crowd of protestors with their signs held high gathered on the stairs. He needed to be careful when he passed them, not to draw their attention.

He found the perfect spot halfway down the block, shielded from the friendly mob on the stairs, and from the street, with the trident maples as cover.

And then he watched. And waited. At some point, she would have to move, and then he would follow, and strike.

To hell with Heath Stover. He had a rendezvous ahead with someone much more enticing.

CHAPTER 2

The homicide offices in Nashville's Criminal Justice Center had been quiet all day. It was the first Monday off daylight savings time, and even though it was barely 5:00 p.m., the skies outside Lieutenant Taylor Jackson's window were an inky black. The lights over the Jefferson Street Bridge glowed, warm and homey, and she could just see the slice of river flowing north to Kentucky. It was a moonless night; the vapor lamps' illuminations reflected against the black waters.

Her detectives were gone for the day. Paperwork had been completed; cases were being worked to her satisfaction. She'd stuck around regardless—the B-shift detectives would be here shortly, and she could hand off the department to her new sergeant, Bob Parks. He was a good match for the position and had the respect of her team, who'd worked with him for years. Parks had no illusions about moving up the ladder; he was content to be her sergeant until his twenty was up in two years and he retired. His son, Brent, was on the force now, too. Taylor suspected Parks had opted to get off the streets to give his son some room. Classy guy.

Her desk phone rang, cutting through the quiet, and she shifted in the window, suddenly filled with premonition.

"Lieutenant Jackson."

It was Marcus Wade, one of her detectives.

"Hey, Loot. We've got a problem."

"What kind of problem?"

"The kind that comes with the chief of police attached."

"I thought you went home."

"I was heading that way, but saw a cordon by Legislative Plaza where the protestors have been camped. Looked like something we might be called in on. I was right."

Taylor took a seat, opened her notebook. "What's going on?"

"They found one of the Occupy Nashville folks dead, right at the steps to the War Memorial Auditorium. Stab wound to the chest. Nice and neat, too."

Taylor groaned.

"It gets better."

"What?"

"The victim? It's Go-Go Dunham."

"Oh, son of a bitch."

"Yep. You wanna head on down here?"

"I'll be there in ten. Who all's there?"

"A shit load of protestors right now. Someone got in touch with her dad, so he's on his way. I called you first. I know you're gonna want to tell the chief."

"Oh, Marcus, you're just too kind."

"You know it," he said, and clicked off.

Normally Taylor's captain, Joan Huston, would be handling the chief, but she was out on paid leave—her first grandchild had just been born, and she'd taken some time to go be with her daughter.

Taylor hung up the phone and grabbed her leather jacket from the peg behind her door. She shrugged into the well-worn coat, retied her hair in a ponytail, grabbed her radio and set off. She took the stairs to the chief's office two at a time.

Virginia "Go-Go" Dunham was the twenty-two-year-old daughter of Joe Dunham, founder of one of the biggest healthcare companies in Nashville. His latest headline-grabbing venture was building environmentally-friendly dialysis centers, ones designed to be both pleasing to the patients and capture major tax breaks from the government. The trend had caught on—his designs had been patented and utilized to build similar centers across the country. Dunham was a pillar of the community, a regular at all the major charitable events, a contributor to the mayor's election fund, and an all-around connected guy. His one and only daughter, Virginia, known as Go-Go, had felt living up to her dad's squeaky-clean image too much trouble, and, as a difficult youngster, quickly mired herself in the social drug scene. She'd earned her moniker at fourteen, when she'd been busted dancing at the Déjà Vu strip club. This was before the new ordinance forbade touching the dancers, and nubile, blond, busty Go-Go had taken full advantage of the situation. She was pulling down three grand a night, and putting the vast majority of that cash right back up her nose.

Several stints in rehab and a few busts later, she was supposed to have cleaned up her act. No longer a regular fixture on the nightclub scene, she'd gone back to school, earned a degree and taken a job working for her dad.

If she were still straight, how in the world had she managed to get herself dead?

Lights were on in the chief's office. This wasn't going to go over well. He was a close personal friend of the victim's father. As close and personal as anyone could be when they were involved in political endeavors together. Dunham and the mayor were fishing buddies; she knew the chief tagged along on occasion.

The offices were empty and quiet, the admin gone home for the day. Taylor was about to knock on the chief's closed door when he called out, "I hear you lurking out there, Lieutenant. Come in."

She followed his instruction.

Chief DeMike was a veteran of the force, promoted to the head spot from within, and a welcome change from the previous incarnation, a man as corrupt as the day was long. DeMike's hair was white, his face ruddy, with cheeks and jowls that would swing in a stiff breeze. He looked a bit like an overweight Bassett hound masquerading as Santa Claus in dress blues. But he was good police, and had always been fair with her.

"You're here about the Dunham girl?"

"You already know?"

DeMike pulled a cigar out of his humidor and started playing with it. "Sugar, I know everything in this town."

Taylor raised an eyebrow.

"Sorry." He snipped off the end of the cigar, then rammed it into the corner of his mouth. He couldn't smoke it in here, not that he hadn't before, but Taylor knew it was only a comfort gesture.

"Joe's been notified. We need to head down to the scene. He's going to meet us there. He's expecting a full show, so you should be prepared."

"I am. Not a problem. But tell me, who made the call to Mr. Dunham? Seems a bit quick to me."

"Already investigating, Lieutenant? Good. I like that. He told me one of her friends called him. Apparently, she's been camping out down there with the protestors."

He stood, the bulk of his weight tossing his chair backward against the windowsill with a crash.

"I thought she'd been walking the straight and narrow of late."

"I don't know, Lieutenant. Head on down there and find out. I'll arrive with due pomp and circumstance in a few."

Taylor nodded gravely, trying not to smile. "Yes, sir."

CHAPTER 3

When the first siren lit up the night, he was four blocks away, at Rippy's on Broadway, sipping a Yuengling, a pulled pork sandwich smothered in sweet and tangy BBQ sauce and corn cakes with butter on order, waiting for Stover to show. The high-pitched wail made pride blossom in his chest.

It had gone gloriously. She'd never seen him coming. As he predicted, after an hour, she'd shuffled off toward the port-a-potties, and when she'd drawn near, he'd straightened his spine, let the knife slide into his hand, and stepped from the bushes. He'd become so adept at his trade that the contact he'd had with her was, on the surface, just an incidental bump. As he'd said, "Excuse me," he'd slid the knife right up under her breastbone directly into her heart. A clean cut, in and out, no twisting or sawing. Precision. Perfection.

He was half a block down the street before she hit the sidewalk.

He was so good at this. Granted, practice does make perfect, and he'd had quite a bit of practice.

He allowed himself a smile. He'd managed to salvage a very annoying day, and give himself something wonderful to think about tonight. Something to chase away the annoyance of having to play charades with Stover the fat ass tonight.

Stupid bastard. Who was more successful in their *chosen* fields?

Now, JR, stop worrying about that. Think about what you just did, how you're sitting right under their noses, having a nice little Southern dinner. Think about the edge of the blade, colored a grimy rust by the girl's blood, sitting in your pocket. Think about the way the tip fed into her flesh, and her eyes caught yours, and she knew it was you who was ending her life. These are appropriate thoughts. You can't look back to the bad things. Just stay focused on the here and now.

Stover arrived with a bellow.

JR played his part—accepting the rough handshake, making small talk, eating, drinking, pretending—all the while sustaining himself with thoughts of his light-eyed beauty, lying on the sidewalk, her heart giving one last gush of blood to her body.

After what seemed like hours, Stover called for the bill, belched loudly without covering his mouth and announced, "We need women."

The idea was repugnant to JR. Women were not for defiling one's self with, they were for the glory of the knife. Glory be. Glorious. Glory glory glorious.

Perhaps he'd had one beer too many.

But this event presented his best chance of escape. So he acquiesced, and followed Stover into the night. The street outside the restaurant was hopping, busy with tourists and revelers even on a Monday. Downtown Nashville was a twenty-four/seven world, and they slipped into the throngs without causing a second glance. Because JR fit right in. He always fit in now.

CHAPTER 4

Taylor arrived at the crime scene ten minutes after Marcus's call. The site was just down the street from the CJC; she could have walked it if she wasn't in too much of a hurry. But tonight she was. Containment would be key. The Occupy Nashville protestors had been causing an uproar downtown for two weeks now. Bills were being passed to stop their ability to gather freely, face-offs between the protestors and other groups had turned the mood on the steps sour, and even the people of Nashville who agreed with their agenda were beginning to turn against them.

The real beneficiaries of their protest were the homeless who spent their time hanging out in the little park on Capitol Boulevard, burrowed in between the downtown Library and Legislative Plaza. Strangely enough, the hippies and the homeless looked remarkably alike, and do-gooders answering the call of the protesters by traveling downtown to bring food and blankets didn't necessarily know the difference. The homeless weren't stupid; they took full advantage of the situation. They were being fed, clothed, and warmed daily, sharing smokes and tents with the protestors. Taylor didn't think that was such a bad thing, but she did wish the folks who'd rallied to the call would think to provide this kind of succor to those less fortunate on a more regular basis. If Twitter could take down a despot, surely it could help keep Nashville's homeless clothed and fed.

But that wasn't her problem right now. She needed to contain a huge local story before it got blown into a political mess.

She was an experienced detective—fourteen years on the job with Metro—so she knew better than to jump to conclusions. If Go-Go was with the protestors and had been stabbed, chances were she'd been murdered by one of her fellow demonstrators. And that news was going to go national.

As she parked, she took in the scene, one she'd been privy to too many times. Sixth Street was blockaded between Church and Charlotte, blue and white lights flashing crazily on the concrete buildings, reflecting off the black glass of the Tennessee Performing Arts Center. Thankfully TPAC didn't have anything playing tonight, the building's lobby was dark and gloomy. She could see the focus of all the attention was midway up the street, just below the steps to the Plaza.

"Lieutenant!"

Tim Davis, the head of Metro's Crime Scene unit, waved to Taylor. She waved back and headed his way, watching the crowd as she walked down Sixth. The area had been cordoned off—that's what Marcus had seen driving home—but a large crowd had gathered on either side of the crime scene. Yellow tape headed them off, but frightened eyes peered down from the Plaza, and across from TPAC a small horde of people had formed, staring curiously up the street in hopes of seeing something tawdry.

Tim was overseeing the evidence gathering. She was glad to see him on duty. Tim was meticulous, and if there was evidence to find, he'd make sure it was bagged and tagged.

"Hey, man. What's up?"

"Marcus told you it was Go-Go?"

"Yeah. Damn shame. What's the evidence telling us?"

"Single stab wound to the chest. I've been collecting everything around, but the ground's littered with crap from the protestors. Messy bunch of people." His nose wrinkled in disapproval. Tim liked things straight and clean. It's what made him so good at spotting objects that were out of place.

"We've got cameras here, don't we?"

"Yeah. I've got a call into TPAC. Their security footage will give us the best chance of seeing what happened."

"Good. Let me know if you find anything else. Is that Keri working the body?"

"Yeah. Sure do miss Sam."

"You and me both, my friend." Sam was Dr. Samantha Owens, Taylor's best friend and the former head of Forensic Medical, the lead medical examiner for the Mid-State of Tennessee. She'd recently moved to Washington, D.C., and Taylor missed her dreadfully. She understood. God knew she understood. If she'd been faced with the kind of loss Sam experienced, she'd have run away, too. But she couldn't help missing her like hell.

"Have you heard from her?"

"I did, a couple of days ago. She's doing well. Found a place she likes in Georgetown."

"Good. Next time you talk to her, give her my best. I'm going to start running some of the evidence we collected. I'll shout if we get anything that looks relevant."

Taylor glanced at her watch—5:15 p.m. The chief would be down here soon. She needed to hurry up and get him some info he could use for a presser. The chief did so love to be on air, and if they hurried, he could make the 6:00 news.

Keri McGee was on her knees next to the body. Taylor joined her.

"Yo," Keri said.

"Yo back. What do you have for me?"

"A whole lot of nothing. No trauma to the body, outside of the stab wound, of course. I'm about finished here, actually. She's only been dead for a little while, no more than an hour. She was found quickly. Was she living on the streets?"

"Why do you ask?"

"Newspaper in her shoes and socks. They do that for warmth. And she hasn't bathed in a while. Not that that's any real indication, a bunch of these folks have been camping down here for days."

Taylor took her own inventory of Go-Go. That the girl hadn't bathed recently was quite evident. She looked like she'd been living rough: her skin was brown with dirt, she had no jewelry on, no watch, just a small red thread tied around her right wrist. From her matted hair to her grubby clothes, Go-Go was downright filthy. She didn't look much like the other protestors, who, despite their attempts to blend in, still glowed with health.

"I want to talk to whoever found her."

"Over there," Keri said, pointing at a young man who was hovering nearby. "I'm about ready to take her back to the morgue. Fox will autopsy her in the morning, along with everyone else we loaded up on today."

"Sounds good. Thanks."

Taylor took her turn with the kid who'd found the body next. He couldn't be a day over twenty, with a snippet of a beard, dark hair and dark eyes, shoulders hunched into a hooded North Face fleece. Taylor appreciated the irony. The kid was protesting capitalism wearing a two-hundred-dollar jacket. His face was streaked with tears.

"Hey there. I'm Lieutenant Jackson, homicide. What's your name?"

"Derek Rucka."

"How do you know Go-Go?"

"She's my girlfriend."

"Really? You're dating? She doesn't seem to be in very good shape for a girl with a man."

He looked down. "She *was* my girlfriend. We broke up a few weeks ago. She took off, and I hadn't seen her until today. I was down here with the gang and I saw her smoking on the steps. We chatted."

"About what?"

"Her coming home. She, well, if you know her name, you know her history. Go-Go is bipolar. She's been doing really well, too, working for her dad. That's where we met. My mom is on dialysis.

But she stopped taking her meds about a month ago, and things went downhill pretty quickly."

"So you were out here trying to save her?"

He shook his head miserably. "No. Not at all. I didn't know she was out here. I certainly didn't know she was on the streets. I'd have come looking sooner."

"So today of all days, you just happen to run into her, and then boom, she's dead? Is there something you want to tell me, Derek?"

The boy's face flushed with horror, and his mouth dropped open. "What? No. I didn't do anything to her. We just talked. Shared a bowl. That's it."

"So you admit to doing drugs with the deceased?"

The kid nodded, his head moving vigorously on its slender stalk. "Yeah. But I promise, that's all we did."

"I think you should probably come down to my office and talk to me some more, Derek. Okay?"

The bowed shoulders straightened and the tears stopped. His voice grew cold. "Am I under arrest?"

"Not right now. We're just going to have a little chat."

"I know my rights. You can't detain me unless you have cause."

Taylor narrowed her eyes at the boy.

"Don't give me a reason, kid. I'm not in the mood. We can do this hard, or we can do this easy. You just admitted to using an illegal substance on state property. You want to go down on a drug charge, I'm happy to make that happen for you. Or you can come in and have a nice friendly chat. Your call."

She stepped back a foot and fingered her cuffs. Rucka swallowed and shoved his hands in his pockets, head cast downward in defeat.

"Okay then. Come with me." Taylor led the kid to her car, put him in the back seat. "I'll be back in a minute. You just hang out."

Of course, one of the reporters saw this, and shouted across the tape at Taylor frantically. "Lieutenant, do you have a suspect in custody?"

Taylor ignored her. She wasn't about to get in a conversation with a reporter, not when the chief was on his way. No sense stealing the old man's glory. She returned to the body, watched as Keri McGee took samples and bagged the girl's hands.

"Anything?" Taylor asked.

"Not really. Nothing that's leaping out. I have hairs that don't match the body, debris, but that's not a surprise, considering she's out in the crowd like this. She's wrapped up like she's wearing a sari. I'll get her back to the morgue, and we can get her peeled down to her skin, run everything and see what's out of place."

One of these things is not like the other...

Oh, great. Now she was going to be singing that stupid song for the rest of the night.

Taylor didn't blame Keri for wanting to get the girl out of the limelight as quickly as possible, especially with the chief on the way. It was practically record speed for a homicide investigation, but Keri was a stellar death investigator. Taylor trusted her to know when it was time to move on to the next step.

Go-Go would be posted in the morning, along with any other unfortunates who found their way to the tables of Forensic Medical. In the meantime, Taylor had a job to do. She'd started toward the perimeter when Keri shouted to her.

Taylor turned and saw Keri waving her back.

"What's up?"

Keri handed Taylor a small leather wallet. "Found it under her layers of blanket. Don't know why I didn't see it when I rolled her."

"Hers?"

"Not unless her name is James Gustafson."

Taylor flipped the wallet open. It was all the standard stuff: a driver's license and a few credit cards, plus some cash. The photo showed a pale man, forty-one, blue on brown, five foot ten inches. His address showed him to be from Virginia.

"Keri, tell me if I'm crazy. Maybe we just caught a break, and this is our killer's wallet. Go-Go tried picking his pocket, he got pissed and stabbed her, then was spooked and ran before he retrieved it?"

"Would you leave your wallet if you had just stabbed someone?"

"No one said these guys were geniuses."

Keri laughed, then a frown crossed her face. She had her purple-nitrile-gloved hands in the grubby folds of Go-Go's blankets. "Ick. Now that's weird."

"What?" Taylor asked.

Keri produced three more wallets, all very similar to the first, and four cell phones.

"Well, well, well," Taylor said. "Our Go-Go is quite the little pickpocket."

"Bet there's some folks up on the plaza who will be happy to get their stuff back."

"No kidding. Good job, Keri. I'll have Parks Jr. do some canvassing, see which phone and wallet belongs to which person. They can all come in and have a chat. At least we have some suspects. Maybe we can crack this one tonight. Later, 'gator."

Taylor headed back to the perimeter tape, planning out the evening, and trying to formulate exactly what she was going to say to Go-Go's father about his wayward, now dead daughter.

What a damn shame.

CHAPTER 5

"Whoo-eeeee!"

Stover had decided to ride the mechanical bull at the Cadillac Ranch. He was spinning in circles, whooping and hollering and generally making an ass of himself. Two bleached blond bimbos had attached themselves to him about an hour earlier, and they gazed adoringly at their man for the evening, salivating over his generosity and the size of his wallet.

JR couldn't stand this much longer. He glanced at his watch; it was past midnight. When had that happened? Granted, he'd been drinking. Keeping up with Stover was a challenge for a man who generally didn't allow himself to indulge in more than the occasional adult beverage, and only then as a reward. Funny, he'd broken his own rules twice in a month. What did that say? Was he getting lax? Tired? Old?

No. Never old. Not in that way. He was certainly aging, like any normal person would, but he was far from staid and predictable.

Stover, now he was predictable. Out of town, away from his wife—and his mistress—looking to grab the first piece of tail that would bite, throw back as much drink as his protruding gut would allow, then fuck and pass out in a strange room without a second thought.

JR was better than that. Cleaner. Seemlier. And certainly more temperate. Stover drew attention to himself like a five-year-old throwing a tantrum—everyone around was aware of him. JR never could handle that level of attention from strangers. Not that he wanted to. God, if he were this indiscreet, he'd have landed in a jail cell years ago. No, prudence and moderation were the keys to his longevity.

Almost as if Stover could read his mind, the man started yelling in a drunken slur. "JR." The name came out *Jar.* "Ca'mere. Get yer bony ass up here."

The blondes twittered and simpered.

JR waved him off, then realized how incredibly intoxicated Stover was. After his invitation, he'd closed his eyes and started to slide off the back of the bull.

It was time to go.

He turned and walked to the bar to settle the bill. Stover had given the bartender his credit card to hold to keep the tab open. JR asked for the tab, and told the bartender to keep it on the card. He figured Stover might as well pay for the drinks, considering how inconsiderate he was being.

But the bartender came back and told JR the card had been declined. Cursing silently, he reached for his own wallet. He'd just give the man some cash, and be done with it.

His back right pocket was empty.

Son of a bitch.

He glanced over to the women who'd latched on to them, but couldn't see either of them in the crowd.

Fury began to build in his chest, so hard and fast that the bartender reared back when he saw the look on JR's face. He'd been ripped off. The worthless bitches had stolen his wallet and run.

He went to Stover, who'd just tripped off the bull, and grabbed him by the shirtfront.

JR hissed the words. "They stole my wallet, you fat fuck."

"Sucks for you." Stover began to laugh, the hysterical giggles of a drunken hyena, which just pissed JR off more. He dragged the man to the bar, pushed him roughly against the wooden rail.

"Your card was declined. Pay the tab."

Something in JR's voice registered with Stover. He obeyed immediately, pulled his wallet out—he still had his, the shit—and paid for their drinks with two crisp $100 bills.

Satisfied, JR stalked away. He needed to find those women. The last thing he wanted was his name getting out. Granted, it wasn't his real name on the license and credit cards, but a variation, a pseudonym, if you will, something he used to assure his anonymity as he cruised the country. He'd adopted the name when he failed out of med school. Employers wouldn't be inclined to hire a man who they perceived wasn't even competent enough to finish school. That wasn't it, wasn't it at all. He could have done the work if he wanted to, but he'd found another hobby, one that satisfied him in ways being a doctor never would. He made a show of struggling with the work so his classmates would think he was just incapable, and he could fade away from their lives.

But Stover was his Achilles heel. He knew JR's real name. The idiot had spied him in the hotel in New Orleans and remembered.

JR pulled up short at the door to the street. The women became secondary. That was a problem, but it wasn't fatal. He knew what he needed to do. There was only one way to really fix this mess.

Stover had to die.

He felt a tingle of excitement go through his body.

Two in one day? In one city? Dare he?

His mind answered in the affirmative, with a caveat.

Don't use the knife.

JR waited for Stover to catch up to him, his mind racing. So many ways to die. Fall in front of a car, trip and hit your head on a light pole…

He thought about his drive around the city earlier and it hit him. The river was only a block away. There were three bridges, too, one of which was solely for pedestrians.

JR assessed the man beside him. He was drunk enough. He'd never be able to swim.

It wouldn't have the satisfaction of the knife—nothing could top that—but this would solve one very large, loud, nagging problem.

He turned to his old friend.

"Come on, Heath. Let's go for a walk."

Stover fell into step beside him, yammering away. God, did the man ever shut his trap?

Well, JR, give him this. It is his last will and testament, after all.

It only took five minutes to mount the bridge and cross halfway to the highest point. He stopped to admire the view. They were standing over the murky river water, the lights of Nashville shining majestically in the darkness.

Time to say goodbye.

He didn't mean to do it. He really didn't. JR gave Stover a push, and the drunken fool began to struggle, and there was nothing to be done for it. The blade was in his hand before he even gave it a second thought. JR shoved the knife in quickly, then drew it out. The pain was enough to stop Stover's cries. He didn't move for a moment, looking vaguely surprised, then toppled over the edge of the bridge himself, with no effort whatsoever.

JR did something he'd only done once before, in another moment of extreme distress. He tossed the knife off the bridge after Stover's body. It killed him to do it—my God, what a prize for his collection, a blade that took not one, but two lives, in a single day—but he'd been forced into impulsivity here in Nashville, and like any animal who knew it had just survived a close call, he needed to retreat to his bolt hole and lick his wounds.

He would call the conference organizers first thing in the morning and plead a bad case of food poisoning. In the meantime, he needed to cut his losses and get the hell out of Dodge.

Nashville had been a little too good to him.

CHAPTER 6

Taylor spent Monday evening keeping the wheels in motion on Go-Go's murder. She had a long, sad chat with Joe Dunham, promised him she'd do everything in her power to bring Go-Go's killer to justice as quickly as possible. It wasn't an empty promise; she had several solid leads already. She was confident she'd have her man soon.

Derek Rucka's interrogation gave her absolutely squat, outside of the fact that Go-Go had been known to suffer from a wee bit of kleptomania, and going off her meds had exacerbated the syndrome. She was a pack rat, indiscriminately lifting whatever she could get her hands on: wallets and phones mostly, but brushes, lipsticks, pens—anything that could be separated from its owner. According to Rucka, it was purely for fun; she took a perverse pleasure in getting away with it.

The kid's story checked out, and a canvas of the protestors confirmed that he was on the other side of the memorial when Go-Go went down. Taylor cut him loose just after midnight.

They'd also found all the wallet and cell phone owners, save one: Gustafson. Everyone else checked out. Taylor had that niggling feeling in the back of her head that there was something to this guy. It was something in his eyes. Alone at her desk, she stared at his license photo for a few minutes, then ran him through the system. Clean. She found a phone number and called, but the phone just rang and rang and rang.

Instinct is vital for every homicide detective, and hers was on fire. She called the local precinct that serviced the area where Gustafson lived in Virginia, but it was late, and they were busy working their own cases. Someone would get back to her tomorrow, supposedly. She knew well enough that she'd have to call back in the morning, made a note of it on her list.

She'd lock him down tomorrow. Frustrated, she headed home.

John Baldwin, her fiancé, an FBI profiler, was in Minnesota working a case, so Taylor had the house to herself. Sleep never came easy for her, with or without Baldwin's presence, but she'd grown accustomed to having him in her bed while she gazed at the ceiling, at the very least to warm her chilly feet. With both he and Sam gone, she was a bit lonely.

But instead of wallowing, she grabbed a beer from the fridge, racked up a game of nine-ball and expertly shot the balls down one by one, until she finally began to weary around three. She slept a couple of fitful hours, then got up, showered and headed to Forensic Medical for Go-Go's autopsy.

Taylor attended herself so the chief could have instant updates to share with his high-profile friends. It was an unremarkable event and only served to make her miss Sam more. Dr. Fox was a good ME, quick and to the point, but he lacked that little bit extra, the sixth sense Sam seemed to have for making a murder come to life.

The girl had been stabbed once, the knife most likely a seven-to-eight-inch, double-bladed stiletto, sliding right past her ribs, under her breastbone, and into her heart. THC showed on the tox screen; a more complete report would take weeks. Exsanguination was the official cause of death, and it was ruled a homicide.

Taylor felt sorry for Go-Go. She was obviously a very troubled girl, but not one who deserved to die on the street at the wrong end of a blade.

It was still early when Fox finished the post. Taylor debated stopping at Waffle House and getting breakfast, but decided to go back to the office first, which ended up being a good call. The videos from TPAC were waiting on her, with a note from Tim: "Check out 3:47 p.m. Think we may have a shot of our guy. I'm in court, will be over as soon as I'm done."

Taylor popped the disc into her laptop and hit Play.

The footage was surprisingly clear, though in muted black and white. She dragged the bar to the spot Tim suggested and hit play. It took three replays to see it. Damn, Tim had a good eye.

There was a flash of white in the bottom right edge of the screen, which Taylor figured must be the bill of a hat. Her theory was confirmed a moment later when a man walked through the full frame, wearing a white baseball cap. He stepped right into a bundle of rags that Taylor assumed must have been Go-Go, then disappeared out of the frames. Go-Go dropped to the ground, and that was it. A fraction of a second. And the bastard's back to the camera the whole time.

Well, the tapes had at least narrowed her search down to the male species. That cut out fifty percent of the suspect pool.

She did some quick mental measuring, putting the guy against the stone wall that led to the auditorium and figured he wasn't over six feet. That Gustafson fellow was about that height as well.

She played the tape several more times, but couldn't find anything more. The idea that Go-Go had managed to pick the man's pocket as he stabbed her looked incredibly remote. It was a blitz attack, fast, clean. Professional even. And if it was his wallet, he certainly didn't attempt to retrieve it. He hit the girl, knocked her down and was gone in the blink of an eye.

Maybe Taylor was barking up the wrong tree here.

Her phone rang, interrupting her thoughts, and she glanced down to see the cell number of her new sergeant. She answered, "Jackson."

"Hey, Loot. It's Parks. I'm down here on River Road boat ramp. We have a floater. ID on him says his name is Heath Stover, late of the Big Easy."

"Bully for you. Call Wade, he's on. I'm working Go-Go."

Parks said, "I know you are. I've already got Wade here. But this is something you might want to see. Our New Orleans dude? He's been stabbed. Right in the same spot as Go-Go."

CHAPTER 7

Heath Stover's overweight torso bore a familiar mark, just under his sternum, a slash in the flesh that allowed the yellow subcutaneous fat to squish out around the edges of the wound. The water had washed the blood away. Fox got on the autopsy immediately once the body arrived at Forensic Medical, and Taylor stood to the side, watching, arms crossed, tapping the toe of her boot on the floor while Fox measured and murmured and inserted a special ruler into the slit to determine its depth. He finally stood and nodded.

"Same kind of blade. Double edged, sharp as hell. See how there's no hesitation, or wiggle room? Went straight in, under the sternum and into the heart." Fox stood up and looked at Taylor, his brown eyes troubled. "I have to tell you, Lieutenant, whoever did this knew what he was doing."

"Is it the same person who killed Go-Go?"

"I can't tell you that. But he—or she—knew exactly where to place the blade for maximum effectiveness. This isn't your every day stabbing. It's clean, precise, and done with amazing skill. And Go-Go's was exactly the same."

"I think we're safe saying *he*. I believe we have Go-Go's murder on tape. If she hadn't gone down I'd have thought he just bumped into her. It was quick. Here, help me run this through."

They played out the scenario she'd seen on the tape a few times, and Fox confirmed that based on Go-Go's wound, the stabbing could definitely work the way Taylor had seen on the videotape.

Fox turned back to his newest guest. "But Stover here, he got stabbed, then went in the river somewhere. Wasn't in the water too long, and there is water in his lungs, just a bit. He was on his last legs when he went in, but he was alive. Could be your blitz attacker hit him and he went in the water, or he killed him by the bank and pushed him over the edge. Radiographs show he does have a few broken bones, so he either got in a fight, or fell—"

Taylor stopped tapping her foot. "Off one of the bridges. That would explain the broken bones. We can do a current analysis from last night, see where he might have gone into the river."

"That makes sense to me. Huh. If this is the same killer, he did two in one day. Dude's got a serious problem."

"No kidding. Thanks, Fox. Now I have to go put Stover and Go-Go together, find out what they have in common. Then I can figure out who did this to them both."

The words floated to her head again, this time slightly altered.

One of these things is *too much* like the other.

CHAPTER 8

Taylor spent the drive back to the office in deep thought. Two kills, exactly alike, with two people who, on the surface, had absolutely nothing in common. A quick investigation on Stover found that he was in town on business, had checked into the Hermitage Hotel in the late afternoon, asked directions to Rippy's BBQ on Broadway, then, around six the previous evening, set off on foot toward LoBro. Marcus Wade was down there now, nosing around. Hopefully there'd be a lead.

In the meantime, Taylor set to work getting in touch with the Fairfax County Police in Virginia. A few annoying false starts later, she was finally connected to a detective named Drake Hagerman. Taylor laid out the story and asked for his help tracking down Gustafson. He promised to get back to her within the day. Satisfied, Taylor hung up and called Marcus to see what was shaking on his end.

What was shaking, apparently, was pay dirt. Marcus answered in a huff.

"I was just about to call you. Can you send me a picture of the guy whose wallet Go-Go had, the one we didn't find last night?"

"I'll bring it down myself. Why? You got something?"

"Stover was in here last night, dining with another guy. Description sounds an awful lot like that photo on the license. If it's him…"

Taylor felt that flash of excitement she got when a case was about to break wide open. Less than twenty-four hours. Impressive. Her people were damn good at their jobs.

"I'll be there in five."

She called Chief DeMike and let him know what was happening, then set off down to Rippy's.

The bar was packed full, the lunch crowd rolling in food and drink and overly loud country music. Taylor would love to know how much they pulled down in a year; Rippy's was always packed to the gills.

She found Marcus at the back bar, chatting with a ponytailed, jean-clad waitress. He looked quite pleased with himself. Marcus was adorable, and his good looks sometimes helped loosen tongues. Taylor gave him a look; he cleared his throat and became completely professional.

"Lieutenant, Brandy served Mr. Stover last night. She said he was with another gentleman."

Taylor pulled a six-pack of photos she'd put together out of her jacket pocket and handed it to the waitress. "Do any of these men look familiar to you?"

Gustafson was on the top row, third photo.

Brandy didn't hesitate.

"That's the guy," she said, pointing to Gustafson.

"You're one-hundred-percent certain?"

"Absolutely. Gave me the creeps. He smiled too much. And didn't tip. They were going honky-tonking. The fat one asked me the best place to go. I sent them to Tootsies, of course, and suggested the Cadillac Ranch, too."

Taylor met Marcus's eye. "Thank you, ma'am. Please keep this to yourself. You may be called on again to provide information. Are you willing to do that?"

"I am. If he's a creep, I don't want him back in here. Hey, I gotta go. My manager's giving me the evil eye." She glanced coquettishly at Marcus. "Shout at me sometime."

Marcus blushed red, and Taylor gave him a smile.

"You're such a charmer."

"You know it. So this is our guy, huh?"

"Looks that way. You keep on this trail, see if you can nail down exactly what might have happened. I'm rather amazed, actually. Either this guy dropped his wallet while he was stabbing Go-Go, or she managed to slide it out of his pocket. Pretty incredible presence of mind for a girl who's stoned and dying."

"But she was an accomplished pickpocket. Maybe she targeted him just as he targeted her. And they both got screwed."

Taylor nodded. "That makes sense. Well done, Go-Go. She practically handed us her killer on a platter. I'm heading back to the office and hitting up the Internets."

"All right. See you later."

Taylor watched Marcus stride away, thankful to have his keen investigative mind at her disposal, then walked back to her vehicle. She had a date with a computer.

The email notification on her iPhone chimed just as she turned the engine over. It was Hagerman, from Fairfax County. According to him, there was no one named James Gustafson in the Virginia DMV system, and the address on the license was a vacant lot. Her killer was a ghost.

CHAPTER 9

ViCAP, the Violent Criminal Apprehension Program, could be a homicide detective's best friend, if they knew exactly how to use it. It wasn't as easy as inputting your crime and the system spitting out a match to similar crimes. You had to know what to ask for. Taylor had unfortunately availed herself of its services many times in the past, and had the level of expertise needed to run the appropriate request chain into the queue. Hopefully the results would come back quickly, but the service wasn't fully automated. A real person had to do some of the legwork, and the FBI was backed up three ways to Sunday on requests. So she inputted the parameters, taking great care with the specifics of both Go-Go's and Heath Stover's murders—the exactness of the stab wounds, all the similarities she could find—crossed her fingers, and went on to the next component of her investigation: figuring out who this Gustafson man really was.

The ViCAP results came back several hours later, much quicker than she expected. She read the email in her inbox with trepidation, then sat back in her chair, let the realization wash over her. There were matches in the system from several places around the country, the most recent a homeless woman in New Orleans. Gustafson, whoever the son of a bitch really was, had been a busy, busy boy.

Taylor knew it was time to start raising the red flags. Too many jurisdictions, too many victims. She filled the chief in on her plan, got an *atta-girl*, then went to the source. Her fiancé was a profiler, after all.

Baldwin answered on the first ring. "Hey, love. How are you?"

"Hi, babe. I've been better. Two unsolved cases on my desk from yesterday alone, and just got a report back from ViCAP. I think I've got a serial on my hands." She gave him all the details, then emailed him the ViCAP report. She waited while he accessed it and read the findings. A few minutes later, he agreed.

"You might be right," he said. "What did you say this guy's name is again?"

"The license said James Gustafson, but Fairfax County just confirmed that no one by that name exists in the system, and the address is a fake. The license, the cards, all of it, they're either excellent identity theft or really sophisticated forgeries. Who is this guy?"

"An excellent question."

"My theory is he's been killing off the radar for years. And he broke his MO with this latest victim. He's been preying on homeless until now. Go-Go was a fuck up, she certainly looked the part, but hitting a well-established surgeon from New Orleans? One mistake could be an accident, sure, but the other... there's a tie to his past, I'm sure of it. The waitress got the impression they two men were friends, out for a night on the town. Maybe Stover knew the real identity of the killer, and Gustafson felt threatened."

"That's a solid theory. He killed a different type of victim out of sequence. The back-to-back kills, I'd bet he's in some sort of trouble and is decompensating."

"Well, he's screwed up. Now we know about him. He's on the radar, and I'm about to make his world hell."

"He sounds like someone who has spent his life being very, very careful. Listen, I'm totally wrapped up in this case, or else I'd help you myself. But I know who to call. I've worked with her on cases before. She's sharp. I think you should have a chat with her."

"What's her name?"

"Maggie O'Dell. Hold on a sec, let me get her number for you." He rattled off the numbers and she wrote them down.

"I'll call her right now. Thanks, honey. Call me later, okay?"

"Will do. Love you."

"Love you, too."

Taylor hung up the phone, waited a moment, then dialed. Even if O'Dell couldn't help, at least the FBI would be aware that something was hinky with the so-called James Robert Gustafson.

The call went to voicemail. Taylor left a message, told the agent who she was, her connection to Baldwin, that she had a significant ViCAP match and wanted to touch base. She hung up the phone, leaned back in her chair and put her boots on the desk.

She'd get some justice for Go-Go, and for Stover. Their deaths would not go unpunished. No matter what. And for the moment, that was the best she could do.

EPILOGUE

The lights of Washington D.C. greeted JR. Luminous, beautiful; the city was home. He always felt secure once he crossed into Fairfax County, knowing he was just miles from his basecamp. It had been a long trip, exhausting in its way, but so, so worth it.

Sated, he was calm again, the fury of the past month's excess slaking the thirst in his blood. Now he would lay low. Fit back into his life. Go to work like a good little boy. Recharge his batteries. Maybe a small vacation, somewhere in the mountains, where he could watch the snow fall, listen to birds chirp and water run and feel the cool air pass over his skin.

And remember. Always, always remember.

ABOUT THE STORY

BLOOD SUGAR BABY is the middle part of a triad of stories that first appeared in SLICES OF NIGHT with my dear friends Erica Spindler and Alex Kava. To see where JR came from, and where he's headed next, I highly encourage you to get the full book, SLICES OF NIGHT.

WHITEOUT

A TAYLOR JACKSON NOVELLA

"The wise man in the storm prays to God, not for safety from danger, but deliverance from fear."

– Ralph Waldo Emerson

CHAPTER 1

October 9, 1987
Annecy, France
1900 Hours

My father's screams echo in the small car.

"Monte, vite, vite. Angelie, baisse-toi! Baisse-toi!"

My head hits the floor just as the window shatters. Blood, thick and hot, sprays my bare legs. I wedge myself under my mother's skirts, her thighs heavy against my shoulders. Somehow I know she is already dead. We are all dead.

Flashes of black.

Their voices, two distinctly male, one female. Another, a stranger's call, silenced abruptly with a short fusillade of bullets. The would-be savior's bicycle smashes into the side of our aging Peugeot. His body catapults across the hood onto the pavement beyond and his head hits the ground; the crack sounds like the opening of a cantaloupe, ripe and hard.

My father, his life leaving him, slides down in the seat like a puppet cut from its strings. He's whispering words over and over, faintly, and with the cacophony in the background I can barely hear him. I risk a glance, wishing I'd not. The image shall never leave me. Red, pulpy and viscous. He is missing half his face, but his full lips are moving.

"Si toi survivrais, cherchér ton Oncle Pierre. Je t'aime de tout mon cœur."

I hear nothing but the first words. Panic fills me. Though I recognize what is happening, the reality has just crept in.

Si toi survivrais. If you survive.

I want to take his hand, to comfort him, to tell him I am there, that I, too, love him with all my heart. I reach for him as he dies. He shakes his head, trying to implore me to stay hidden, not to move. He isn't even speaking now, but I can hear his words in my head, like he has transferred his soul to my body for these last fluttering moments, has given himself up early to crowd into my body and try to save me.

Undeterred, my hand steals across the gearshift. I touch the cold skin of his thumb.

A roaring in my ears. There is pain beyond anything I've ever felt, and I go blank.

CHAPTER 2

October 8, 2013
Nashville, Tennessee
0415 Hours

Homicide never sleeps. At least that's what Taylor Jackson told herself when the phone rousted her from a moderately deep slumber, the first decent shut-eye she'd had in a week. She'd finally crashed at 3:00 a.m., succumbing to the two-to-three hours she normally managed on a good night. The sheets were tangled around her legs, so she rolled to Baldwin's side of the bed, used a long arm to snake the phone off the hook.

"Who, what, where, when, and, most importantly, why?"

Homicide detective Lincoln Ross didn't miss a beat.

"Me. Your wake up call. Your phone. 4:15 a.m. Because you told me to get you up so you didn't miss your flight."

"You're fired."

"Excellent. I'll charter a plane to the Bahamas right now. See ya."

She yawned. "Okay, okay. I'm up. You downstairs?"

A faint horn sounded.

"On my way."

At least no one was dead. Not yet, anyway.

Jeans, boots, black cashmere T-shirt, leather jacket, ponytail,

Carmex. Three minutes flat. Take that, Heidi Klum.

Two hours and three Diet Cokes later, her somewhat caffeinated body in an exit row window seat, the 737 rushed into the sky. She watched the ground fall away and asked herself again why she'd agreed to do this. The invitation had been the fault—*now, Taylor, be nice*—the *inspiration* of her fiancé, John Baldwin, whose place she was taking at the Freedom Conference, a small foreign intelligence initiative that met annually to hear about the latest tools for cyber intelligence and information gathering. The professional makeup of the conference was specific to clandestine services, but some civilian law enforcement officials attended as well. Baldwin had been set to speak about using behavioral profiling as a predictive analysis for terrorist attacks against the United States, and was featuring the case of the Pretender, a nasty serial killer who'd killed dozens in his bid to ruin all of their lives.

To ruin her life, as well.

Two years in the past, the moniker conjured chills and made her throat tighten.

Dead. He's dead. Stop it.

Baldwin had been called off at the last minute to deal with a skinner in Montana—what was it about these freaks who liked to remove their victims' skin?—and Taylor had agreed to take his place at the conference. She had his notes, his slideshow, though she was thinking of skipping that—there were crime scene photos from Nashville that showed her own bloodstains, and pools of her best friend's blood. She didn't know if she was quite ready to see them at all, not to mention plastered, bigger than life, on a presentation screen for an entire audience to see.

It had been interesting to see his analytical write-up about the case. It was so cut and dried. Like there were no other options. In Baldwin's world, everything that transpired was a foregone conclusion based on several psychological metrics. His evaluation made her feel better about what had happened. Taylor had lost her head. She'd hunted the man down, gone off grid in order to kill him, nearly lost her own life in the process, but in the end, it was

Baldwin's finger that pulled the trigger.

He'd done that for her.

A foregone conclusion.

She settled deeper into the seat, shut her eyes. The least she could do was give his speech for him.

CHAPTER 3

October 7, 2013
London, England
0000 Hours

The phone in my flat bleats to life as I am leaving for the airport.

My phone never rings, and this is purposeful. It is there for emergencies: fires, break-ins, unanticipated scenarios that could lead to my death. It is not for casual conversations, and it never rings, because only one person has my number.

My heart speeds up, just a little. *Why is he calling? Why now?*

I pick up the receiver. "*Oui?*"

"Angelie. What have you done?"

"*Je ne sais pas de quoi tu parles.*"

"In English, Angelie. How many times have I told you?"

"*Alors*, Pierre. Fine. I don't know what you're talking about."

"Angelie, you know exactly what I'm talking about. A couple of *gendârmes* just pulled Gregoire Campion's body out of a duffel bag that was stashed in his bathtub. He was in pieces."

This news is both good and bad. Good, because the smug bastard is dead, at last. Bad, because if my Uncle Pierre is telling the truth and the body has been found so soon, the borders will be under extra scrutiny. Pierre has given me a gift without even knowing.

"That means nothing to me. I must go, *Oncle. À bientôt.*"

I hear his cry of protest as I drop the receiver. I must hurry.

From my closet I pull the necessary gear. A quick change of undergarments gives my thin body curves; tinted contacts turn my eyes blue; a beautifully made wig transforms me into an elegant blonde. I trade my jeans and trainers for a cashmere dress that clings perfectly to every inch of my altered body. A pair of knee-high leather Frye boots with specially made lifts adds a good three inches to my five-foot-four frame.

My name is now Alana Terbraak. I have been this woman before. Alana is fearless, a predator disguised as a Dutch-Canadian travel agent. She is the perfect cover for crossing borders; it is her job to scope out areas she sends her clients to. No one questions Alana's travel. She is one of my better identities.

I place several remaining identities in the bag, under a secure flap that is impossible to see with the naked eye, and pull the worn Canadian dollars from my safe. I mix them in with my Euros and pound notes, wipe down the small flat, lock everything up, and leave.

My plane departs in two hours, and I will not miss it.

CHAPTER 4

October 8, 2013
Washington, D.C.
1400 Hours

An early snow greeted Taylor when she landed in D.C. As promised, a man was waiting for her by Baggage, holding an iPad; the screen spelled out her name. He took her bag silently and led her to a black sedan. Flakes danced around her, floating generously from an icy sky. She was glad for the warmth of the car.

When they were on the road, he offered her a drink. "There's bottled water, Scotch, and vodka in that cooler by your feet."

"Thank you." Taylor took a water. It was too early to drink, even though it might warm her from the inside out.

The snow continued to cascade down as they drove to the west, getting heavier the closer they got to the Chesapeake Bay. Charles, the driver, slowed, taking it easy; the roads were getting slick.

Taylor gave up, turned up the heat in the backseat. "Too bad you don't have hot chocolate in here. I didn't know snow was in the forecast."

"It wasn't. We've got an Alberta Clipper that snuck up on us, same storm that's wreaking havoc back in the Midwest and down in Florida. It's a good thing you flew in today. Tomorrow you'd be stuck at the airport, shivering your skinny self off. Gonna get bad, that's what they're saying. Big blizzard, storm surge up the bay, power lines down from the ice. Hope you brought a sweater."

"I did. My friend Maggie O'Dell—she's an FBI agent—called last night and warned me that the storm was going to be bad. When Maggie speaks, I listen."

Forty minutes and several white-knuckled slips and slides later, Charles deposited her at the front steps of the Old Maryland Resort and Spa. "I'll bring up your bag. You're to meet the conference folk at the desk."

"Thanks, Charles. And thanks for getting me here in one piece." Taylor tried to hand him a tip, but he brushed it off with a shy smile. She shivered in her leather jacket and mounted the stairs to the resort's reception area. A woman waved at her the moment she walked in the door. She was small to the point of being elfin, gray hair cut into a chic chin-length bob, cornflower blue eyes, and a friendly smile. Taylor felt a bit like a linebacker on her approach.

"Welcome to Maryland, Lieutenant Jackson. I'm Cherry Gregg, the chair of the Freedom Conference. We are so glad to have you here. Was the ride from the airport okay?"

"It was great, thank you. I appreciate you sending a car for me." That was a lie; Taylor had wanted to rent a car, not liking the idea of being stuck an hour out of D.C. on the Chesapeake Bay without her own transportation, but it was all part of the speaker gig—getting coddled and treated like royalty. Samantha Owens, her best friend, lived in Georgetown, and was planning to come down at the end of the weekend and ferry Taylor back to D.C. for a night of catch-up. She could live for two days without a car, especially because the conference was being held at a lavish spa resort that seemed to have every amenity she might need.

"If you're anything like me, you hate not having your own car, but we are at your service this weekend. Anyplace you'd like to go, just call down to the desk, and your driver will ferry you about like a queen."

Taylor didn't even bother trying to hide her surprise. "You read my mind. How did you know?"

Gregg answered with a slight laugh. "Lieutenant, I was a CIA field agent for twenty years, and COS—sorry, Chief of Station—in four different countries. Reliable transportation was always my number-one priority. If you get completely desperate, there's an Enterprise car rental four blocks south."

Taylor laughed, liking Gregg immediately. "I'll remember that. Is the weather going to hold up?"

"It's not. Thankfully, you're the last one to arrive. We've got everyone else safely here already. We're told they have backup generators and enough fuel to hold us for at least a week, should we be so unlucky as to lose power, and the kitchens are fully stocked. There are fireplaces in many of the rooms with plenty of wood, too. One of the treats of this place, and it's going to work in our favor this weekend."

"Sounds like they thought of everything."

"Oh, they did, I assure you. Most importantly, the bar is prepped and ready, too. They laid in an extra ration of grog for us all."

"Priorities. I like it."

"You bet. I'm so happy you could join us, Lieutenant. You're very kind to take over Dr. Baldwin's spot. Would you like to settle into your room, then meet me back here in two hours? We've got a cocktail reception we'd like you to attend—it's business dress. We'll get you introduced to the other panelists, and there's a fair amount of people who'd like to meet you. Your story, your history... well, let's just say folks are interested."

Folks were always interested. Taylor attracted trouble like dust on black furniture. Inevitable.

"I don't know if that's good or bad, but you're too kind. Thank you."

"Here's your key—you're up on the fifth floor, in the Maryland Suite. I've been told they used to call it the Crab Cake Suite, but people complained."

They shared another laugh, and Taylor set off for the elevators. The room was at the end of a long, narrow hallway. She held her pass to the door, and it unlocked.

Her first impression was a blizzard of white—white walls, white furniture, white bedding, white carpeting. The cleaning bills must be astronomical. There was a fireplace at the far end of the suite, and the bathroom walls were clear glass, with a hot tub that had a perfect view of the fire.

She started to giggle, took a picture and texted it, then dialed Baldwin's cell. He answered on the first ring.

"I would suggest you plan to drink champagne instead of red wine."

"I know, right? The picture doesn't do it justice."

She went to the windows, pulled back the heavy curtains. "Baldwin, you should see this place. The view of the Chesapeake Bay is spectacular, or would be in the summer—right now it's just snowing. But you saw that hot tub and fireplace. It's like the sex bomb suite or something."

"Sounds more like a honeymoon suite. I'm sorry I have to miss it." There was a note in his voice that made her stomach hitch.

"I'm sorry too. Though I am wondering why, exactly, they reserved this particular room for *you*."

"I'd told them you were coming," he replied.

She started to laugh then, and he joined her.

"You're naughty. Everything moving along with your skinner?"

"Don't tell anyone, but we're serving a warrant in an hour. I think we've nailed the psycho."

"That's my guy. Always gets his man. Good job."

"Thanks, hon. Just glad to get another monster off the streets. Listen, there's a really bad storm heading your way. So stay inside, stay warm and dry, and if you get stuck there, I'll come and rescue you. And we can see what the real view is from that hot tub. Okay?"

"Sounds wonderful. Love you. Bye."

She unpacked her suitcase. Business casual for the cocktail party— she guessed jeans wouldn't work. She pulled a black wool skirt from the bag, and switched her motorcycle boots for knee-high cognac leather. A black cashmere sweater set and her grandmother's pearls completed the outfit. She glanced in the mirror.

"You look entirely too respectable."

She took her hair down, let it hang loose around her shoulders.

"Better. Much less uptight."

And the woman in the mirror grinned back.

CHAPTER 5

Chesapeake Bay, Maryland
1700 Hours

Taylor allowed herself a second glass of wine. The cocktail party was in full swing, the stories flying fast and furious. After the initial round of introductions, and a few awkward questions answered blithely, she'd stuck to listening, watching. There was a beautiful brunette built like a brick shithouse across the way who'd garnered the attention of practically every man in the place. She had a wonderfully exotic accent, a loud voice, and was telling stories about Sudan's second civil war in the '80s. Something about Gaddafi switching sides to support Mengistu, and a microfiche that she'd planted to thwart a southern attack.

"...But he never thought to look in the lid of the teapot, and believe you me, I've never looked at cinnamon tea the same way again," and the crowd roared with appreciative laughter.

Taylor smiled to herself and crossed the room to watch the storm. Snow on water fascinated her. Nashville wasn't a bastion of winter weather; it just got cold, and rarely snowed more than an inch or two. This was a full-fledged blizzard, and it was monstrously beautiful.

"Intelligence officers. We're like bees: we can only speak in one language, and if you don't know it, there's no manual for translation."

Taylor turned to see the man who'd spoken. He was in his late fifties, small and dapper, with short gray hair and a sad smile, and the barest hint of an accent. French, she thought, though it was very refined.

"Oh, we cops are the same way. Our stories are usually bloodier, though."

"Give them time. A few more pops, and they'll be into Afghanistan. Plenty of bloody stories there. I'm Thierry Florian. I know your fiancé. He's a good man. We worked together in Argentina last year."

"Ah, Argentina. So that's where he was. I knew it was South America, but Baldwin is always very careful not to disclose too much of his... private work."

"Nature of the beast. Helps to have a spouse in the business. No awkward questions at two in the morning."

"We're not married. Yet."

"There's time." His head was cocked to the side like a spaniel. "Your photos don't do you justice. Your eyes are different colors. Your right is darker than your left. I've never seen heterochromia with gray like that. *C'est trés jolie.* Very pretty."

He wasn't hitting on her, just noticing. It still felt weird, so she changed the subject. "Are you still clandestine service then, Thierry?"

"I retired from the DGSE in November after thirty years in. I run the Macallan Group now. Do you know who we are?"

"I know you're not a bunch of Scotch enthusiasts."

He laughed. "That's right. We grew out of the Futures Working Group, but we are a privately held company. Very dedicated, and very much off book." He winked.

"Baldwin's told me about your work. You've assembled an interesting gang of people."

"We have people from every section, multiple countries. From CIA to Mossad and military to police. We even have a couple of novelists, brilliant men and women whose sole purpose is to dream up the most unfathomable situations for us to scrutinize, because real life always imitates art."

"Doesn't it though."

His shoulders shrugged, a perfectly Gallic gesture Taylor had never seen an American man master. "*Oui*. It is strange, life. Any time you want to join us, say the word. You have just the right temperament to fit in. I was hoping to discuss it with you this weekend."

Taylor raised her eyebrows. "What, you want me to come to a meeting or something?"

She envisioned pipes and dark smoky rooms, green computer screens and cables spitting out from teletype machines. Romantic thoughts of spies long past—which was silly, because she'd seen Baldwin at work, and it wasn't cool and dreamy. It was brutal, and watching him in that element always gave her a chill down the spine. When he shut down his compassion, his became another person entirely.

Florian gave a small laugh. "So to speak. The meeting in question would be of a more permanent nature."

"Oh. Are you offering me a job?"

"I am. I would like to hook Baldwin, too. He understands our mission, that our work is vital to the safety of all of our countries. Like the intelligence services, we collect and analyze data, only act when necessary. We share with many of them if we see they are behind the curve ball."

Act when necessary. Again, she was getting into a shadow world she didn't like to think of. Some would see it as breaking the law, something she was vehemently opposed to. But for the greater good, as Baldwin always liked to point out—for the greater good, rules were sometimes meant to be bent and broken. And if it saved lives? Absolutely.

"I think you mean behind the eight ball."

"*Alors*, my English. Yes. The eight ball. But more importantly, we use the information we collect to anticipate. Anticipate, and avoid. The problem with the FBI, with your police forces, with law enforcement, in general, is the very nature of the work. React, react, react. The CIA is better, but even they are stymied by their political ties. Black ops hardly exist anymore. There is no funding for special programs, and no balls on your politicians.

"Our work is entirely independent and very proactive. We want to prevent the attacks before they start, rather than hunt down the perpetrators after the fact. You talk John Baldwin into coming along, and you can name your price. You are both worth it."

"That's very kind, but it's not about the money—"

"Of course not. You are, I believe the right word is, an idealist. You fight for justice, because every fiber of your being screams that it is the right thing to do. Just think, Taylor Jackson, what power there would be in *preventing* the attacks you investigate, *before* they occur. That is our job. And your unique abilities are worth a great deal to me.

"You both come from money; you have also earned enough to retire comfortably. So think of this salary as a cushion. You can buy his-and-hers Ferraris, or give it away to starving African children, I do not care. I need your minds. You are instinctive, and smart, and you could do a lot of good for your country. Think about it. *Santé.*"

He clinked her glass and walked away.

She took a sip of wine to cover her discomfiture. *Well. That was interesting.*

She dismissed the conversation. She was perfectly happy working homicide for Metro Nashville. She didn't like change. She especially didn't like the idea of abandoning her team.

And preventing murder? Preventing attacks? No one could do that, not effectively. Someone evil would always slip through the cracks.

The snow was heavier than ever, coming down so hard she could barely see the lights of the cars passing by on the street below. She checked her phone; the forecast was now calling for twenty inches. A small bloom of panic started in her chest. The last time she'd been snowed in, a blizzard of epic proportions in Scotland, not-so-great things had happened.

Florian caught her eye from across the room and smiled politely. He was clearly watching her, and she resented it, though she didn't know why. He'd made an offer. She'd gotten them before. It was what it was.

But....

She'd be forty in a few years, and as far as her career was concerned, she would need to make a decision about her role going forward. It was already being whispered that she'd make Captain soon, would be in charge of Nashville's entire Criminal Investigative Division, and that meant she'd be off the streets and on to the paperwork and political glad-handing. Captain Jackson. A few more years, then further up the brass ladder. Maybe even Chief in ten years. More bureaucratic nonsense. And then what? Run for office? No, thank you. She had too many opinions and not enough reserve to stop her from sharing them freely.

Baldwin wanted her to join the FBI, which would be a logical step. And though she admired everything he did, she knew she wouldn't fit in. The culture was too restrictive. She had enough bossing around at Metro that drove her mad. Having to follow the kind of dictates that the federal government imposed on law enforcement was a recipe for disaster.

The Macallan Group. Proactive rather than reactive. Huh.

She looked around the room again for Thierry Florian, but didn't see him. She sent him a mental *thanks a lot*. There would be no sleep for her tonight.

CHAPTER 6

October 9
Chesapeake Bay, Maryland
0000 Hours

The cameras are on for my safety. I made sure before we began. They will catch everything. Just in case.

The kisses are going a mile a minute. Our clothes are gone, my slip is rucked up over my hips. I skipped panties, hopeful for this moment. It makes things so much easier. His hands rush over my body, grasping my skin, kneading my buttocks, hands hurrying to my thighs and then my back, up and down and around, and I whisper, "Too fast, too fast."

He slows, smiling, his right palm lingering along the curve of my hip, then sliding to my breast, his mouth featherweight, following his touch.

Better.

It has been too long. I should stop him before it goes much further, but it feels so good to be touched, to be loved.

His hand slips down between my thighs, and a moan escapes my lips. *Stay in control, stay in control*, but I am losing it. He is too good, too skilled, and I hit the point where I don't care anymore. I am just an animal, needing, wanting. His finger is deep inside me, and we are still standing, skin-to-skin, glued together. And it feels so good.

Fuck it. I inch up, and he catches the movement, effortlessly lifts me, and my legs wrap around his waist. He is breathing hard, ready to go. Pushing against me. Waves of pleasure shudder through me. I think I might faint, take a deep breath to clear my head.

He catches my lips, kissing, sucking, staring into my eyes. He moves his hand, and I can't help but respond.

Recognizing it is time, he lays me down on the bed and slows his movement further, stroking, caressing, gentling when I want it rough, the mistake of a new lover. "Now," I urge, and he smiles and spreads my legs wide, one palm on the inside of each thigh, and thrusts into me, hard. I cry out, go right over the edge into the bliss, and he comes with me.

I lose time; I always do after sex. Hazardous, but inescapable. Hence the cameras. An old habit, hard to break.

When our breathing slows, he rolls off me, to the side, and I rise from the bed.

"Don't get up," he says, leaning on an elbow, beckoning me back.

Too late. I am already at my purse, the bag open, the cold steel in my hand. My favorite companion, the only one I truly trust. I turn to him, a brief smile playing on my lips.

"Thank you," I say, and fire. The suppressed round sounds like a sigh in the darkened room. It takes him between the eyes, and he collapses back onto the bed.

Another means to an end.

I replace the weapon, dress, brush my hair, enjoy the flush of color on my cheeks. I wipe down the room, grab my cell phone, turn off the video camera. Face the connecting door to the room next to my newly dead lover.

A moment twenty-five years in the making. Finally here.

I jimmy the lock, silent as possible. The door opens, and there he is. Asleep, quiet. Far from innocent. He looks older in his sleep.

Older, and soon to be very, very dead.

CHAPTER 7

0110 Hours

Taylor showered and changed, then stalked around her suite, wishing for something to do. No pool table, as the bar was closed for the night. Baldwin was getting some well-earned sleep, having made a successful arrest. She'd forgotten to pack a book, though there was probably a library on the hotel grounds.

Truth be told, nothing would distract her enough. She was worried about the storm. The gathering winds were howling past her window; a small piece of siding had come loose and was rattling. She could just make out people moving around outside—workers, most likely, sent out into the storm to batten down the hatches. They worked in twos, probably tied together so they wouldn't get lost.

A scene from a Laura Ingalls Wilder book pranced into her head, something she'd not thought about since she was a child. The rope between the shed and the house, followed to feed the animals, so Pa wouldn't get lost. Or Laura. She couldn't remember exactly who was meant to be saved by the slender thread, but it had worked, and all ended well.

She had no tether to keep her safe, and it worried her.

The television gave no succor, either. The whole country seemed to be in the grip of this massive and mercurial storm. The Weather

Channel was covering the huge, multi-state event causing chaos across the country. The mega-storm had swooped down from Canada, slicing through Illinois, where Rockford had received record-breaking snow totals, and people were still lost, stuck on highways and in houses inaccessible to rescue crews. She sent her friend Mary Catherine Riggio a text, checking on her, knowing the Rockford P.D. homicide detective would be out helping the emergency prep folks, but didn't hear back. And poor Maggie was down in Pensacola, Florida, which was flooded out after twenty inches of rain, and still experiencing thunderstorms and high winds. Major damage. The radar clearly showed the catastrophic storm heading right toward the Washington, D.C., area, which meant Taylor was now directly in its path.

The Weather Channel's anchor warned everyone to hunker down, because it was going to get worse before it got better. The snow totals were going to break records all up the Eastern seaboard, the storm surges would cause widespread flooding up and down the Chesapeake Bay.

Great.

As a first responder herself, Taylor wasn't used to sitting in a hotel room waiting for a storm to hit. If this were Nashville, she'd be in the command center at Metro, giving instructions, helping the city cover all the quadrants to minimize the danger to its citizens. She gave a moment's thought to calling the Calvert County Sheriff, offering her services, but realized she'd be as wanted as a wart.

She lit the fire, grabbed a beer from the mini-fridge, snuggled into the bed, and watched the flames dance while she listened to the warnings. When she could take no more, she flipped off The Weather Channel, found *The Princess Bride* on one of the movie channels, and turned down the lights. She knew the words practically by heart, but it was better than nothing.

The R.O.U.S., Rodents of Unusual Size, were beginning to lurk when the power went off.

The fireplace was down to coals as well. She'd burned through more logs than she'd realized, and the stash was getting low.

Taylor picked up the room phone, heard nothing. She pressed a few buttons, but no dial tone started. Thankfully, she'd thought to charge her cell phone. She called down to the front desk. Nothing. The lines were dead.

She knew the hotel had generators, she just needed them to kick in. It would get cold in the room quickly—the fireplace didn't put off that much heat—so she grabbed the extra blanket from the armoire and tossed it on the end of the bed.

Nothing to do but wait, and try to sleep. After an hour of tossing and turning, she managed to drift, her rest disturbed by terrible dreams. She was cold, so cold, hiking through the snow, with no one in sight, just the expanse of white spreading in all directions. She knew it was the end; she wouldn't survive. And the voice of the Pretender whispered in her ear.

CHAPTER 8

0200 Hours

It was two in the morning when the fire alarms went off. She scrambled from the bed, shaking off the chill, not sure if it was the temperature or the dreams, and threw on her jeans. It was cold in the room, her fingers fumbled with the buttons. After shrugging into her jacket, she pocketed her cell and wallet, and opened the door to the hallway with care. She could smell smoke.

Other guests were streaming from their rooms. Her hand went absently to her waist, reaching for the comfort of her Glock. Nothing there. She hesitated for a fraction of a second. Better safe than sorry.

She went back into her room, made sure the door was latched, then retrieved her Glock 27 from its case in the interior of her suitcase. The key to the lock shook in her hands—damn, it was cold. She had only brought the small backup gun, certainly hadn't planned to get it from its case. She hadn't expected to need it, not at a conference in a swanky hotel.

She slapped a magazine in place, put two more in her jacket pocket, and stowed the weapon in a small belt-clipped holster. She felt sure she wouldn't be the only one armed out of this crew—cops and counterintelligence officers weren't that different.

More comfortable with the familiar weight on her hip, she left the room, followed the remaining stragglers to the stairwell.

"What's the matter?" she called out to the nearest man.

"Dunno," he replied. "Guess it's a fire. Wish they'd turn that bloody alarm off though, it's breaking my eardrums."

"No kidding. It's deafening."

Down the five flights, carefully picking their way, with cell phones giving the only decent light. There was emergency lighting on the walls, but the lights were dim, as if they weren't getting proper connections.

The stairwell exited into the lobby. A crowd of people had gathered in the dark. They weren't being evacuated, just left to mingle in the cavernous space.

Taylor didn't like this at all. She bumbled around in the dark a bit, saw Cherry, her face underlit by a flashlight, making her seem like a ghoul. She was pale and carrying a clipboard. Just as Taylor reached her, the alarm stopped, leaving her ears ringing.

Cherry gave her a wan smile. "Oh, good, Lieutenant Jackson. I can mark you off the list."

"What's going on? Is there a fire?"

"When the power went out, the generators to the rooms failed. A small fire started on the roof, and they're trying to contain it. There's a skeleton staff on the night shift, plus several people couldn't—or wouldn't—make the drive in, and the roads are blocked now, so the fire trucks can't get here. They're doing the best they can."

"Should we be evacuating people?"

"No, not yet. Thankfully, the lobby is on a separate generator, and the heat will stay on in here for a while. As soon as they give the word, we can send people back to their rooms. Might as well settle in until they give the all clear."

"You need to put me to work, I'm going bonkers. What can I do to help?"

Cherry flashed the light on her list. "We're still missing a few people. Would you be willing to take a flashlight and hike back upstairs, knock on doors? Be very careful, we wouldn't want you getting hurt."

"Absolutely. Who are we missing?"

"Let's see… Ellis Stamper—he's in 4880. And Thierry Florian, right next door in 4900. Hildy Rochelle, as well, the brunette woman who was charming everyone tonight. She's on the fifth floor, 5380."

The man nearest them said, "Cherry, I saw her earlier. She's down here somewhere."

"Oh, good. Thanks for letting me know, Ron." She turned back to Taylor. "Just the two gentlemen, then."

"Got it. On my way."

"Thank you, Taylor. I appreciate it."

Cherry handed Taylor an extra flashlight. She headed back to the stairwell.

Now that it was silent and empty, Taylor had to admit it was a little creepy. She climbed the stairs, enjoying the burn in her thighs that started on the third floor. It warmed her up. The faint scent of smoke was stronger up here, but no worse than when she'd exited her room.

The fourth floor was deserted. Taylor turned on the flashlight—it was amazing how dark the hallway had become. She heard nothing but the whistling wind.

Room 4880 was halfway down the hall. She knocked on the door.

"Excuse me, Mr. Stamper? You're needed downstairs."

Nothing.

She banged a few more times. He must have passed her in the night. She walked down to the room next door. "Mr. Florian, it's Taylor Jackson. The generators are out to the rooms, and there's a fire on the roof. They want everyone downstairs. Cherry sent me up to find you."

Silence again.

They must have already made their way down. A wasted trip.

She'd just started back toward the stairwell when she heard the noise.

She stopped dead in her tracks, listened for it. Yes, there it was again. It sounded like crying. She pulled open the stairwell door and let it slam closed, then stepped lightly back to the two men's rooms.

Stamper's room was still dead quiet, but she could swear there were hushed voices coming from Florian's.

She knocked again. "Mr. Florian? Are you in there?"

Nothing. The silence was pervasive, complete. False alarm?

She shook it off. Must have been the wind. Or, better yet, this old place was probably haunted, and she'd just been tricked by a ghost.

Not that she believed in ghosts.

Not really.

She went for the stairwell, made her way back down to the lobby. She found Cherry in the spot she'd left her.

"Nobody home. They must already be down here, and you just missed them."

Cherry's brow creased.

"They're not here, Taylor. I've talked to everyone, they are all in the room behind the lobby's entrance. There's a giant wood-burning fireplace in there, and plenty of logs. They've opened the bar, there's some water boiling for tea and hot chocolate. But everyone who went in passed by me, and I didn't see them."

"Well, that is weird. Let's go do a lap, see if they came late."

It took five minutes of flashing lights in strangers' eyes to see that there was no trace of either man.

CHAPTER 9

0230 Hours

Too close. Surely the woman won't come back, she will assume the bastard has already vacated his room.

I remember seeing her at the cocktail party, tall, blond, aloof. Looked frigid as hell. Pretty, if you liked the ice princess type. She gave off a whiff of danger, her eyes watching every move in the room. A cop, for sure. I've seen too many in my day not to be able to pick them from the crowd.

Florian is whimpering again. I kick him in the ribs. "Shut up, old man. We are not finished."

He is missing part of a finger, a play I wasn't planning to have to employ so early in our friendly chat. But he was not taking me seriously, so I had to make a point. It was the tip of his pinky, just a quick snip of the shears, but bloody, for all that.

I flash the light in his eyes, his pupils hurriedly shrink. He moans again.

"I will take the gag out if you promise to cooperate. To tell me what I want to know."

A nod.

"If you don't cooperate, there will be more fingers. Then toes, and hands, followed by your feet. *Tu comprends*? Do you understand?"

Another nod. I swear his skin pales—perhaps I've finally made my point.

I remove the gag, dragging it down over his chin. He gulps for air. "They will come back. You can't get away with this."

"How disappointing. *Crétin. Maudite vache.* Do you not know who I am?"

He looks, uncomprehending. He does not know me in the darkness, in his confusion. Granted, I'm still in the brown wig from earlier, the dark contacts. A small adjustment to my nose.

I pull the wig from my head, and he gasps.

But it is not in recognition, it is in pain. He has passed out. I forget his age. He will not last the night at this rate. I must slow down.

His words penetrate. *They will come back.*

They will. I should move him. But where?

My finger taps against my thigh, and I hear his intake of breath. He is awake, and recognizes that small movement. Finally, he knows who he is dealing with.

"*Mon dieu.* Angelie. Angelie Delacroix. Is that you?"

"*Oui, Thierry. C'est moi. Je suis vivant, et tu êtes mort.*"

The knife slides into his ribs with ease, just above the kidneys. Not deep enough to be fatal. Not yet.

I whisper in his ear, the words harsh, metallic on my tongue. The question I've been waiting two and a half decades to ask.

"Why did you kill my father?"

CHAPTER 10

0400 Hours

Unintended consequences. The fire was contained, and everyone was given the okay to go back to their rooms. But without power, the electronic key cards wouldn't work. The generator that powered the rooms was damaged in the fire. Until the power was restored, they were stuck. The hotel staff was forced to gather everyone back in the lobby near the fireplace.

The generator to the first floor lobby ran out of fuel just after 4:00 a.m.

The depth of the snow was overwhelming. In just eight hours, there were at least four feet pushing up against the hotel's front door, and it was still coming down. Ice crackled along the windows, the moaning wind fighting to gain entry into the hotel. Cracks sounded in the distance, tree limbs collapsing under the sudden weight.

There was talk of evacuation, but Taylor knew that was a pipe dream—what were they going to do, bring a bus in? And where would they go? The entire eastern seaboard was caught in the grip of the storm. Nothing was moving. They were stuck here.

Cherry was waiting for a maintenance man to arrive with an override master key that would allow them access to rooms 4880 and 4900. She paced the lobby, staring out into the snow. Taylor figured she knew deep down there was no help coming.

Everyone knew something was wrong, that Thierry Florian and Ellis Stamper were missing. Whether they were in their rooms, or had left the premises and weren't able to return, no one knew. The idea of the two men caught out in that blizzard was unthinkable.

Stamper, it turned out, was also a member of the Macallan Group. He was Thierry's assistant, though that term was a misnomer. *Right-hand* would be more appropriate. *Bodyguard* might even come into play.

Their relationship had even been speculated about once or twice, though Florian put those vulgar rumors to rest quite openly, taking a beautiful young lover who'd ended up as his wife three years earlier. Stamper had married a year later as well.

It was their habit to get two-bedroom suites at hotels, ostensibly so Stamper could watch out over his boss. But for this event, the suites were booked, and they'd been forced into adjoining rooms instead. The front desk clerk remembered their conversation clearly, and the manager had sent a fruit basket to Mr. Florian to apologize for the mix-up.

There was no way to call either wife, to ask if she'd heard from her husband. No power, no cell service, no landlines. They were an island, in the dark and cold.

Taylor was chomping at the bit to get into the rooms. She wasn't in her jurisdiction, or she'd be ordering people around. Instead, the hotel staff was waiting for a representative from the Sheriff's office to show up before they opened the doors.

Precious moments ticking away. Modern technology was fantastic until the world was plunged into the dark, and then the Middle Ages again reigned supreme.

Taylor watched the minutes pass on her TAG Heuer watch, catching Cherry's eye every once in a while.

It took people who'd become accustomed to death to sense that this situation was very, very bad.

CHAPTER 11

0500 Hours

"Angelie. You must know, I did everything in my power to stop the murder. Your father, he would not listen. We begged him to stay put in Paris, that we had him covered, but he loaded up your mother and sister and you into the caravan and drove south. He thought he could protect you better than I. He was wrong."

"He was not wrong. He died protecting us. It was your job to keep him safe, to keep us all safe. He stole secrets for you, and you let him be gunned down. They killed my sister first, did you know that? Beatrice was six. Six, Florian—dead in my mother's lap. Her blood dripping into my hair."

"Is that what you're doing, Angelie? Systematically murdering all of the people involved in your father's case? Yes, I heard tonight about poor Gregoire Campion. I didn't realize you were capable of such an atrocity. You cut him into pieces and stowed his body in a duffel in his bathtub. The man was your friend, Angelie. How could you do that to him?"

I laugh. "A friend? Campion was never my friend. He used me, for years. Like all of you. His death is not on my conscience, Thierry. I did simply what I must to gain the truth, at last."

"*Alors*, Angelie, this is a pointless exercise. Murdering the minders will not bring your father back. It will not bring your family back. We did everything we could to protect them. In the end, the cause was simple. Your father trusted the wrong people."

Fury crowds into my chest. This is the lie Campion spewed when he was at the end. I slap Florian's face, hard.

"Lies. Don't even try to justify yourself. Oncle Pierre has shared the file with me, Thierry. I know exactly what happened. I know how you sold my father out to the Iraqis. He was the only one who had the capability to help them build their bloody bombs, and you told them where he would be that day."

His voice is soft in the darkness. "No, Angelie. That is wrong. We would never give your father to them. Never."

Florian goes silent. Something is not right here, I can feel it. I take a lap around the dark room, trying and failing to gather my temper. The cover-up is secure; all involved have the same story. How to get the truth? What will I have to do to this master of spies to find the answers I seek?

"Angelie. You've served your country admirably for fifteen years. You're one of the best assets we've ever had. Your future is bright. Why are you doing this? Why now, after all these years?"

I pull the crumbled paper from my purse. So many lives, so many sacrifices, all to procure this single sheet of paper.

I put it in front of his face, play a flashlight over the words.

He reads, then chews on his lip before he calmly sits back on the floor.

"Don't do this," he says, and there is no pleading in his voice, not like the others, who begged for their lives. Florian won't beg. He will find a way to go down swinging. He taught me that, at least.

I can't keep the tears from my voice. "I know, Thierry. I know it all."

CHAPTER 12

0600 Hours

The skies outside were dark gray. No power yet, but it wasn't the dead-of-night blackness from earlier. The mood in the room lightened, especially when the staff began handing out apples and bananas and granola bars, and stoked up the fire. If they just had some marshmallows, this would be more like a damn camping trip.

Taylor looked at her watch for the millionth time. "It's nearly six, Cherry. There's no more time to waste. It's been too long."

Cherry had dark circles below her eyes. She was clearly exhausted. But she came to life at Taylor's words, almost in relief. "I agree. I'm worried sick. Let's get the manager on duty, find out what the hell is happening."

At her wave, the hotel's manager on duty, a burly man named Fred, approached.

"Ma'am? Bad news. Our mechanic isn't going to make it. The Sheriff's office is responding to a huge wreck—buncha cars on the highway crashed, they can't spare anyone for at least an hour. We're stuck, I'm afraid."

"Fred, I'm sorry, but we need in those rooms. The Freedom Conference will pay for the damages we're about to incur."

"What?"

Taylor chimed in. "Can you let us into your maintenance room? We're going to need some tools. A wrench and a screwdriver, for starters. A crowbar, if you have it."

Fred's brown creased. "Um, ma'am, just what are you planning to do?"

Taylor smiled. "Easy. Bust the locks off the doors."

"I can't let you do that. Those locks cost—"

"It doesn't matter. There could be two lives at stake in there, and we're not going to wait any longer."

"I gotta talk to the main hotel property managers, they're in Denver. They own the resort. I can't let you—"

Taylor got in his face, her voice stern. "Fred, we aren't going to wait. We will take responsibility. I'm a cop. You place the blame squarely on my head, and I'll cover your back. The tools, now."

People always backed down when she used that tone. Fred grabbed a flashlight, and, without a word, headed toward the back stairs.

"I've got this, Cherry. I'll be back for you in a minute."

It took five minutes to gather the tools she thought she'd need. Fred wasn't talking, just shined the big industrial flashlight where Taylor asked. She'd scared him enough that he was keeping his mouth shut; she assumed he probably had a record he hadn't disclosed, something minor, and didn't want his bosses getting wind of his issues. She met guys like him in her investigations all the time. DUIs, late on their child support, warrants for traffic violations, gambling debts. Stupid stuff that should just be handled. Instead, they furtively tried to hide their misdeeds.

"Let's go up. I might need your muscle," she said, and Fred sullenly shined the light on the stairs for her. When they reached the first floor lobby, he stopped cold.

"You know what? You're on your own from here. I ain't going up there. I'm not going to be held responsible for this."

Of course not.

"A noble speech, Fred. Thanks for doing the right thing."

She left him gaping after her and found Cherry warming her

hands near the fireplace. "I've got everything. Are you ready?"

"Yes," she said simply, and fell in line behind Taylor. The whispers started as they left the room.

As they climbed the stairs, the wind shrieked harder around the building, and its violent passage heightened the echoes of their footfalls in the darkened stairwell. It was even creepier than last night—Taylor sensed the storm was peaking. Hopefully, this would be the worst of it.

The fourth floor was eerily quiet. Once the stairwell door was shut, the wind's fury was muffled a bit.

The two women walked quickly down the hall. They stopped at Stamper's room first.

Taylor didn't move for a moment, just breathed deeply. All the hair stood up on the back of her neck. Something was different. Something was wrong.

"Do you smell that?"

Cherry nodded. She'd been around enough destruction, enough death, to recognize the scent.

"Blood," she whispered.

Taylor nodded. This wasn't going to end well, she could just feel it.

She took the crowbar to the door, not caring about the damage she was inflicting. With a great wrenching groan, the lock pulled free of the door. The metal warped, and Taylor used the screwdriver to wedge the tongue out of the bolt. It still didn't free, so she gave it a strong kick, and the door latch popped free.

She drew her weapon, took a flashlight from Cherry, and cross-armed the light under her shooting hand, the outside corners of each wrist meeting in a kiss.

The room was dark, the curtains pulled closed. Taylor swung the light around the room until she saw the body. The coppery tang of blood, a scent Taylor was much too familiar with, grew stronger the nearer she got to the bed.

Their worst fears, confirmed.

Cherry gasped aloud when she saw the neat hole in Ellis

Stamper's forehead. The greatest damage was to the back of his skull, which had a massive hole in it where the bullet exited.

"Jesus. He's been executed."

Taylor said nothing, just moved the flashlight around the room, taking in the scene. He was naked on the bed, the sheets twisted. Underlying the blood was the scent of musk. Taylor approached the body, shined her flashlight up and down the length of him. There was a spent condom in the trashcan next to the bed.

"He had company."

Cherry joined her. "Conference sex. Happens all the time. We should make sure this doesn't get back to his wife." She reached for the condom; Taylor stopped her.

"What are you doing? We don't touch anything. If you persist I'll escort you from the room. Do you understand?"

Cherry gave Taylor a sad little smile. "I was COS for twenty years. My first responsibility is to my people."

"Not to the law, not to justice? You're willing to cover this up? Whoever he screwed most likely killed him."

"This will ruin him. His family, his honor—"

"Cherry, the man's dead. I daresay he's already ruined. Let's worry about soothing hurt feelings if the time comes. There's DNA on that condom, a piece of the puzzle we can't pretend doesn't exist. Get it?"

"Cops. Always afraid to do the right thing." There was a note of exasperated humor in Cherry's voice, which was a good thing, but Taylor gave her a baleful eye anyway, and she moved away from the bed.

The flashlight pummeled the darkness once more, and Taylor spied the connecting door to the next room. She thought about the room set up, realized it went to 4900.

"Cherry, look. This goes into Florian's room. Easier to get through this than tearing the electronic lock off the other door."

"I agree. But Taylor, be careful."

"*Careful* is my middle name."

Taylor eased the door open with her shoulder; it wasn't locked, or fully closed. Unlocked she could understand; if Stamper was Florian's bodyguard, he would need access to the room. And if the rumors were true, and they *were* lovers? That logic was sound; the used condom spoke volumes. Could Florian have shot his lover in a fit of rage, then left the hotel?

On the surface, that felt plausible, though not exactly right. Taylor hadn't gotten the violent vibe from Florian; he seemed more like an earnest schoolteacher than a bully.

She shone the flashlight closer on the lock. There were scratches, like an impatient thief had jimmied it open. So much for that theory.

She took a deep breath and called his name quietly.

"Mr. Florian?"

Silence.

"Shine the light around, Taylor."

She did, and wasn't surprised to find the room empty.

CHAPTER 13

0615 Hours

Florian has fainted, again. Before he succumbed to the pain, he was talking, but not saying the things I needed to hear. There are answers here, I know it. My father was not a traitor. My family did not have to die.

Many years of espionage have taught me well; eventually, everyone breaks. Watching Florian bleed and cry and lie isn't enough. I will speed up the process.

I go to the bathroom, gather a handful of water from the sink. The stream sputters and runs out as I watch. The room is cold; my hands are clumsy in the dark. Without the power, this is more difficult than I planned. The leads tied to Florian's chest and testicles will not work without electricity, and the fear of pain will not suffice. There has to be actual stimulus to coerce statements. Which means I'm back to the knife.

I splash the meager handful of water in his face, but it is enough. He sputters and his eyes open. I stand with my arms crossed, waiting for him to again register who I am, and why we are here.

"Angelie," he moans.

I drop to my knees, cajoling now, friendly.

"Talk to me, Thierry. Tell me what I need to know."

I wrap his wounds, binding them against the bleeding. It will feel better that way. He head lolls against me. I smell his fear. The infamous Thierry Florian, helpless and scared.

"That is all I have, Angelie. I know nothing else."

Kneeling back on my heels, I watch him. The letter tells me he is still lying.

"Thierry, they'll come for you soon. You must tell me the rest. Tell me, and this pain will stop." I tug on a lead attached between his legs, and he gulps a breath. His head bobs side to side, a metronome of hurt.

He whispers, "I would tell you you're wrong, but you will not believe me. "

"No, I won't believe anything less than the truth. You've been lying to me this entire time. For fifteen years, you've looked me in the face, knowing you killed my father. How could you? I thought you were my friend. I thought you were my father's friend."

He sighs, a great, dragging breath. "Dear Angelie, I am not lying. Your father panicked. We had a safe house prepared, guards to keep him safe, but someone got to him. Convinced him he was being double-crossed. Angelie, I do not know who this person was."

"Whoever it was, he told the truth. You double-crossed my father. You left him out in the cold to die."

I toy with the knife at the edge of his groin. A lesser man would beg, plead, promise me anything, just to get the sharp edge away from their skin. Florian merely shakes his head.

"No, no, Angelie. I would never do that to him. He was my friend, yes, but I will be honest. He was too valuable. He was the greatest asset I'd ever trained. But the others, they had no compunction about lying to him to get what they wanted. And he chose to believe their faint words of promise, rather than follow my protocols.

"I wanted you all in the safe house in Annecy, he chose to buy the caravan and stay in the campgrounds. There was no way to protect him, he was too exposed. He exposed you all, and panicked when they came for him."

"More lies. This letter is dated three days before his death. He says he knew you were working for the Soviets. That you were a double agent. That's why he didn't trust you." I catch my tone, a petulant child. I add a sneer. "You dishonored your vows, Thierry, and their blood is on your hands."

CHAPTER 14

0630 Hours

Taylor's theory about Florian being the shooter changed when she saw the blood by the window.

"Cherry, over here."

"Oh, no. This goes from bad to worse."

"It does, but don't lose hope just yet. There's not enough blood to assume the worst, not by a long shot. This is just a thimbleful, really." Taylor stared at the blood drops. They were drying around the edges, though the centers were still wet. Not fresh, but not old, either.

"The storm kicked into high gear at midnight. A time of death on Mr. Stamper would go a long way toward telling us whether Florian is still on site or was taken from the hotel."

Cherry shook her head. "You're not making me feel better. I have one man down, and one missing. Where the hell could he be?"

Taylor tucked her weapon back into its holster.

"I don't know. Anywhere—this campus is huge. But if he's still here, you're missing the bigger picture."

"The bigger picture?"

"It's entirely possible we're locked in this hotel with a cold-blooded murderer."

Cherry sat down hard on Florian's bed. "Oh, Lieutenant, trust me, I am well aware of this."

There was something in her tone, in the self-defeated flop on the bed.

Taylor squatted on the floor in front of the woman. "You sound like a woman who needs to get a load off her chest."

"I've screwed up. I didn't protect him. It's my fault."

"What do you mean, you've screwed up? Cherry, talk to me. What's really going on here?"

"You know who Thierry Florian is, I suspect?"

"He's worked with my fiancé, but I don't know him. I just met him tonight. He told me he's the head of the Macallan Group, and former clandestine services. The French, right, DGSE?"

"Always shy with his accomplishments, Thierry. That's what makes him such an excellent spy. His father was a leader in the French *Résistance* during World War II. When the French needed information about the Germans, François Florian would put himself in the worst possible situations, get arrested, then find ways to keep himself alive while he gathered information. When he had what he needed, he would escape and bring the information back to the resistance."

"An impressive man."

"Yes. Thierry was his youngest child, born well after the end of the war, but the tales his family told were intoxicating. While the rest of his siblings went into safe positions as doctors and lawyers, Thierry followed in his father's footsteps and joined what was then known as the DGSE—the Directorate-General for External Security."

"The French version of our CIA."

"Correct. He had an illustrious career. When he retired, he was the equivalent of our Director of Counterintelligence. But it was an especially covert side job that put him on his current path. Before he left he worked with the Alliance Base—do you know what that is?"

"An international cooperative of intelligence agencies, right?

Working against Al Qaeda and other terrorist organizations?"

"Yes." She smiled, a little sadly. "Thierry has always ruffled feathers in the intelligence community with his theories. He feels cooperative intelligence is vital to deter more terrorist attacks on the Western world. But putting a bunch of spies together—well, friction was inevitable. He saw the ways the organization worked, and the ways it didn't. He was determined to perfect the mix. Hence, The Macallan Group."

"Why are you telling me this, Cherry? The man's CV isn't necessary for me to want to help."

"Bear with me a few moments more, Taylor. Thierry has made many enemies, and he is a target. It is entirely possible we have been infiltrated by someone he pissed off back in the day, and they're taking their chance at retribution."

"You handpicked the conference members, though, didn't you? Surely you wouldn't be so careless as to let a known combatant in."

She gave a little moan. "Spies, Taylor, we're all spies. Everyone working at cross-purposes. It's why I don't work with Thierry at Macallan. I have a clearer head than he when it comes to the simple fact that for centuries, we've been working against each other. It's all well and good to hope for cooperation, but ultimately, someone will want to get payback for some perceived grievance, and it all collapses."

"So who here had a vendetta against Thierry?"

"I don't know."

"Cherry, think. If you truly believe the killer is a part of the conference, think!"

Cherry went quiet, then, in a small voice, said, "There's one other person unaccounted for. Not from the conference, from our lives. I've known her for years. She is a friend, of sorts. Used to be a protégé of Thierry's before she went out on her own. We've worked in some pretty hairy places together. She went off grid a year ago, just when Thierry formed The Macallan Group. He wanted to recruit her, came looking, but I hadn't heard from her in several months. We put out some feelers, to see if anyone knew where she was. She was for hire, you see, a black market baby, very hush-hush."

Taylor knew what *for hire* meant. "She's an assassin."

Cherry leapt from the bed at the word, shaking her head. "I was silly to bring it up. There's no way she could be involved in this. She fights against evil. That's what drives her."

"I take it the feelers came up empty?"

"Yes. Nothing. She's gone gray."

"Gray?"

"Blending in. Hiding in plain sight. She's most likely setting up for a major job."

Taylor's voice rose. "A major job? Come on Cherry, talk to me. What kind of major job would this woman have to disappear for a year to prepare for?"

Cherry just shook her head. "I don't know. Before she left, she'd been... reckless. Taking on jobs that were out of character."

A sense of foreboding crept into Taylor's stomach. International assassins on the loose made her very uncomfortable—she'd come face to face with one herself a year earlier and hadn't enjoyed it a lick. A different tact was necessary; she could see Cherry was shutting down.

"Tell me this. Something about this set-up makes you think of this woman. What is it?"

Cherry pursed her lips. "Thierry alluded once, only once, that there was history between them. She still worked for DGSE then, was being groomed to move up the ladder. Something set her off and she went freelance, and I've never known what it was. But Thierry did. He must have. That's what he meant when he told me she'd become a black widow."

Ah. Interesting. "She'd get physically close to her prey, then kill them."

"Exactly. And she's one of the best at what she does. She's a legend, Taylor."

A legendary assassin. A wicked snowstorm. No power. One dead, one missing. This was just getting better and better.

"I take it the scene in Stamper's room looks familiar?"

"Very."

Taylor took the flashlight, went to the door, unlocked the bolt. Opened it into the dark hallway, then shined the light back into the room. There was no more time to lose.

"I need a name, Cherry."

The harsh light caught Cherry's face. She looked frightened and old, defeated, a pale specter in the darkness. She sat back down on the bed as if exhausted.

"She goes by many names, Taylor. But I believe her given name is Angelie Delacroix."

"That's a start. Let's go. We need to—"

Cherry shook her head, clearly the truth of the matter was finally sinking in. "No, Lieutenant, we have a bigger problem."

"Worse than one dead and one missing? Seriously?"

"Angelie's uncle is active MI-6. And he's downstairs."

CHAPTER 15

0640 Hours

I sit down on the floor near Florian. "Oncle Pierre told me the whole story last year. You were on the scene. You were the one who saved me, who took me to the hospital. But first you smashed me on the head so I wouldn't recognize you. Why did you kill my father, Thierry? My family? Why would you kill them and save me? *Pourquoi? Pourquoi?*"

I am shouting, losing control. I resist the urge to hit him again.

"Angelie. Angelie, it wasn't me. You have the story wrong."

I am beginning to believe Thierry Florian may be telling the truth. He is a proud man, one I've watched interrogate a hundred men. He is brave. And as he sits here bleeding, exposed, I must believe I know him well enough to recognize when he is telling the truth.

"Then what is the story, Thierry?"

"Don't make me tell you. Please."

This last word is spoken as softly as a lover's kiss. Finally, after hours of pain and fury, the great man is begging.

I tuck the muzzle of my Sig Sauer against his chin, and I raise his head so he is forced to meet my eyes.

"Tell me, and I will end your suffering."

He leans into the gun, his voice the harshest I've ever heard.

"Kill me, and you will never get justice."

I stand and whirl away. Florian breathes out a sigh.

"You will not stop, will you? Ah, Angelie. I trained you well."

I run back to him, wrench his head back. Spit the words. "The truth, now. I am sick of playing this game."

"Pierre," he says, speaking out loud a terrible reality I've never fathomed. "It was Pierre. Your uncle killed your father."

Nausea overwhelms me. I drop my hand. "You're lying."

Florian shakes his head. He is disheveled, bloody, has absolutely nothing left to lose.

"I have never lied to you, Angelie. I have protected you, all along. I did not want you to suffer the pain of this knowledge. Indeed, I sheltered you from it since you were a child. Yes, it was I who rescued you. I got wind of your uncle's plan the day before the attack, though at the time I did not know he was behind it. I was in Germany. I drove all night to reach you, to take you all to safety.

"Your father ignored our attempts to get him into the safe house in Annecy. He was fleeing back to Paris on Pierre's orders. He believed Pierre was trying to help. He listened to him, and drove directly into the trap."

I stagger against the wall, tripping on something in the darkness. A pain I have not felt in twenty-five years rises in me, tears through my body, my brain, leaving me breathless.

"This cannot be the truth."

"It is the truth. I arrived on the scene moments after the shooting. Gregoire Campion was riding his bicycle down from the safe house, he met me on the westbound street. We were too late to save them, Angelie, too late by five minutes. But you were still alive, clinging to your mother's skirts, covered in your parents' blood. I couldn't leave you there, and I could not let you see our faces. I did the only thing I could, which was rescue you and get you to a hospital. And I spent the next twenty years trying to determine what happened that day."

I try to digest this information.

"Why did you not tell me the moment you determined Pierre was behind the execution?"

"Ah. Angelie. And cause you that much more pain? Your uncle raised you, taught you well. He knew where your heart lay, knew you would try to avenge your parents someday. He is the reason you were hired into the DGSE. Gregoire Campion was worried about you from the first because he suspected Pierre's involvement, kept an eye on you, eased your path in the service. And you killed him. The man who watched over you, dead by your hand. Angelie, you disgrace yourself."

Campion, on the side of the angels?

I harden myself against Florian's words. "Pierre told me Campion was the one who let my parents' path slip, that he told the Iraqis where my father was going to be that day."

"That was Pierre, *mon cherie*. Pierre was receiving money, so much money, that he was willing to sacrifice his brother and his family. He has lied to you, Angelie, about many things. I am not a double agent. And I did not kill your father."

There is great finality to his words. I know he is telling the truth.

I slide down the wall, the pistol dangling between my legs.

Mon dieu. What have I done?

CHAPTER 16

0645 Hours

Taylor hustled down the four flights of stairs, Cherry on her heels. The minute they reached the bottom floor, Taylor asked, "What does he look like?"

"Mid-sixties, silver hair, six feet or so. He was wearing a blue suit last night, no tie, but I don't remember what he was wearing this morning. It was dark, and I was too concerned for Thierry and Ellis."

They burst into the lobby, raced to the room where everyone was staged. The room was still shrouded in darkness, and there was no more time to waste.

"Stay here. I'll find him."

"But you don't know what he looks like."

Taylor flashed the light on the ceiling a few times, creating a strobe effect that caught people's attention.

"Pierre Matthews. Are you in here?" she called.

Murmurs from the crowd, then one man stood, Taylor could see the outline of his bulk against the window.

"I'm here. Whatever is the matter?"

Taylor crossed the room, weaving between people, and took him by the arm. "Come with me, please, sir. There's a problem. We need your help."

The lobby was filled with natural light, the darkness finally easing in the early morning sun. The snow, she noticed, had stopped. Taylor turned off the flashlight, tucked it into her back pocket.

"What is this about?" Matthews asked.

"Sir, I'm Lieutenant Taylor Jackson, and you know Cherry Gregg. We have reason to believe you may be in danger. Would you please come with us?"

Matthews was nonplussed, but nodded. Taylor took the lead, Cherry flanked. They got him across into the bar, and Taylor got him into a corner where she felt he would be safest.

"You two have been scurrying in and out all night. What's happened? Where are Thierry and Ellis?"

Cherry spoke plainly. "Ellis is dead, and Thierry is missing."

"Bloody hell. Are you sure?"

"Do you know a woman named Angelie Delacroix?" Taylor asked.

Matthews sucked in a breath, and Taylor raised an eyebrow. "I'll take that as a yes."

She saw him debating with the answer. Finally, he replied, "She's my niece. Why are you asking about her? Is she all right?"

Cherry grabbed the man's forearm. "Pierre, she killed Ellis. She's taken Thierry."

Pierre froze. "Angelie is here? Are you sure?"

"Yes. She knows."

Taylor gave Cherry a sharp look. "She knows what?"

Cherry and Pierre were locked in a staring contest, no words needed. Taylor recognized there was a bigger issue, something major they were keeping from her.

"Tell me right now what's happening, or I'm out. I'll go warm my hands by the fire and let Fred shoot me dirty looks."

Cherry nodded to Pierre. "You tell her."

"Ah, bugger me." He rubbed his hands over his face, the whiskers on his chin rasping loudly against his palm. "Angelie started acting up about two years ago. She didn't like the politics within the DGSE anymore, didn't want to play by the rules. We were all working together at the time, on the Allied project. The greater good. CIA, MI-6, DGSE, Freedom Forum, Futures Working Group—hell, even Pakistan's ISI was along for the ride. In the middle of the fuck-up in Benghazi, she got a bug up her bum about some old case, took off for parts unknown. All we've heard from her since has been at the end of a gun—she's left a trail of bodies all over Europe, the last one found just two days ago in London."

"Gone rogue?" Taylor couldn't help the skepticism that slipped into her tone.

"That's right. You must understand, Lieutenant, Angelie is marked by tragedy. Her parents were killed in an ambush outside Annecy, France, twenty-five years ago. She was the only survivor, and she spent her whole life searching for the killers."

Taylor heard the past tense. "*Spent* her whole life? She's found her parents' murderers?"

He cut his eyes at Cherry, who nodded imperceptibly. "She found him at last. Gregoire Campion, her latest victim, the body from two days ago. She found a letter with the details. He sold out her parents, my own brother, and for what? Money? Security? Who can know the true heart of a man like that, Lieutenant? I am sure his death assuaged many of Angelie's troubles."

Taylor processed that for a moment. "If she found the man who did it, then why would she come here and kill Ellis Stamper? Why kidnap Thierry Florian?"

"Stamper was most likely collateral damage. Florian worked with Campion back then. He was the DGSE equivalent of a station chief in Geneva, Switzerland, just north of Annecy. She must think he was a part of the plot."

"Was he?" Taylor asked, trying to reconcile this information against her brief meeting with Florian and Cherry's praise-filled backgrounder. He didn't seem capable of that level of treachery. Taylor prided herself on being able to read people; she hadn't caught a whiff of evil from Florian.

"I don't know. He denied it, said he was there trying to protect them, but I never got the whole story. My brother's death was a terrible time for us all. I took Angelie in, raised her as my own daughter. She had a massive memory block on what happened that day—after the head injury, it was all gone. She took a hard blow, probably pistol-whipped. It was a miracle that she survived. Florian had his eye on her from the very beginning. You know what they say: keep your friends close, but keep your enemies closer."

Taylor didn't like Pierre Matthews. He was slick; the answers were too pat, too prepared, and something in her gut told her he was lying. Granted, a situation like this, about family, so personal, there was no reason to tell her the whole truth. Yes, he was lying. She'd bet her life on it. About what, she didn't know, and that made him very dangerous to her in this situation. And she realized Cherry knew more than she was letting on, too.

"Are you armed, Pierre?"

"My weapon is in my room. Why?"

Thank God for small favors.

"Well, your friend, or your enemy, is missing, and Cherry believes it's likely your niece is prowling around this hotel with her own loaded weapon. We need to figure out where Thierry Florian is, and take your niece into custody while we assess what happened last night."

Cherry came back to life, finally. "Without lights for those dark hallways, or the ability to open multiple doors without tearing this place apart, how do we search?"

Taylor shrugged. "We need to find a way to get the lights turned on."

CHAPTER 17

0650 Hours

I unbind Florian's ties, my fingers working quickly. It would have been so easy to simply kick his chair, let him fall into the pool. He would have been gone, his storied life a sudden footnote, the weight of the chair keeping him under.

There will be no more deaths, save one.

Florian stands cautiously, rubbing his wrists.

"Clothes?"

I gesture to the right, by the hot tub, where his clothes are folded in a neat pile. He says nothing, simply turns his back on me and dresses. I walk slowly, carefully, around the edges of the pool. It would be so easy to fling myself into the dark water. It is salt water; I can smell the brine. Like floating in an ocean, sinking deep beneath the waves. My parents used to take us to the sea, to Le Lavendou, and we'd stay at the Beau Rivage and prune ourselves in the azure water from sunup to sundown.

I did not know these holidays were paid for by secrets. Blueprints and plans for rapidly-developed forms of kinetic energy, stolen by my father from his employer, and sold to the Iraqis. Or the Russians. Syrians and Pakistanis. Whoever was paying at that particular moment.

My father was a mole. An asset. Turned for the DGSE's use, a puppet on a string, only useful while he could help in the race to nuclear proliferation supremacy.

And me? I became the very person my father hated. The nameless, faceless people he put his trust in, the mechanics of his dead drops and microfiche holders and tradecraft.

I could not help it. *Mon oncle*, he showed me how valuable this work was. How I could change the world, one turned asset at a time.

If my father lived, would that have changed? Would I have been so heavily recruited? So well-trained? Honed into a weapon of immeasurable worth?

I think not.

Florian is watching me. "Angelie. You must leave."

My toe yanks back from the water. I stare into Florian's eyes, unable to see clearly for the lack of light.

"Go. I will handle this situation. Get away from this place."

"Why would you have me save myself, Thierry Florian? Why should I not turn myself in? Suffer the consequences of my actions? I have killed this night. Taken your friend from you. You should want my head."

He smiles, the tiniest lift of the corners of his mouth. And I know what he will say next.

"What a curious turn of phrase. *Oui, cherie*, I very much want your head. And I shall have it. You work for me now, Angelie. Again. Again and forever. Now, go."

I am defeated. For a moment I think to kill him anyway. Then I can be free. But I listen.

I stash the gun in my waistband, gather my tools, and without a word, head for the door. There is a storm. I know this; I see the piles of snow against the door. How I will get away isn't clear. I had no plans for escape. This was intended to be my last hurrah. A suicide mission. But now that I know the truth? As they say, the show must go on.

The hallways are still dark and quiet. The blueprint of the hotel plays through my head. I need to turn left at the gym, it will lead me to the basement, which has an exit onto a back expanse of land. There is a shelter one hundred yards from the hotel, a place I can regroup until I can reach my exit.

A voice from the other side of the pool. "Hey. Hey, stop!"

My weapon is pointed at the voice before I can form a coherent thought.

CHAPTER 18

0700 Hours

A fuel truck, riding slowly behind a snowplow, arrived at seven in the morning to everyone's cheers. The fuel was pumped into the basement generators, the lights flickered to life, and a semblance of normality restored. People scattered back to their rooms to get some sleep and check in with loved ones.

Taylor was glad of it; now they could do a proper search, and run a crime scene unit through Stamper and Florian's rooms.

Cherry and Pierre had been huddled together in a corner of the bar for the past fifteen minutes, backs to the wall, eyes darting to the entrance every few moments, and Taylor wondered what sort of story they were concocting. Self-preservation, preparation, a cover-up, she didn't know, only that they were both acting like Angelie Delacroix was going to burst through the wall yelling *yippie ki-yay* and shoot up the place.

Taylor left them alone, paced the bar. Florian's disappearance was gnawing at her. She wanted to strike off and look for him, but knew how foolish that was, especially if the über-assassin was still on site. They needed manpower, backup, K9 units, the works. Sure enough, fifteen minutes later, the Calvert County Sheriff, a decent-looking man named Evans, arrived, summoned by the report of a murder.

Taylor and Cherry explained the situation. To his credit, he took down their stories with a raised eyebrow and only a few head shakes. He went upstairs, came down with a grim expression, asked Taylor several probing questions, then said, "Lieutenant, glad you were here. Situation might have gotten further out of control. There are more people coming, State Police, FBI, K9. Storm's holding everyone up. We're going to need you to give your official statement, so get comfy."

"Can't I help? I don't want to sit around doing nothing."

"It's going to take more than two of us to search this place." He smiled, kindly enough. "You've done your part. Why don't you head to your room and get some rest? I'd lock my door, though my guess is Florian and this Delacroix woman are long gone. Timing wise, the streets were still passable until after midnight. The hotel lobby's videotape wasn't recording, so that's useless. Just need to bring in the troops and get this place searched and processed. You know how it goes."

Taylor did, and knew her role in the situation was finished. With the jurisdictional cops on scene, she was relegated back to conference attendee and witness. Which was weird.

But Evans had a point. A little sleep wouldn't go amiss.

She interrupted another confab between Pierre and Cherry.

"Cherry, I'm going to go up to my room. Call me if they find Florian, okay?"

CHAPTER 19

0730 Hours

Taylor had to detour to her room—though the power was back on, the elevators were still off-limits. She pulled a site map off the concierge desk and glanced at it. The back staircase would be closer to her room. She took the hallway toward the gym, the scent leading her toward the pool and the hot tub. Ah, a hot bath in that giant tub upstairs would be lovely, though she doubted the water heaters were going to get suitable power from the generators to pump water hot enough for her taste.

She pushed through the pool doors and immediately knew something was wrong. Instinct, coupled with the chair at the edge of the pool, ropes coiled neatly by its legs. She drew her weapon and went into a defensive stance. The glass windows in the place were wavy, giving weak light that shimmered against the pool water. She went slowly, searching, until she saw the open door to the life-guard office. And inside was Thierry Florian, eyes closed, leaning back on a longue chair. Blood soaked his shirt, and he was pale as a ghost. Asleep, or dead?

She rushed to him, put her fingers against his carotid. A steady beat, and her breath whooshed out. He started, eyes opening. "Angelie, I told you—"

He cut himself off when he saw Taylor.

"Where is she?"

"I don't know what you're talking about."

"Mr. Florian, please. Ellis Stamper is dead. You've obviously been tortured. I know all about Angelie Delacroix. Cherry and Pierre Matthews filled me in. Where is she?"

He licked his lips, which were cracked and bloody. "Gone," he whispered.

She helped him sit up.

"Why aren't you dead? It looks like she gave you quite a working over."

He smiled, though the action obviously caused him pain. "You are blunt, aren't you, Lieutenant? Angelie didn't want me dead. She just wanted information."

"Somehow, I don't believe that is the whole story. The Sheriff is here, and there's about to be a whole wad of law enforcement on his tail. Is she still here, Thierry? Tell me the truth."

"She left ten minutes ago. You won't catch her."

Taylor met his eyes. "Watch me."

CHAPTER 20

0735 Hours

Taylor called Cherry, told her to share what was happening with the Sheriff, and to send backup immediately. She shoved her cell phone in her pocket and press checked her Glock. It was habit, a cop's unconscious movement.

Florian tried to stop her. "You're wasting your time."

He tried to rise, but the blood loss had taken its toll.

"You stay here and guard the pool. When the Sheriff's people come, show them the way."

"On your head be it," Florian said. "Don't say I didn't warn you."

Taylor gave him a smile and started off.

One thing Taylor had gathered about Angelie Delacroix, there would be signs of her passage. Morbid signs. Since Taylor hadn't seen any on her way in, she exited opposite the door she'd originally come through, toward the north end of the pool, right out into the hallway that led to the back entrance of the hotel. The light was startling here, she had to blink to adjust.

She took in the whiteness outside, knew there was no way anyone could get out of there without leaving a mess.

It didn't take long to find the trail. Footprints led toward a small outbuilding about fifty yards away. Backup was moments behind, so Taylor stepped out into the freezing cold.

Her hands went numb almost immediately, but she kept the weapon up and ready. The going was slow, the snow drifting to her waist in places. The chill wind was rising again, Taylor recognized the feeling. This was a temporary reprieve; there was more snow on the way.

Her feet were snug in her boots, but snow was sliding down the calf and into the leather. A fine shiver started, and with it, her common sense.

You're an idiot, Taylor. Go back inside and let the locals freeze their asses off.

She could hear them now, closing in. She started edging backwards. As she turned, there was a woman, standing in her path.

Taylor froze.

The woman was small—Taylor had a good six inches on her—but her weapon was pointed right at Taylor's head.

"And who might you be?" the woman asked, her accent clearly French.

"Police. Put the gun down, Angelie. You can't rack up any more bodies today, you're already going away for a very long time."

The woman cocked her head to the side. The gun didn't waver.

"I think you are the one who needs to disarm yourself, Lieutenant Jackson. Yes, I know your name. It's next to that smiling photograph on the program in Thierry's room. A profiler, are you?"

"Homicide. You're under arrest. Put the damn gun down, now."

"I think not," Angelie said, then before Taylor could blink, she took off, through the snow, toward a stone wall that barely peeked out under its white blanket.

"Shit!"

Taylor ran after her, amazed at Angelie's prowess in the snow.

Taylor was too tall, too ungainly, to make quick progress. There was only one thing to do.

Taylor stopped and fired, and the bullet found its target. Angelie spun to the side, and Taylor heard her cry out.

"Drop the weapon, Angelie, and I won't do that again."

Shouts rang out from the building to her left, the Sheriff's deputies were coming. Angelie heard them as well, didn't hesitate. She fired off several rounds, spraying them wildly behind her, forcing Taylor face down in the snow.

Taylor rolled to her right, flipped over and up onto her knees and aimed again.

Angelie's left arm was dragging by her side, but she kept running, a dead sprint through the heavy snow. She reached the stone wall before Taylor could get off a second round, and disappeared behind it.

It took Taylor a full minute to scramble to her feet and reach the spot.

"She's here," she called to the deputies, who were wading through the snow well behind her.

Carefully, slowly, weapon first, Taylor looked over the edge of the wall. Beyond it was a steep slope. It was terraced, a vineyard in the summertime, staggered levels that ran down the hill, demarcated by stone barriers. One section dropped off into the beach below. Taylor figured it must be a forty-foot drop.

Angelie Delacroix was crouched against the stone barrier above the beach, back to the ocean, watching Taylor. She was trapped, and bleeding.

Their eyes met.

Taylor edged closer. *Take the shot, Taylor, take the shot. You can end this, right here.*

She took a breath to steady her hands, shaking in the cold. Her finger rested on the trigger. Just a fraction of movement, and the bullet would take Angelie Delacroix in the forehead.

And in that moment, Angelie raised her weapon toward Taylor in a sort of salute and smiled, crooked, knowing, then jumped off the ledge, toward the sea.

Taylor gritted her teeth and scrambled over the wall. *Damn it. Damn it all.* She'd had a clear shot. She shouldn't have hesitated. But she recognized something in the woman's eyes. Something dark, and unimaginable to those who hadn't been faced with taking a life. And Taylor had chosen that route, too many times.

The first bullet had hit Angelie in the shoulder. Taylor had shot to maim, not kill. She made a choice, right or wrong, and now her prey was gone.

She pointed the weapon at the barrier, just where the woman had disappeared. Listened, but heard nothing.

"Police!" she shouted. "Show me your hands."

Silence. The waves crashed below, a seagull cried. Silence amplified by the dizzying expanse of white before her, her voice echoed slightly. To her right, disturbed by the deputies making their way closer, a bird took wing, startled by the noise, sent her heart right to her throat.

Taylor ducked her head, took a deep breath in through her nose, and leading with her Glock, looked over the edge. She was prepared for what she found.

Nothing.

There was no sign of Angelie Delacroix.

All that was left of her was a spattering of blood drops on the snow, like a shower of rubies dashed onto white velvet.

When Taylor had hesitated, that split second when she decided she couldn't kill, not again, something like realization had dawned in Angelie's eyes. She had recognized that Taylor would not fire again.

That knowing smile would haunt Taylor's dreams.

A choice. Right or wrong, Taylor had let her get away.

She slumped against the stone. The deputies finally reached her, Sheriff Evans at their head.

"Where is she, where is she?"

"She jumped."

Evans looked slightly relieved, holstered his weapon.

"Then she's dead. That's a fifty-foot fall. We'll find her body on the beach."

"I don't think so," she said, and he looked at her queerly.

"Of course we will. What the hell were you doing, out here chasing her down alone? I thought I told you to stand down."

Taylor turned to face him, the wind whipping her hair around her face.

"I was doing my job."

And the sun broke through the clouds.

EPILOGUE

January 15, 2014
London, England
0300 Hours

I stand over his bed. He sleeps with one arm tossed over his head. I recognize the position; my father, his brother, also slept in this way—careless, with abandon.

He is quiet. No snoring, just deep, rhythmic breaths.

I want him to see. I want him to know. I rub my shoulder, warding off the pain from the ghost of a bullet that lodged against my scapula, courtesy of the blonde ice queen. I'll never forget, and she knew that would be the case. But I will leave her alone. I have learned a hard truth in the past few months.

Not all scores are meant to be settled.

But some… some beg for closure.

I slide his covers down with the end of my weapon, and lean close, so I can whisper in his ear.

"Oncle Pierre, time to wake up."

ABOUT THE STORY

WHITEOUT is the last of a triad of stories that first appeared in STORM SEASON with my dear friends Erica Spindler and Alex Kava. To see the rest of the havoc this storm wreaked, I highly encourage you to get the full book, STORM SEASON.

ACKNOWLEDGMENTS

A lot of credit for this collection goes directly to my friend Del Tinsley, who, many years ago, talked me into trying my first short story, something I swore I couldn't, wouldn't every do. Little did I know that first foray into the short form would turn into something real and everlasting. Because I love writing shorts, as Del long assumed I would.

Many thanks to Bryon Quertermous, who published my first story, along with a bevy of online publications from *Flashing in the Gutters* to *Mouth Full of Bullets* who featured my work in the early days.

Thanks also to the divine Amy Kerr, who's put so much work into building this collection and Two Tales Press in general. Couldn't do it without you!

I'm surrounded by incredible friends and sounding boards—Laura, Ariel, Paige, Jeff, Allison, Toni, Jason, Catherine—who keep me humble and looking ever-forward. My parents are always there to listen whilst I run through story ideas and plot points, a gift for which I am forever grateful. I simply wouldn't be the writer or person I am without my partner in crime for more than two decades, my darling husband Randy, who is not only the plot whisperer, but the source of my greatest joy.

I shouldn't leave out the thriller kittens, Jameson and Jordan, since they inspired the Two Tales Press title and colophon. See the shadow? That's the ghost of our original thrillercat, Jade.

And finally, thank you. For reading, for cheering me on, for buying the books and keeping me writing. Without you, none of this would happen.

SNEAK PEEKS

(you lucky reader!)

For your enjoyment, I've included three excerpts for you. The first is from my newest Taylor Jackson novel, FIELD OF GRAVES, which is actually a prequel to the series. The next is a peek at my first standalone thriller, NO ONE KNOWS, which came out earlier this year. Last but not least is an excerpt from one of my favorite writers, Laura Benedict, who is writing a brilliant Southern Gothic series called Bliss House. The excerpt is from her latest novel, THE ABANDONED HEART, available now. I hope you love them all!

FIELD OF GRAVES

Exclusive Excerpt

FIELD OF GRAVES
Copyright © 2016 by J.T. Ellison

MIRA Books
a division of Harlequin
225 Duncan Mill Road
Toronto, Ontario M3B 3K9
Canada

PROLOGUE

Taylor picked up her portable phone for the tenth time in ten minutes. She hit Redial, heard the call connect and start ringing, then clicked the Off button and returned the phone to her lap. Once she made this call, there was no going back. Being right wouldn't make her the golden girl. If she were wrong—well, she didn't want to think about what could happen. Losing her job would be the least of her worries.

Damned if she did. Damned if she didn't.

She set the phone on the pool table and went down the stairs of her small two-story cabin. In the kitchen, she opened the door to the refrigerator and pulled out a Diet Coke. She laughed to herself. As if more caffeine would give her the courage to make the call. She should try a shot of whiskey. That always worked in the movies.

She snapped open the tab and stood staring out of her kitchen window. It had been dark for hours—the moon gone and the inky blackness outside her window impenetrable—but in an hour the skies would lighten. She would have to make a decision by then.

She turned away from the window and heard a loud crack. The lights went out. She jumped a mile, then giggled nervously, a hand to her chest to stop the sudden pounding.

Silly girl, she thought. *The lights go out all the time. There was a Nashville Electric Service crew on the corner when you drove in earlier; they*

*must have messed up the line and a power surge caused the lights to blow. It
happens every time NES works on the lines. Now stop it. You're a grown
woman. You're not afraid of the dark.*

She reached into her junk drawer and groped for a flashlight.
Thumbing the switch, she cursed softly when the light didn't
shine. Batteries, where were the batteries?

She froze when she heard the noise and immediately went on
alert, all of her senses going into overdrive. She strained her ears,
trying to hear it again. Yes, there it was. A soft scrape off the back
porch. She took a deep breath and sidled out of the kitchen, keeping close to the wall, moving lightly toward the back door. She
brought her hand to her side and found nothing. Damn it. She'd
left her gun upstairs.

The tinkling of breaking glass brought her up short.

The French doors leading into the backyard had been breached.
It was too late to head upstairs and get the gun. She would have to
walk right through the living room to get to the stairs. Whoever
had just broken through her back door was not going to let her
stroll on by. She started edging back toward the kitchen, holding
her breath, as if that would help her not make any noise.

She didn't see the fist, only felt it crack against her jaw. Her eyes
swelled with tears, and before she could react, the fist connected
again. She spun and hit the wall face-first. The impact knocked
her breath out. Her lips cut on the edge of her teeth; she tasted
blood. The intruder grabbed her as she started to slide down the
wall. Yanked her to her feet and put his hands around her throat,
squeezing hard.

Now she knew exactly where her attacker was, and she fought
back with everything she had. She struggled against him, quickly
realizing she was in trouble. He was stronger than her, bigger than
her. And he was there to kill.

She went limp, lolled bonelessly against him, surprising him
with the sudden weight. He released one arm in response, and she
took that moment to whirl around and shove with all her might.
It created some space between them, enabling her to slip out of his

grasp. She turned quickly but crashed into the slate end table. He was all over her. They struggled their way into the living room. She began to plan. Kicked away again.

Her attacker lunged after her. She used the sturdy side table to brace herself and whipped out her left arm in a perfect jab, aiming lower than where she suspected his chin would be. She connected perfectly and heard him grunt in pain. Spitting blood out of her mouth in satisfaction, she followed the punch with a kick to his stomach, heard the *whoosh* of his breath as it left his body. He fell hard against the wall. She spun away and leapt to the stairs. He jumped up to pursue her, but she was quicker. She pounded up the stairs as fast as she could, rounding the corner into the hall just as her attacker reached the landing. Her weapon was in its holster, on the bookshelf next to the pool table, right where she had left it when she'd gone downstairs for the soda. She was getting careless. She should never have taken it off her hip. With everything that was happening, she shouldn't have taken for granted that she was safe in her own home.

Her hand closed around the handle of the weapon. She pulled the Glock from its holster, whipped around to face the door as the man came tearing through it. She didn't stop to think about the repercussions, simply reacted. Her hand rose by instinct, and she put a bullet right between his eyes. His momentum carried him forward a few paces. He was only five feet from her, eyes black in death, when he dropped with a thud.

She heard her own ragged breathing. She tasted blood and raised a bruised hand to her jaw, feeling her lips and her teeth gingerly. Son of a bitch had caught her right in the jaw and loosened two molars. The adrenaline rush left her. She collapsed on the floor next to the lifeless body. She might have even slept for a moment.

The throbbing in her jaw brought her back. Morning was beginning to break, enough to see the horrible mess in front of her. The cat was sitting on the pool table, watching her curiously.

Rising, she took in the scene. The man was collapsed on her game room floor, slowly leaking blood on her Berber carpet. She peered at the stain.

That's going to be a bitch to get out.

She shook her head to clear the cobwebs. What an inane thing to say. Shock, she must be going into shock. How long had they fought? Had it been only five minutes? Half an hour? She felt as though she had struggled against him for days; her body was tired and sore. Never mind the blood caked around her mouth. She put her hand up to her face. Make that her nose too.

She eyed the man again. He was facedown and angled slightly to one side. She slipped her toes under his right arm and flipped him over with her foot. The shot was true; she could see a clean entry wound in his forehead. Reaching down out of habit, she felt for his carotid pulse, but there was nothing. He was definitely dead.

"Oh, David," she said. "You absolute idiot. Look what you've made me do."

Now the shit was absolutely going to hit the fan. It was time to make the call.

CHAPTER 1

Three months later
Nashville, Tennessee

Bodies, everywhere bodies, a field of graves, limbs and torsos and heads, all left above ground. The feeling of dirt in her mouth, grimy and thick; the whispers from the dead, long arms reaching for her as she passed through the carnage. Ghostly voices, soft and sibilant. "Help us. Why won't you help us?"

Taylor jerked awake, sweating, eyes wild and blind in the darkness. The sheets twisted around her body in a claustrophobic shroud, and she struggled to get them untangled. She squeezed her eyes shut, willed her breathing back to normal, trying to relax, to let the grisly images go. When she opened her eyes, the room was still dark but no longer menacing. Her screams had faded away into the silence. The cat jumped off the bed with a disgruntled meow in response to her thrashing.

She laid her head back on the pillow, swallowed hard, still unable to get a full breath.

Every damn night. She was starting to wonder if she'd ever sleep well again.

She wiped a hand across her face and looked at the clock: 6:10 a.m. The alarm was set for seven, but she wasn't going to get any more rest. She might as well get up and get ready for work. Go in a little early, see what horrors had captured the city overnight.

She rolled off the bed, trying hard to forget the dream. Showered, dressed, dragged on jeans and a black cashmere T-shirt under a black motorcycle jacket, stepped into her favorite boots. Put her creds in her pocket and her gun on her hip. Pulled her wet hair off her face and into a ponytail.

Time to face another day.

She was in her car when the call came. "Morning, Fitz. What's up?"

"Morning, LT. We have us a body at the Parthenon."

"I'll be right there."

It might have become a perfect late-autumn morning. The sky was busy, turning from white to blue as dawn rudely forced its way into day. Birds were returning from their mysterious nocturnal errands, greeting and chattering about the night's affairs. The air was clear and heavy, still muggy from the overnight heat but holding a hint of coolness, like an ice cube dropped into a steaming mug of coffee. The sky would soon shift to sapphire the way only autumn skies do, as clear and heavy as the precious stone itself.

The beauty of the morning was lost on Lieutenant Taylor Jackson, Criminal Investigation Division, Nashville Metro Police. She snapped her long body under the yellow crime scene tape and looked around for a moment. Sensed the looks from the officers around her. Straightened her shoulders and marched toward them.

Metro officers had been traipsing around the crime scene control area like it was a cocktail party, drinking coffee and chatting each other up as though they'd been apart for weeks, not hours. The grass was already littered with cups, cigarette butts, crumpled notebook paper, and at least one copy of the morning's sports section from *The Tennessean*. Taylor cursed silently; they knew better than this. One of these yahoos was going to inadvertently contaminate a crime scene one of these days, sending her team off on a wild-goose chase. Guess whose ass would be in the proverbial sling then?

She stooped to grab the sports page, surreptitiously glanced at the headline regaling the Tennessee Titans' latest win, then crumpled it into a firm ball in her hands.

Taylor didn't know what information about the murder had leaked out over the air, but the curiosity factor had obviously kicked into high gear. An officer she recognized from another sector was cruising by to check things out, not wanting to miss out on all the fun. Media vans lined the street. Joggers pretending not to notice anything was happening nearly tripped trying to see what all the fuss was about. Exactly what she needed on no sleep: everyone willing to help, to get in and screw up her crime scene.

Striding toward the melee, she tried to tell herself that it wasn't their fault she'd been up all night. At least she'd had a shower and downed two Diet Cokes, or she would have arrested them all.

She reached the command post and pasted on a smile. "Mornin', kids. How many of you have dragged this crap through my crime scene?" She tossed the balled-up paper at the closest officer.

She tried to keep her tone light, as if she were amused by their shenanigans, but she didn't fool anyone, and the levity disappeared from the gathering. The brass was on the scene, so all the fun had come to a screeching halt. Uniforms who didn't belong started to drift away, one or two giving Taylor a sideways glance. She ignored them, the way she ignored most things these days.

As a patrol officer, she'd kept her head down, worked her cases, and developed a reputation for being a straight shooter. Her dedication and clean work had been rewarded with promotion after promotion; she was in plainclothes at twenty-eight. She'd caught a nasty first case in Homicide—the kidnapping and murder of a young girl. She'd nailed the bastard who'd done it; Richard Curtis was on death row now. The case made the national news and sent her career into overdrive. She quickly became known for being a hard-hitting investigator and moved up the ranks from detective to lead to sergeant, until she'd been given the plum job she had now—homicide lieutenant.

If her promotion to lieutenant at the tender age of thirty-four had rankled some of the more traditional officers on the force, the death of David Martin—one of their own—made it ten times worse. There were always going to be cops who tried to make her life difficult; it was part of being a chick on the force, part of having a reputation. Taylor was tough, smart, and liked to do things her own way to get the job done. The majority of the men she worked with had great respect for her abilities. There were always going to be detractors, cops who whispered behind her back, but in Taylor's mind, success trumped rumor every time.

Then Martin had decided to ruin her life and nearly derailed her career in the process. She was still clawing her way back.

Taylor's second in command, Detective Pete Fitzgerald, lumbered toward her, the ever-present unlit cigarette hanging out of his mouth. He'd quit a couple of years before, after a minor heart attack, but kept one around to light in case of an emergency. Fitz had an impressive paunch; his belly reached Taylor before the rest of his body.

"Hey, LT. Sorry I had to drag you away from your beauty sleep." He looked her over, concern dawning in his eyes. "I was just kidding. What's up with you? You look like shit warmed over."

Taylor waved a hand in dismissal. "Didn't sleep. Aren't we supposed to have some sort of eclipse this morning? I think it's got me all out of whack."

Fitz took the hint and backed down. "Yeah, we are." He looked up quickly, shielding his eyes with his hand. "See, it's already started."

He was right. The moon was moving quickly across the sun, the crime scene darkening by the minute. "Eerie," she said.

He looked back at her, blinking hard. "No kidding. Remind me not to stare into the sun again."

"Will do. Celestial phenomenon aside, what do we have here?"

"Okay, darlin', here we go. We have a couple of lovebirds who decided to take an early morning stroll—found themselves a deceased Caucasian female on the Parthenon's steps. She's sitting up there pretty as you please, just leaning against the gate in front of the Parthenon doors like she sat down for a rest. Naked as a jaybird too, and very, very dead."

Taylor turned her gaze to the Parthenon. One of her favorite sites in Nashville, smack-dab in the middle of Centennial Park, the full-size replica was a huge draw for tourists and classicists alike. The statue of Athena inside was awe-inspiring. She couldn't count how many school field trips she'd been on here over the years. Leaving a body on the steps was one hell of a statement.

"Where are the witnesses?"

"Got the lovebirds separated, but the woman's having fits—we haven't been able to get a full statement. The scene's taped off. Traffic on West End has been blocked off, and we've closed all roads into and around Centennial Park. ME and her team have been here about fifteen minutes. Oh, and our killer was here at some point too." He grinned at her lopsidedly. "He dumped her sometime overnight, only the duckies and geese in the lake saw him. This is gonna be a bitch to canvass. Do you think we can admit 'AFLAC' as a statement in court?"

Taylor gave him a quick look and a perfunctory laugh, more amused at imagining Fitz waddling about like the duck from the insurance ads quacking than at his irreverent attitude. She knew better, but it did seem as if he was having a good time. Taylor understood that sometimes inappropriate attempts at humor were the only way a cop could make it through the day, so she chastised him gently. "You've got a sick sense of humor, Fitz." She sighed, turning off all personal thoughts, becoming a cop again. All business, all the time. That's what they needed to see from her.

"We'll probably have to go public and ask who was here last night and when, but I'm not holding my breath that we'll get anything helpful, so let's put it off for now."

He nodded in agreement. "Do you want to put up the chopper? Probably useless—whoever dumped her is long gone."

"I think you're right." She jerked her head toward the Parthenon steps. "What's he trying to tell us?"

Fitz looked toward the doors of the Parthenon, where the medical examiner was crouched over the naked body. His voice dropped, and he suddenly became serious. "I don't know, but this is going to get ugly, Taylor. I got a bad feeling."

Taylor held a hand up to cut him off. "C'mon, man, they're all ugly. It's too early to start spinning. Let's just get through the morning. Keep the frickin' media out of here—put 'em down in the duck shit if you have to. You can let them know which roads are closed so they can get the word out to their traffic helicopters, but that's it. Make sure the uniforms keep everyone off the tape. I don't want another soul in here until I have a chance to be fully briefed by all involved. Has the Park Police captain shown up yet?"

Fitz shook his head. "Nah. They've called him, but I haven't seen him."

"Well, find him, too. Make sure they know which end is up. Let's get the perimeter of this park searched, grid by grid, see if we find something. Get K-9 out here, let them do an article search. Since the roads are already shut off, tell them to expand the perimeter one thousand outside the borders of the park. I want to see them crawling around like ants at a picnic. I see any of them hanging in McDonald's before this is done, I'm kicking some butt."

Fitz gave her a mock salute. "I'm on it. When Sam determined she was dumped, I went ahead and called K-9, and pulled all the officers coming off duty. We may have an overtime situation, but I figured with your, um, finesse... " He snorted out the last word, and Taylor eyed him coolly.

"I'll handle it." She pushed her hair back from her face and reestablished her hurried ponytail. "Get them ready for all hell to break loose. I'm gonna go talk to Sam."

"Glad to serve, love. Now go see Sam, and let the rest of us grunts do our jobs. If you decide you want the whirlybird, give me a thumbs-up." He blew her a kiss and marched toward the command post, snapping his fingers at the officers to get their attention.

Turning toward the building, she caught a stare from one of the older patrols. His gaze was hostile, lip curled in a sneer. She gave him her most brilliant smile, making his scowl deepen. She broke off the look, shaking her head. She didn't have time to worry about politics right now.

CHAPTER 2

Taylor approached Sam cautiously, making sure she followed the ME's path to the body. They wouldn't be able to blame any loss of evidence on her. Pulling on her latex gloves, she tapped Sam lightly on the shoulder. Sam looked up. Anticipating Taylor's first question, she shook her head.

"There's no obvious cause of death—no stab wounds, no gunshot wounds. Evidence of rape. There's some bruising and tearing, a little bit of blood. He got her pretty good. There's some dirt on her, too. Wind probably blew some stuff around last night. I'll get a better idea when I get her open."

She rocked back on her heels and saw Taylor's face for the first time. "Girl, you look like crap. When's the last time you slept?"

"Been a while." The sleepless nights were catching up with her. She was almost thankful when a new case popped like this; the past slid away briefly when she could focus her attention elsewhere.

Sam gave her one last appraising glance. "Hmmph."

Dr. Samantha Owens had shoulder-length brown hair she always wore back in a ponytail, feminine wisps she couldn't control framing her face. She often joked that she'd rather look like a girl than a ghoul when she met someone new so the first impression wasn't one of horror. Taylor was always amused to see people scatter like rats when they found out the beautiful and composed woman was a professional pathologist. Most run-of-the-mill people didn't want to hang out with a woman who cut up dead bodies for a living.

Unlike many of the women she and Taylor had grown up with, Sam didn't join the Junior League, have beautiful babies, and lunch at Bread & Company. Instead, she spent her time perched over Nashville's endless supply of dead bodies, a position she was in much too often. She was also Taylor's best friend and was allowed liberties where others weren't.

"I've been telling you, you need to get some help."

"Hush up, Sam, I don't want to hear it. Tell me about our girl." Taylor let the knot in her stomach and the ache in her temples take complete hold. She had warmed up in the early-morning heat, but looking at the dead girl was giving her the chills. "Fitz said she was dumped?"

Sam traced an invisible line around the body with her finger. "Definitely. She wasn't killed here. See the livor pattern? The bottom of her legs, thighs and calves, her butt, the inside of her arms, and her back. The blood pooled in those areas. But she's sitting up, right? The lividity wouldn't present this way unless she had been chilling out on her back for a while. She was definitely dead for a few hours before she was dumped."

Taylor looked closely at the purplish-red blotches. In contrast, the front of the girl's body looked as pale and grimy as a dead jellyfish.

"No blood, either. Maybe he's a vampire." Sam leered briefly at Taylor, made fangs out of her fingers, hissed. Her morbid sense of humor always popped up at the most inappropriate times.

"You're insane."

"I know. No, he did her someplace else, then dumped her here." She looked around and said quietly, "Seriously, this feels very staged. She was put here for a reason, posed, everything. He wanted her found right away. The question is, why?"

Taylor didn't comment, but tucked Sam's remark into the back of her mind to be brought out and chewed on later. She knew it was worth thinking about; Sam had sound instincts. She turned back toward the command center. Seeing Fitz, she peeled the glove off her right hand, put two fingers in her mouth, and whistled sharply. He turned, and she shook her head. The helicopter definitely wasn't going to be needed.

Taylor looked back at the girl's face. So young. Another, so young. "Give me something to work with. Do you have a time of death?"

Sam thought for a moment. "Looking at her temp, she died sometime before midnight. Let's say ten to twelve hours ago, give or take. Rigor's still in, though she's starting to break up."

"Gives him time to kill her and get her here. Okay. Semen?"

"Oh yeah. It's all over the place. This guy really doesn't care about trying to be subtle. Not terribly bright. It shouldn't be too hard to match him up if he's in CODIS. He's certainly not holding anything back." She laughed at her pun, and Taylor couldn't help a brief smile.

"How about under her nails? Did she fight back?"

Sam lifted the dead girl's right hand. "I looked pretty closely, but I didn't see anything resembling skin or blood. I'll have them bag her hands and do scrapings back at the shop, but it doesn't look like she got hold of anything. We didn't find any ID with the body, so we'll print her and send them over to see if you can find a match. They'll be clear enough to run through AFIS."

Taylor was hardly listening. She stared at the girl's face. *So young,* she thought again. Man, there was going to be major fallout when they held this press conference. The statement started percolating in her head. *At six o'clock this morning, the body of a Caucasian female was discovered on the steps of the Parthenon...*

She looked back to Sam. "So no idea what killed her, huh?"

Sam relaxed, sitting back on her haunches. She stripped off her gloves and watched Taylor leaning in on the body.

"Hell if I know. Nothing's really jumping out at me. Give me a break, T, you know the drill."

"You'll get me all the pics yesterday, right? And do the post right now. I mean—" she attempted a more conciliatory tone, "—will you do the post right now?"

"I'll bump her to the top of the guest list. There's something else... Do you smell anything?"

"Just your perfume. Is it new?"

"See, that's the weird thing. I'm not wearing any. I think the smell is coming from the body. And I'll tell you, Taylor, this would be my first sweet-smelling corpse, you know?"

Taylor had noticed the scent. She inhaled sharply through her nose. Yes, there were all the usual stinks that came with a dead body: the unmistakable smell of decay, the stink of fear, the tang of stale urine and excrement. But overlaying all these olfactory wonders was a tangy sweetness. She thought hard for a moment, searching for the memory the smell triggered. The scent was somehow familiar, almost like—That was it!

"Sam, you know what this smells like? The spa across the way, Essential Therapy. Remember, I gave you a gift certificate for a massage there for your birthday? They have all those lotions and soaps and essential oil candles... "

"Wait a minute. You're right. She smells like incense." She stared at the body. "What if... Okay, give me a second here." Sam reached into her kit and extracted a small pair of tweezers. She bent over and started picking through the dirt on the body.

"What are you doing?" Taylor watched Sam put a few pieces of leaves and sticks into a small white paper bag. Somewhat disgusted, she watched Sam shove her nose into the bag and breathe in deeply. "Ugh, Sam."

"No, here." Sam's eyes lit up, and Taylor was tempted to back away. But Sam grabbed her hand and shoved the bag toward her face. "Really, smell."

Taylor wrinkled her nose, swallowing hard. It was one thing seeing the body and smelling it from a few feet away, but sticking her nose into the detritus that came from the body itself was totally gross. Grimacing, she took the bag and inhaled. The scent was smoky and floral, not at all unpleasant.

Sam's eyes were shining in excitement. "This isn't dirt, Taylor. These are herbs. She has herbs scattered all over her body. Now what the hell is that all about?"

Taylor shook her head slowly, trying to absorb the new discovery. "I don't know. Can you isolate which herb it is?"

"Yeah, I can let a buddy of mine at UT in Knoxville take a look. He's head of the university's botany department and totally into all this stuff. I don't think it's just one herb, though. The leaves are all different sizes and shapes. Oh man, this is too cool."

"Sam, you're awful." Taylor couldn't stop herself from smiling. "You like this job too much."

"That's why I'm good at it. Tim's our lead 'gator today. I'm going to get him set up here to bag all this stuff, and I'll have a runner take it up to UT ASAP. You know, it would be a lot simpler if that idiot mayor would help us get our own lab capable of handling this kind of stuff. Hell, it'd be nice if we could even do tox screens in-house."

Sam continued grumbling under her breath and stood up, signaling the end of the conversation. She waved to her team, calling them over. The body was ready to be moved.

"Wait, Sam. Did Crime Scene pick up anything else? Clothes, jewelry?"

"Not yet, but you're in their way. She's got enough of this crap on her that it's gonna take them a while to collect it all. Why don't you go back and try to find out who this girl is for me, okay? Y'all need to catch this guy, 'cause once the press gets a hold of this, they're gonna freak the whole city. It's not every day I have to come to the middle of Centennial Park to collect a body, much less for a staged crime scene. Look at the vultures hovering already."

She swept her hand toward the media trucks. Their level of activity had picked up, excitement palpable in the air. Techs were setting up lights and running around on the street by the duck pond, with cameras and portable microphones in tow. The news vans were lined up around the corner. Taylor watched Fitz and the patrol officers struggle to keep the reporters from rushing the tape to gather their precious scoops. Nothing like murder in the morning to start a feeding frenzy.

"Seriously, Taylor, you know how they are. They'll find some way to spin this into a grand conspiracy and warn all the parents to keep their girls at home until you catch whoever did this." She started grumbling. "It should be frickin' illegal for the chief to have given them their own radios. Now every newsie in Nashville hovers over my shoulder while I scope a body."

Taylor lowered her eyelids for a second and gave her best friend a half smile. "Well, honey, if it makes you feel any better, all the talking heads and their cameramen are squishing through goose poo trying to get their stories. Guess Lake Watauga has its purposes after all. Call me as soon as you have anything."

Sam laughed. "Yeah, yeah. Split. You're making me nervous."

**Like what you've read so far?
FIELD OF GRAVES is available from your
favorite print, ebook, or audiobook retailer!**

NO ONE KNOWS

Exclusive Excerpt

CHAPTER 1

Aubrey
Nashville
Today

One thousand eight hundred and seventy-five days after Joshua Hamilton went missing, the State of Tennessee declared him legally dead.

Aubrey, his wife (or former wife, or ex-wife, or widow—she had no idea how to refer to herself anymore), received the certified letter on a Friday. It came to the Montessori school where she taught, the very one she and Josh had attended as children. Came to her door in the middle of reading time, borne on the hands of Linda Pierce, the school's long-standing principal, who looked as if someone had died.

Which, in a way, they had.

He had.

Or so the State of Tennessee had officially declared.

Aubrey had been against the declaration–of–death petition from the beginning. She didn't want Josh's estate settled. Didn't want a date engraved on that stupid family stone obelisk that loomed over the graves of his ancestors at Mount Olivet Cemetery. Didn't want to say good-bye forever.

But Josh's mother had insisted. She wanted closure. She wanted to move on with her life. She wanted Aubrey to move on with hers, too. She'd petitioned the court for the early ruling, and clearly the courts agreed.

Everyone was ready to move on. Everyone but Aubrey.

She'd felt poorly this morning when she woke, almost a portent of the day to come, but today was the last day of school before spring break, so she had to show, and be cheery, and help the kids with their party, and give them their extra-credit reading assignments.

From the second they arrived, her students buzzed around her. It didn't take long for Aubrey to catch the children's enthusiasm and drop her previous malaise. It was a beautiful day: the sun glowed in the sky, dropping beams through the windows, creating slats of light on the multihued carpet. The kids spun through the light, whirling dervishes against a yellow backdrop. She didn't even try to contain them; watching them, she felt exactly the same way. Breaks signaled many things to her, freedom most of all. Freedom to go her own way for a bit, to explore, to read, to gather herself.

But when her classroom door opened unexpectedly, and Principal Pierce came into the room, the nausea returned with a vengeance, and her head started to pound. Aubrey watched her coming closer and closer. Her old friend's face was strained, the furrows carved into her upper lip collapsed in on each other, her yellowed forefinger tapping against the pristine white-and-blue envelope. She needed to file her nails.

What was it about moments, the ones that start with a capital *M*, that made you notice each and every detail?

Aubrey reminded herself of her situation. The children were watching. Trying to ignore the stares of the more precocious ones scattered about the classroom, gifted youngsters whose sensitivity to the emotions of others was finely honed, Aubrey took the letter from Linda, handed off the class into the woman's very capable, nicotine-stained hands, and went to the ladies' room in the staff lounge to read the contents.

The letter was from her mother-in-law. Aubrey knew exactly

what it contained.

She tried to pretend her hands weren't shaking.

She flipped the lid down on the toilet, locked the door, then sat and ripped open the envelope. Inside was a piece of paper folded into thirds, topped with a handwritten note on a cheery yellow, daisy-covered Post-it. Aubrey felt that added just the right touch. Her mother-in-law always had been wildly incapable of any form of tact.

There was no denying it now; her hands trembled violently as she unfolded the page. She looked to the handwritten note first. The words were carefully formed, a schoolgirl's roundness to the old-fashioned cursive.

Aubrey,
For your records.
Daisy Hamilton

Scribbled in print beneath the painstakingly properly written note were the words:

Joshua's Mother

Well, no kidding, Daisy. Like I could forget.

The sticky note was attached to a printout of an email. It was from Daisy's lawyer, the one who'd helped put this vehicle in motion last year, when Daisy decided to petition the courts to have Josh declared legally dead.

Aubrey fingered the scar on her lip as she read.

Dear Daisy,
Per our earlier conversation, attached please find a copy of the Order entered from the civil court today by Judge Robinson. As I explained to you on the phone, this Order directs the Department of Vital Statistics to issue a death certificate for your son, Joshua David Hamilton, as of April 19 of this year.

Now that this Order has been officially entered, we should take another look at the estate plan. Josh's life insurance policy will be fulfilled as soon as the declaration is received, and I'd like you to be fully prepared if you plan to contest the contents. I will be forwarding you a final bill for my services on this matter in the next couple of days.

Best personal regards,

Rick Saeger

And now it was official.

In the eyes of the law, Joshua David Hamilton was no longer of this earth. No longer Aubrey's husband. No longer Daisy's son.

No longer.

Aubrey was suddenly unable to breathe. Even though she'd been expecting it, seeing the words in black-and-white, adorned by Daisy's snippy little missive, killed her. Tears slid down her face, and she crumpled the letter against her thigh.

Daisy was a bitch, always had been, and Aubrey got the message loud and clear.

Get over it. Get on with your life. And watch out, kid, because I'm coming for that life insurance money.

But just how do you move on when you can't bury your husband? Five years later, there were still no good answers to the puzzle of Josh's evaporation. One minute there, the next gone. Poof. Disappeared. Missing. Kidnapped, hit over the head, and suffering from severe amnesia, or—worse than the idea of his heart no longer beating—he'd chosen to leave her. Dead, but not dead. Without a body, how could they know for sure?

Damn you, Josh.

He *was* dead. Even Aubrey had to admit that to herself. It had taken a year to formulate that conclusion, a year of the worst possible days imaginable. As much as she hated to believe he was really gone, she knew he was.

Because if he wasn't, he would have let her know. He was the other half of her. The better half. The responsible half. The serious half.

For him to be taken, or to have run away—no. He would never leave her of his own volition.

Which meant he *must* be dead.

The circle that was her life, a snake forever eating its tail.

Aubrey didn't know the answers to the riddle. Only knew that one thousand eight hundred and seventy-five days ago, Josh had been nagging at her to hurry up and get in the car because they were late for one of his closest friend's joint bachelor/bachelorette party. That they'd had a serious fender bender on the way to the party, which resulted in the small white scar that intersected Aubrey's top lip in a way that didn't detract from her heart-shaped face. That they'd arrived at the hotel over an hour late, and Aubrey had offered to get them checked in while Josh went to find the groom and join the party. That he'd kissed her deeply before he went, making the cut on her lip throb in time with her heart. That he'd glanced back over his shoulder and given her that devastating half smile that had been melting her insides since she was seven and he was nine and he'd pushed her down on the hard playground asphalt and made her cry.

That she'd repeated the words of this story so many times it had become a mantra. To the police. To the lawyers. To the media. To Daisy. To herself.

Her world was broken into thirds.

Seven and seventeen and five.

Seven years before he came into her life.

Seventeen in-between years when she'd seen Josh almost every day. Seventeen years of joy and fury and love and sex and marriage and heartache and happiness. Of prepubescent mating rituals, teenage angst, young-adult dawning realization, the inescapable knowledge that they couldn't live without each other, culminating in a small wedding and three years of marital bliss.

Five years of After. Five years of wondering.

She thought they were happy. Late at night, in the After time, Aubrey would lie in their bed, still on her side, wearing one of his white oxford shirts she pretended held the lingering bits of his scent, and wonder: *Weren't we? Weren't we happy?*

What was happiness? Where did it come from? How did you measure it? She'd always looked at the little things he did—from a sweet note in whatever book she was reading, to bringing her freshly-cut apples when she was vacuuming, or having a travel mug of hot Earl Grey tea waiting for her in the morning as she rushed out the door—as signs that he loved her. That he was happy, too.

But then he was gone, and she had to pick up the pieces of their once life, shattered like the reflective glass of a broken mirror on the floor.

Seven, and seventeen, and then five. Five years of emptiness, solitude, loneliness.

The State of Tennessee didn't care about any of that.

All the state cared about were the cold hard facts: one thousand eight hundred and seventy-five days ago, Joshua David Hamilton disappeared from the face of the earth, and now enough time had passed that a stranger had declared him legally dead.

Want to keep reading?
NO ONE KNOWS
is available wherever books are sold!

THE ABANDONED HEART

LAURA BENEDICT

PRAISE FOR LAURA BENEDICT

Murder, sexual obsession, and misogyny explode in the final scenes, bringing all the simmering evil to the surface in a shocking finale, that, like all good horror stories, is probably not the end. You just can't look away from this bombsite—nor forget it. Dripping with southern gothic atmosphere."

> —*Booklist,* starred review, on CHARLOTTE'S STORY

Set in 1957 in southern Virginia, Benedict's suspenseful, atmospheric follow-up to 2014's *Bliss House* finds housewife Charlotte Bliss devastated by the death of her four-year-old daughter... A satisfyingly creepy tale for a rainy night.

> —*Publisher's Weekly*, on CHARLOTTE'S STORY

An evocative, frightening and flawless gothic, CHARLOTTE'S STORY is guaranteed to send a delicious chill down your spine. Nobody does more for the modern southern gothic than Laura Benedict.

> —J.T. Ellison, *New York Times* bestselling author of
> WHAT LIES BEHIND

Benedict writes with passion and authority. CHARLOTTE'S STORY is not to be missed.

> —Carolyn Haines, author of the *Sarah Booth Delaney Bones Mysteries*, including BONE TO BE WILD

ABOUT LAURA

Laura Benedict is the author of the Bliss House series of dark suspense novels, CHARLOTTE'S STORY, BLISS HOUSE, and THE ABANDONED HEART (Pegasus Crime), as well as DEVIL'S OVEN, a modern Frankenstein tale, ISABELLA MOON, and CALLING MR. LONELY HEARTS (Ballantine). Her work has appeared in Ellery Queen Mystery Magazine, PANK, and numerous anthologies like THRILLERS: 100 MUST-READS (Oceanview), and SLICES OF FLESH (Dark Moon Books). She originated and edited the Surreal South Anthology of Short Fiction Series with her husband, Pinckney Benedict, and edited FEEDING KATE, a charity anthology, for their press, Gallowstree Press. A Cincinnati, Ohio native, Laura grew up in Louisville, Kentucky, and claims both as hometowns. She currently lives with her family in the southern wilds of a Midwestern state, surrounded by bobcats, coyotes, and other less picturesque predators. Find out more, enter her monthly contests, and follow her blog at laurabenedict.com.

PROLOGUE

It was the spring of 1876, and the first families of Old Gate, Virginia, were putting on quite a show for the man from New York who meant to be their new neighbor. The world was not such a large place that someone from a good Virginia family did not have connections in New York who could make *inquiries* about such a man. So everyone in the county already knew that Randolph Hasbrouck Bliss was about thirty years old, the son of a man who was reputed to have made an enormous fortune buying cotton from farmers in the Confederate States (sometimes from the government itself) for resale to the Northern textile mills, and then selling arms and ammunition back to the Confederacy. That he had a wife who was, interestingly, several years older than he, and a young daughter who, it was said, wasn't quite right in the head. That he had been educated at the College of New Jersey, and, after having shown some skill in managing one of his father's import operations (French wines, and more textiles), had decided to try his hand at farming apples and peaches in central Virginia. Those who had made the *inquiries* hadn't been able to find out exactly why he had decided to change careers, but there were whispers that he had *habits* of a nature that embarrassed and displeased his mother, who was from old Dutch New York stock. It was believed that those *habits* involved women. Often much younger women, and women of ill repute.

But the dinner guests at Maplewood, the gracious, pillar-fronted home of Katharine "Pinky" Archer and her husband, Robert, found their prejudices undermined as soon as they met Randolph.

He wasn't a man whom any woman would particularly call handsome, with features that were heavy and decidedly non-patrician: a prominent nose and thick, dark brows. But his jaw was strong and his brown eyes alert and lively. He wore his clothes well, despite having a waist that did not taper much from his broad shoulders, and an overall frame that was more like that of a laborer than of a man who spent his days giving orders to others. Like every other man in the room, he was dressed in a double-breasted evening coat of black, with matching trousers. His silk waistcoat was a rich shade of peacock blue that was at once daring and elegant. They could see that everything he wore was of superior quality, and though his face was rather common, he inhabited his expensive clothes with an easy, animal grace.

After a dinner that included expected delights of smoked oysters, turtle soup, bison, and a French cream tart, the Reverend Edward M. Searle and a couple of the other men of Old Gate watched Randolph with interest as he stood, smiling, surrounded by women. The women, including Edward's wife, Selina, and their hostess, Pinky Archer, preened under Randolph's gaze. His compliments were easy and witty. Was it that gaze that attracted them? As he looked at each woman, he seemed to give her his undivided attention, and when he looked elsewhere, she would wilt a bit. The women's attraction to Randolph was puzzling to all of the men, and, if they had spoken to one another about it, they might have agreed that it had something to do with the juxtaposition of his wealth and his common appearance. Or was it the uneasy sense that he was capable of doing the unpredictable?

When Pinky sat down at the piano, she asked who would be willing to sing "Silver Threads Among the Gold," as she had recently learned it, and Randolph volunteered readily. He sang confidently in a bold, baritone voice, but showed a strong degree of modesty when the group—particularly the women—applauded enthusiastically at the song's end. One of the older women, Pinky's mother, dabbed discreetly at her eye with a handkerchief.

When the singing was done, the party broke into smaller groups. Some played cards, others gathered around the enormous book of drawings of New York scenery that Randolph had sent as a gift to his hostess. With most of the women occupied, Edward, who was the priest at St. Anselm's Episcopal Church, saw his opportunity to speak to Randolph alone.

A servant had brought Randolph a glass of water, and he was finishing it when Edward approached. He spoke quietly. "Randolph, won't you walk outside with me for a moment? The evening is fine, and I like to take a small stroll after a large meal. Maplewood's garden is quite fragrant in the evening."

Randolph smiled, his dark eyes full of mischief. "Are you sure you wouldn't rather take a turn with one of these beautiful ladies, Edward? Your wife looks very becoming. In fact all the women I've met since I arrived in Old Gate are possessed of charms unseen where I come from in New York. And I warn you. I won't sit still if you try to kiss me beneath a rose bower."

Robert Archer, their host, was passing and chanced to hear Randolph's response. He stopped, chuckling. "You can trust Edward. I've known him since we were boys, and he never tried to kiss me once."

A slight look of irritation passed over Edward's face, but he banished it quickly and, with feigned gruffness, said, "But you haven't Randolph's exotic Yankee charm, Robert. Familiarity breeds contempt, as I'm sure you'll agree."

"Scoundrel. Don't be long with your stroll, gentlemen. I fear the ladies will not tolerate Randolph being away from them much longer." He laid his hand on Randolph's broad back in a gesture of camaraderie that was not quite a slap. "You've become quite the favorite already. You'll have to tell me your secret sometime. My Pinky and I have only been married five years, yet sometimes I think that since I've passed the age of thirty she sees me as ready for the ash heap. Beware, Randolph. The young women of the county are a flirtatious set, but we love them dearly, don't we, Edward?"

Edward nodded sagely and guided Randolph to the door.

Outside, the evening was indeed fine, and the cloudless sky above Maplewood was a brocade of countless stars.

"You can't see the sky like this in New York, in the city." Randolph stopped on the garden's path and looked up. "Too many factories, too many lights. My wife, Amelia, will like it here very much. She is reluctant to leave Long Island, but I think she and my daughter will be happy in the end. I have a working design for Bliss House, though it is sure to take more than a year to build."

Edward cleared his throat. "Some would say Old Gate is a bit rough around the edges, but I was happy to come back here after the war and seminary."

"I can't think of a better place to build new traditions for myself and my family. Sometimes a man needs to escape the bonds of family tradition, don't you agree?"

"Then I would say you will find its isolation to your liking. Old Gate is not like other Virginia towns. We are an insular place. The people who settled here, rather than in larger places like Lynchburg or Charlottesville, came here—or come here—because they were either not wanted in those larger societies or had reasons of their own for absenting themselves." He looked closely at Randolph. "What are your reasons for wanting to come to a place as remote as Old Gate?"

Randolph smiled and gave a small laugh. "I suppose I want a change. Nothing wrong with that, is there? As I said, sometimes the bonds of family can become too tight."

Rather than pressing him further, Edward glanced over his shoulder to see if they were being followed and continued walking. "This way, please." When he was satisfied that they were far enough away from the house, he stopped again. He was several inches taller than Randolph, and the moonlight sharpened his patrician profile: a high, Grecian nose, tall forehead, and chiseled chin. His prominent height intimidated many people.

Randolph looked up at him without any sign of anxiety. "Is something troubling you? I'll be of assistance if I can."

"My friends would not thank me for speaking with you. While I am of their society, they hold somewhat more jaundiced views than I on many things." He shook his head. "I would never accuse them of a lack of integrity, but I fear that the trio of individuals who own the property you are about to purchase for your home has not been completely honest with you."

Randolph laughed. "It is business. No business can be conducted in complete honesty. Nothing would ever be settled. Do you think the price they ask is too dear? It seems quite reasonable to me. It's a prime bit of land. Perfect for orchards, and an excellent home site."

"If it is so excellent, is it credible to you that it should be so close to town and as yet undeveloped? We have undergone much improvement since the war."

"Is there some defect I should know of? I have found none. Monsieur Hulot, my architect, has approved the surveyor's report, and will depart with his assistant from France at my telegram. I have spent much time at the site. I am satisfied. What is this, Edward?" Randolph assumed a joshing tone. "Is there some other bidder you want it for? I'm not afraid of paying a bit more to ensure that I have it. Or—" He seemed to consider for a moment. "Is it that my erstwhile neighbors are disturbed because they've learned that the distinguished Monsieur Hulot happens to be a Negro?"

Edward gave a little cough. "I'm sure that has never come up."

"Then just tell me what it is you have to tell me."

"Very well," Edward said. "A lot of the old families struggle to keep up their homes. The ones farming tobacco are just recovering. They need the money. Your money."

"Seems a fair trade."

"That particular farm was never planted with tobacco. It was part of an early land grant, and the owners leased different parts of it to many tenants over the years. When I was a boy, it was home to the Doyle family, a family with Quaker sympathies."

"Quakers? Here?"

"The Doyles were friendly with the Quaker group down in Lynchburg. And as you probably know, the Quakers had no sympathy for slaveholding and subverted it in every way they could. Old Gate was on the route from Lynchburg to Culpeper County, which was a kind of gathering point for runaway slaves headed north."

"Is there anywhere here that isn't touched by that kind of history? We must move past the war, man. It's our duty."

"Please, listen. We need to go back inside soon." Now Edward was brusque. "There was a house and a barn on the property, and the house had a shed attached to it. Sometime in 1847 or '48, the Doyles began to hide runaway slaves who were on their way north, in that shed. It became a kind of open secret among certain people in Old Gate."

Randolph nodded. "That sounds like it was virtuous, but dangerous."

"There are people in this house tonight whose parents didn't like what the Doyles and the Quakers were doing. People who didn't want to lose their own slaves because of such subversion close to home. Randolph, a group of Old Gate men surrounded the property one night and set fire to both the house and shed. When the family and, it's said, two female slaves and their children tried to escape, the men held them at gunpoint until they went back inside the buildings. If they didn't, they shot them dead, right there."

In their own momentary silence, they heard a woman's laughter from the house.

"It's a terrible story, but it has nothing to do with me. I thank you for telling me, Edward. Was anyone prosecuted?"

"Of course not. It was done at night, and there were no witnesses left. No one is really even sure how many were killed. Eight, maybe ten people."

"I see."

"No, I don't think you do. A few years later, another house was built there, on that same site. But no one was able to live in it for more than a few months at a time. Everyone who lived in that house suffered some tragedy, and they were forced to leave. Suicides. Madness. A murder."

Randolph scoffed. "That's bald superstition, and quite ridiculous. You're an educated man. Surely you don't believe in such things. Superstition is the stuff of old women and parlor games. To be honest, I'm amused by the superstitious aspects of the old pagan rites. Why, the Romans were a noble bunch, and the Celtics, too. But ghosts? That's nonsense."

Edward stiffened. "You would put your family at risk?"

"Of course not. There *is* no risk. There's nothing left of any buildings there except traces of a foundation. And that will be dug up before any building begins. I dare any curse to try to cling to me. It would find that I am not so easily cowed."

"I wish you would listen. There are other farms to be had."

"We should go back inside, Edward. It's growing late." Edward's shoulders fell, and he shook his head. They started back to the house. Not wanting to leave his new friend dispirited, Randolph made an effort to acknowledge his obviously genuine concern. "As a priest, perhaps you could perform some sort of blessing on the land. Might that not help obviate any curse, or whatever seems to be going on?"

Edward stopped. "I dislike that the Old Gate parties involved in this sale have not been frank with you. They seem to take it as rather a joke that someone like you—someone from a part of the country that they revile—is paying good money for the site of such an atrocity. You do not have true friends here, I'm afraid, Randolph. I don't know that they will ever be different if you choose to build your house here."

The light from the salon touched Randolph, illuminating his not quite handsome face. When Edward looked down into those eyes, he wasn't sure if the sincerity he saw there was true or skillful manipulation. There was something else, too, something harder, that he hadn't seen when they were in the house.

"I hope I may consider *you* my friend." Randolph rested his hand on the taller man's back, just as Robert Archer had touched *him* in friendship, and Edward felt an unpleasant sensation of cold spread over his body.

An hour later, the party broke up with many promises for future invitations. Randolph was heartily enjoined to write to his new friends just as soon as he knew when he would be returning to Old Gate to begin building his new home.

As he settled into the coach that would take him back to Missus Green's Inn and Boardinghouse near the center of town, Randolph felt in the left pocket of his waistcoat for his matches. The matches were there, but there was something else: a small, folded note, which, when opened and held close to the flame of a lighted match, was revealed to be an invitation of a particularly intimate sort, written in a delicate, well-formed hand. He smiled. It was an invitation he would gladly accept.

He blew out the match and settled back in the seat. Yes. He was very much looking forward to settling in Old Gate.

CHAPTER 1

Lucy
Walpurgisnacht, 1924

Lucy Bliss ran blindly through the moonlit rose garden, thorns grabbing at her as though they would keep her from leaving. As she reached the break in the garden wall that would lead her to the woods, her robe tangled on the last bush, so she tore it from her body with a cry and left it behind. Was someone following? Surely Randolph, who was as frail as a man risen from a grave of five years, could not capture her.

My husband risen from his grave! So much is explained. The voices in the night. The light near the springhouse. How did I not see?

Above the trees the distant lights of Old Gate shone silver on the scattered clouds. Only twenty-five years earlier, before she had married Randolph in 1899, there had been but a dozen gas streetlamps in town, and the night sky had looked endless and cluttered with stars. How different it had been. Walking with her friends to the little theater, or home from a party, her laughing voice louder than she knew was proper. But she hadn't cared. She had been cheerfully rebellious, happy to disregard her mother's constant instructions about minding her behavior, and her father's lectures from both his Episcopal pulpit and the dinner table. Though they were rigid people, and difficult to love, she had loved them both, and had obeyed—to a point. Few things were ever serious to her in those days. It had all been in fun.

Bright. Her life had been so wonderfully bright.

Now she was well into her forties, and her life had dimmed. Her feet were bare, tender from running over the crushed shells on the winding garden paths beside Bliss House, and her breath came in bursts. From moment to moment she wasn't sure if she were dreaming or not. Before she'd gone to bed, Terrance, who had run Bliss House for her these past few years, and was no older than she, had given her the medicine that helped her feel calm, helped her forget. But she had terrible dreams and often woke to find that she had chewed the knuckle of her finger until it bled and there were tears on her cheeks. Now, dreaming or awake, she had fled the house, running, running. For months she had been loath to walk outside. Loath to leave her room. How she had run when she was a child! And when her son, Michael Searle, was young, they had run through the orchards together, playing and racing, far from Randolph's critical gaze.

Michael Searle, my son. But more than a son. A gift.

This very night he was on his way home from North Carolina, where he had been visiting the woman he would marry. She had to get somewhere safe, to warn him—before he arrived—never to return to Bliss House.

Your father is alive! He will steal your happiness, my sweet child.

The path into the woods was crowded with brush and newly red switches of wild blackberry, whose thorns were even more ambitious and brutal than those of the roses. She slowed. Her thin, torn gown was no protection from the cool night, and a layer of sweat caused her to shiver violently. Craving the former safety of her own bed within her flower-covered bedroom walls, she thought of sinking to the ground, nesting in the brambles like an animal. Still, she pushed deeper into the woods, even though no one seemed to be coming after her.

Do they think I am weak, that I will come crawling back?

As a girl, she had thought of Bliss House as a mysterious, magical place, all the more fascinating because her parents had told her to stay away. Now she knew every inch of its shining wood floors and paneled walls. She had danced in the ballroom dozens of times, and hurried up and down the staircases twenty times a day, and aired the rooms, and watered flowers and written letters at her desk in the morning room, and rocked her son to sleep, and wiped his brow, and entertained friends, and listened to the bees drowsing over the roses, and watched her husband, the man who had built Bliss House, go slowly mad. And she had lived in the presence of ghosts, and had even ceased to be afraid of them.

But if Randolph were alive—truly alive—she would have to live in fear.

Again. It didn't matter if she were awake or dreaming. She would rather die than live with Randolph. Again.

Ahead, in the trees, there was a quivering light where there should not have been a light. Lucy glanced again over her shoulder to make sure she hadn't gotten turned around, but there was Bliss House rising tall and threatening behind her, its windows glowing warmly as though it were still a safe place. A place where, sometimes, she was happy.

Thank God Michael Searle is away. I will keep him safe.

Yes. Ahead of her was a light where there was supposed to be nothing, and desperation carried her toward it.

Are you hooked yet?
Devour the rest of THE ABANDONED HEART,
available wherever books are sold!

ABOUT THE AUTHOR

Photo credit: Krista Lee Photography

New York Times bestselling author J.T. Ellison writes dark psychological thrillers starring Nashville Homicide Lt. Taylor Jack-son and medical examiner Dr. Samantha Owens, and pens the Nicholas Drummond series with #1 *New York Times* bestselling author Catherine Coulter. Cohost of the premier literary television show, *A Word on Words*, Ellison lives in Nashville with her husband and twin kittens.

For more insight into her wicked imagination, follow J.T. online and join her email list at jtellison.com/subscribe.

JTELLISON.COM
@THRILLERCHICK
/JTELLISON14

CPSIA information can be obtained
at www.ICGtesting.com
Printed in the USA
LVOW12s1628021116

511367LV00002B/508/P